MIDWINTER MURDER

The Agatha Christie Collection

The Man in the Brown Suit
The Secret of Chimneys
The Seven Dials Mystery
The Mysterious Mr. Quin
The Sittaford Mystery
Parker Pyne Investigates
Why Didn't They Ask Evans?
Murder Is Easy
The Regatta Mystery and Other Stories
And Then There Were None
Towards Zero
Death Comes as the End
Sparkling Cyanide
The Witness for the Prosecution and Other Stories
Crooked House
Three Blind Mice and Other Stories
They Came to Baghdad
Destination Unknown
Ordeal by Innocence
Double Sin and Other Stories
The Pale Horse
Star over Bethlehem: Poems and Holiday Stories
Endless Night
Passenger to Frankfurt
The Golden Ball and Other Stories
The Mousetrap and Other Plays
The Harlequin Tea Set

The Hercule Poirot Mysteries

The Mysterious Affair at Styles
The Murder on the Links
Poirot Investigates
The Murder of Roger Ackroyd
The Big Four
The Mystery of the Blue Train
Peril at End House
Lord Edgware Dies
Murder on the Orient Express
Three Act Tragedy
Death in the Clouds
The A.B.C. Murders
Murder in Mesopotamia
Cards on the Table
Murder in the Mews and Other Stories
Dumb Witness
Death on the Nile
Appointment with Death
Hercule Poirot's Christmas
Sad Cypress
One, Two, Buckle My Shoe
Evil Under the Sun
Five Little Pigs
The Hollow
The Labors of Hercules
Taken at the Flood
The Under Dog and Other Stories
Mrs. McGinty's Dead
After the Funeral
Hickory Dickory Dock
Dead Man's Folly
Cat Among the Pigeons
The Clocks
Third Girl
Hallowe'en Party
Elephants Can Remember
Curtain: Poirot's Last Case

The Miss Marple Mysteries

The Murder at the Vicarage
The Body in the Library
The Moving Finger
A Murder Is Announced
They Do It with Mirrors
A Pocket Full of Rye
4:50 from Paddington
The Mirror Crack'd
A Caribbean Mystery
At Bertram's Hotel
Nemesis
Sleeping Murder
Miss Marple: The Complete Short Story Collection

The Tommy and Tuppence Mysteries

The Secret Adversary
Partners in Crime
N or M?
By the Pricking of My Thumbs
Postern of Fate

AGATHA CHRISTIE

MIDWINTER MURDER

FIRESIDE TALES FROM THE QUEEN OF MYSTERY

wm

WILLIAM MORROW

An Imprint of HarperCollins*Publishers*

This is a work of fiction. Names, characters, places, and incidents are products of the author's imagination or are used fictitiously and are not to be construed as real. Any resemblance to actual events, locales, organizations, or persons, living or dead, is entirely coincidental.

 For information, address HarperCollins Publishers, 195 Broadway, New York, NY 10007.

HarperCollins books may be purchased for educational, business, or sales promotional use. For information, please email the Special Markets Department at SPsales@harpercollins.com.

FIRST EDITION

Library of Congress Cataloging-in-Publication Data has been applied for.

ISBN 978-0-06-303036-7

20 21 22 23 24 LSC 10 9 8 7 6 5 4 3 2 1

CONTENTS

INTRODUCTION

Christmas at Abney Hall

Christmas we used to spend in Cheshire, going up to the Watts'. Jimmy usually got his yearly holiday about then, and he and Madge used to go to St. Moritz for three weeks. He was a very good skater, and so it was the kind of holiday he liked most. Mother and I used to go up to Cheadle, and since their newly built house, called Manor Lodge, was not ready yet, we spent Christmas at Abney Hall, with the old Wattses and their four children and Jack. It was a wonderful house to have Christmas in if you were a child. Not only was it enormous Victorian Gothic, with quantities of rooms, passages, unexpected steps, back staircases, front staircases, alcoves, niches—everything in the world that a child could want—but it also had three different pianos that you could play, as well as an organ. All it lacked was the light of day; it was remarkably dark, except for the big drawing-room with its green satin walls and its big windows.

Nan Watts and I were fast friends by now. We were not only friends but drinking companions—we both liked the same drink, *cream,* ordinary plain, neat cream. Although I had consumed an enormous amount of Devonshire cream since I lived in Devonshire, raw cream was really more of a treat. When Nan stayed with me at Torquay, we used to visit one of the dairies in the town, where we would have a glass of half milk and half cream. When I stayed with her at Abney we used to go down to the home farm and drink cream by the half-pint. We continued these drinking bouts all through our lives, and I still remember buying our cartons of cream in Sunningdale and coming up to the golf course and sitting outside the club house waiting for our respective husbands to finish their rounds of golf, each drinking our pinta cream.

Abney was a glutton's paradise. Mrs Watts had what was called her store-room off the hall. It was not like Grannie's store-room, a kind of securely-locked treasure house from which things were taken out. There was free access to it, and all round the walls were shelves covered with every kind of dainty. One side was entirely chocolates, boxes of them, all different, chocolate creams in labelled boxes . . . There were biscuits, gingerbread, preserved fruits, jams and so on.

Christmas was the supreme Festival, something never to be forgotten. Christmas stockings in bed. Breakfast, when everyone had a separate chair heaped with presents. Then a rush to church and back to continue present opening. At two o'clock Christmas Dinner, the blinds drawn down and glittering ornaments and lights. First, oyster soup (not relished by me), turbot, then boiled turkey, roast turkey, and a large roast sirloin of beef. This was followed by plum pudding, mince pies, and a trifle full of sixpences, pigs, rings, bachelors' buttons and all the rest of it. After that, again, innumerable kinds of dessert. In a story I once wrote, *The Affair of the Christmas Pudding,* I have described just such a feast. It is one of those things that I am sure will never be seen again in this generation; indeed I doubt nowadays if anyone's digestion would stand it. However, *our* digestions stood it quite well then.

I usually had to vie in eating prowess with Humphrey Watts, the Watts son next to James in age. I suppose he must have been twenty-one or twenty-two to my twelve or thirteen. He was a very handsome young man, as well as being a good actor and a wonderful entertainer and teller of stories. Good as I always was at falling in love with people, I don't think I fell in love with him, though it is amazing to me that I should *not* have done so. I suppose I was still at the stage where my love affairs had to be romantically impossible—concerned with public characters, such as the Bishop of London and King Alfonso of Spain, and of course with various actors. I know I fell deeply in love with Henry Ainley when I saw him in *The Bondman,* and I must have been just getting ripe for the K.O.W.s (Keen on Wallers), who were all to a girl in love with Lewis Waller in *Monsieur Beaucaire.*

Humphrey and I ate solidly through the Christmas Dinner. He scored over me in oyster soup, but otherwise we were neck and neck. We both first had roast turkey, then boiled turkey, and finally four or five slashing slices of sirloin of beef. It is possible that our elders confined themselves to only one kind of turkey for this course, but as far as I remember old Mr Watts certainly had beef as well as turkey. We then ate plum pudding and mince pies and trifle—1 rather sparingly of trifle, because I didn't like the taste of wine. After that there were the crackers, the grapes, the oranges, the Elvas plums, the Carlsbad plums, and the preserved fruits. Finally, during the afternoon, various handfuls of chocolates were fetched from the store-room to suit our taste. Do I remember being sick the next day? Having bilious attacks? No, never. The only bilious attacks I ever remember were those that seized me after eating unripe apples in September. I ate unripe apples practically every day, but occasionally I must have overdone it.

What I do remember was when I was about six or seven years old and had eaten mushrooms. I woke up with a pain about eleven o'clock in the evening, and came rushing down to the drawing-room, where mother and father were entertaining a party of people, and announced dramatically: 'I am going to die! I am poisoned by mushrooms!' Mother rapidly soothed me and administered a dose of ipecacuanha wine—always kept in the medicine cupboard in those days—and assured me that I was not due to die this time.

At any rate I never remember being ill at Christmas. Nan Watts was just the same as I was; she had a splendid stomach. In fact, really, when I remember those days, everyone seemed to have a pretty good stomach. I suppose people had gastric and duodenal ulcers and had to be careful, but I cannot remember anybody living on a diet of fish and milk. A coarse and gluttonous age? Yes, but one of great zest and enjoyment. Considering the amount that I ate in my youth (for I was always hungry) I cannot imagine how I managed to remain so thin—a scrawny chicken indeed.

After the pleasurable inertia of Christmas afternoon—pleasurable, that is, for the elders: the younger ones read books, looked at their presents, ate more chocolates, and so on—there was a terrific tea, with a great iced Christmas cake as well as everything else, and finally a supper of cold turkey and hot mince pies. About nine o'clock there was the Christmas Tree, with more presents hanging on it. A splendid day, and one to be remembered till next year, when Christmas came again.

Agatha Christie

Three Blind Mice

It was very cold. The sky was dark and heavy with unshed snow.

A man in a dark overcoat, with his muffler pulled up round his face, and his hat pulled down over his eyes, came along Culver Street and went up the steps of number 74. He put his finger on the bell and heard it shrilling in the basement below.

Mrs Casey, her hands busy in the sink, said bitterly, 'Drat that bell. Never any peace, there isn't.'

Wheezing a little, she toiled up the basement stairs and opened the door.

The man standing silhouetted against the lowering sky outside asked in a whisper, 'Mrs Lyon?'

'Second floor,' said Mrs Casey. 'You can go on up. Does she expect you?' The man slowly shook his head. 'Oh, well, go on up and knock.'

She watched him as he went up the shabbily carpeted stairs. Afterwards she said he 'gave her a funny feeling.' But actually all she thought was that he must have a pretty bad cold only to be able to whisper like that—and no wonder with the weather what it was.

When the man got round the bend of the staircase he began to whistle softly. The tune he whistled was 'Three Blind Mice.'

* * *

Molly Davis stepped back into the road and looked up at the newly painted board by the gate.

MONKSWELL MANOR
GUEST HOUSE

She nodded approval. It looked, it really did look, quite professional. Or, perhaps, one might say *almost* professional. The *T* of *Guest House* staggered uphill a little, and the end of *Manor* was slightly crowded, but on the whole Giles had made a wonderful job of it. Giles was really very clever. There were so many things that he could do. She was always making fresh discoveries about this husband of hers. He said so little about himself that it was only by degrees that she was finding out what a lot of varied talents he had. An ex-naval man was always a 'handy man,' so people said.

Well, Giles would have need of all his talents in their new venture. Nobody could be more raw to the business of running a guest house than she and Giles. But it would be great fun. And it did solve the housing problem.

It had been Molly's idea. When Aunt Katherine died, and the lawyers wrote to her and informed her that her aunt had left her Monkswell Manor, the natural reaction of the young couple had been to sell it. Giles had asked, 'What is it like?' And Molly had replied, 'Oh, a big, rambling old house, full of stuffy, old-fashioned Victorian furniture. Rather a nice garden, but terribly overgrown since the war, because there's been only one old gardener left.'

So they had decided to put the house on the market, and keep just enough furniture to furnish a small cottage or flat for themselves.

But two difficulties arose at once. First, there *weren't*

any small cottages or flats to be found, and secondly, all the furniture was enormous.

'Well,' said Molly, 'we'll just have to sell it *all.* I suppose it *will* sell?'

The solicitor assured them that nowadays *anything* would sell.

'Very probably,' he said, 'someone will buy it for a hotel or guesthouse in which case they might like to buy it with the furniture complete. Fortunately the house is in very good repair. The late Miss Emory had extensive repairs and modernizations done just before the war, and there has been very little deterioration. Oh, yes, it's in good shape.'

And it was then that Molly had had her idea.

'Giles,' she said, 'why shouldn't *we* run it as a guesthouse ourselves?'

At first her husband had scoffed at the idea, but Molly had persisted.

'We needn't take very many people—not at first. It's an easy house to run—it's got hot and cold water in the bedrooms and central heating and a gas cooker. And we can have hens and ducks and our own eggs, and vegetables.'

'Who'd do all the work—isn't it very hard to get servants?'

'Oh, *we'd* have to do the work. But wherever we lived we'd have to do that. A few extra people wouldn't really mean much more to do. We'd probably get a woman to come in after a bit when we got properly started. If we had only five people, each paying seven guineas a week—' Molly departed into the realms of somewhat optimistic mental arithmetic.

'And think, Giles,' she ended, 'it would be our *own* house. With our *own* things. As it is, it seems to me it will be years before we can ever find anywhere to live.'

That, Giles admitted, was true. They had had so little time together since their hasty marriage, that they were both longing to settle down in a home.

So the great experiment was set under way. Advertisements were put in the local paper and in the *Times,* and various answers came.

And now, today, the first of the guests was to arrive. Giles had gone off early in the car to try and obtain some army wire netting that had been advertised as for sale on the other side of the county. Molly announced the necessity of walking to the village to make some last purchases.

The only thing that was wrong was the weather. For the last two days it had been bitterly cold, and now the snow was beginning to fall. Molly hurried up the drive, thick, feathery flakes falling on her waterproofed shoulders and bright curly hair. The weather forecasts had been lugubrious in the extreme. Heavy snowfall was to be expected.

She hoped anxiously that all the pipes wouldn't freeze. It would be too bad if everything went wrong just as they started. She glanced at her watch. Past teatime. Would Giles have got back yet? Would he be wondering where *she* was?

'I had to go to the village again for something I had forgotten,' she would say. And he would laugh and say, 'More tins?'

Tins were a joke between them. They were always on the lookout for tins of food. The larder was really quite nicely stocked now in case of emergencies.

And, Molly thought with a grimace as she looked up at the sky, it looked as though emergencies were going to present themselves very soon.

The house was empty. Giles was not back yet. Molly went first into the kitchen, then upstairs, going round the newly prepared bedrooms. Mrs Boyle in the south room with the mahogany and the fourposter. Major Metcalf in the blue room with the oak. Mr Wren in the east room with the bay window. All the rooms looked very nice—and what a blessing that Aunt Katherine had had such a splendid stock of linen. Molly patted a counterpane into place and went downstairs again. It was nearly dark. The house felt suddenly very quiet and empty. It was a lonely house, two miles from a village, two miles, as Molly put it, from *anywhere.*

She had often been alone in the house before—but she had never before been so conscious of being alone in it.

The snow beat in a soft flurry against the windowpanes. It made a whispery, uneasy sound. Supposing Giles couldn't get back—supposing the snow was so thick that the car couldn't get through? Supposing she had to stay alone here—stay alone for days, perhaps.

She looked round the kitchen—a big, comfortable kitchen that seemed to call for a big, comfortable cook presiding at the kitchen table, her jaws moving rhythmically as she ate rock cakes and drank black tea—she should be flanked by a tall, elderly parlormaid on one side and a round, rosy housemaid on the other, with a kitchen-maid at the other end of the table observing her betters with frightened eyes. And instead there was just herself, Molly Davis, playing a role that did not yet seem a very natural role to play. Her whole life, at the moment, seemed unreal—Giles seemed unreal. She was playing a part—just playing a part.

A shadow passed the window, and she jumped—a strange man was coming through the snow. She heard the rattle of the side door. The stranger stood there in the open doorway, shaking off snow, a strange man, walking into the empty house.

And then, suddenly, illusion fled.

'Oh Giles,' she cried, 'I'm so glad you've come!'

'Hullo, sweetheart! What filthy weather! Lord, I'm *frozen*.'

He stamped his feet and blew through his hands.

Automatically Molly picked up the coat that he had thrown in a Giles-like manner onto the oak chest. She put it on a hanger, taking out of the stuffed pockets a muffler, a newspaper, a ball of string, and the morning's correspondence which he had shoved in pell mell. Moving into the kitchen, she laid down the articles on the dresser and put the kettle on the gas.

'Did you get the netting?' she asked. 'What ages you've been.'

'It wasn't the right kind. Wouldn't have been any good for us. I went on to another dump, but that wasn't any good, either. What have you been doing with yourself? Nobody turned up yet, I suppose?'

'Mrs Boyle isn't coming till tomorrow, anyway.'

'Major Metcalf and Mr Wren ought to be here today.'

'Major Metcalf sent a card to say he wouldn't be here till tomorrow.'

'Then that leaves us and Mr Wren for dinner. What do you think he's like? Correct sort of retired civil servant is my idea.'

'No, I think he's an artist.'

'In that case,' said Giles, 'we'd better get a week's rent in advance.'

'Oh, no, Giles, they bring luggage. If they don't pay we hang on to their luggage.'

'And suppose their luggage is stones wrapped up in newspaper? The truth is, Molly, we don't in the least know what we're up against in this business. I hope they don't spot what beginners we are.'

'Mrs Boyle is sure to,' said Molly. 'She's that kind of woman.'

'How do you know? You haven't seen her?'

Molly turned away. She spread a newspaper on the table, fetched some cheese, and set to work to grate it.

'What's this?' inquired her husband.

'It's going to be Welsh rarebit,' Molly informed him. 'Bread crumbs and mashed potatoes and just a *teeny weeny* bit of cheese to justify its name.'

'Aren't you a clever cook?' said her admiring husband.

'I wonder. I can do one thing at a time. It's *assembling* them that needs so much practice. Breakfast is the worst.'

'Why?'

'Because it all happens at once—eggs and bacon and hot milk and coffee and toast. The milk boils over, or the toast burns, or the bacon frizzles, or the eggs go hard. You have to be as active as a scalded cat watching everything at once.'

'I shall have to creep down unobserved tomorrow morning and watch this scalded-cat impersonation.'

'The kettle's boiling,' said Molly. 'Shall we take the tray into the library and hear the wireless? It's almost time for the news.'

'As we seem to be going to spend almost the whole of our time in the kitchen, we ought to have a wireless there, too.'

'Yes. How nice kitchens are. I love this kitchen. I think it's far and away the nicest room in the house. I like the dresser and the plates, and I simply love the lavish feeling that an absolutely *enormous* kitchen range gives you—though, of course, I'm thankful I haven't got to cook on it.'

'I suppose a whole year's fuel ration would go in one day.'

'Almost certainly, I should say. But think of the great joints that were roasted in it—sirloins of beef and saddles of mutton. Colossal copper preserving pans full of homemade strawberry jam with pounds and pounds of sugar going into it. What a lovely, comfortable age the Victorian age was. Look at the furniture upstairs, large and solid and rather ornate—but, oh!—the heavenly comfort of it, with lots of room for the clothes one used to have, and every drawer sliding in and out so easily. Do you remember that smart modern flat we were lent? Everything built in and sliding—only nothing slid—it always stuck. And the doors pushed shut—only they never stayed shut, or if they did shut they wouldn't open.'

'Yes, that's the worst of gadgets. If they don't go right, you're sunk.'

'Well, come on, let's hear the news.'

The news consisted mainly of grim warnings about the weather, the usual deadlock in foreign affairs, spirited bickerings in Parliament, and a murder in Culver Street, Paddington.

'Ugh,' said Molly, switching it off. 'Nothing but misery. I'm *not* going to hear appeals for fuel economy all over again. What do they expect you to do, sit and freeze? I don't think we ought to have tried to start a guesthouse in the winter. We ought to have waited until the spring.' She added in a different tone of voice, 'I wonder what the woman was like who was murdered.'

'Mrs Lyon?'

'Was that her name? I wonder who wanted to murder her and why.'

'Perhaps she had a fortune under the floorboards.'

'When it says the police are anxious to interview a man 'seen in the vicinity' does that mean he's the murderer?'

'I think it's usually that. Just a polite way of putting it.'

The shrill note of a bell made them both jump.

'That's the front door,' said Giles. 'Enter—a murderer,' he added facetiously.

'It would be, of course, in a play. Hurry up. It must be Mr Wren. Now we shall see who's right about him, you or me.'

Mr Wren and a flurry of snow came in together with a rush. All that Molly, standing in the library door, could see of the newcomer was his silhouette against the white world outside.

How alike, thought Molly, were all men in their livery of civilization. Dark overcoat, gray hat, muffler round the neck.

In another moment Giles had shut the front door against the elements, Mr Wren was unwinding his muffler and casting down his suitcase and flinging off his hat—all, it seemed, at the same time, and also talking. He had a high-pitched, almost querulous voice and stood revealed in the light of the hall as a young man with a shock of light, sunburned hair and pale, restless eyes.

'Too, too frightful,' he was saying. 'The English winter at its worst—a reversion to Dickens—Scrooge and Tiny Tim and all that. One had to be so terribly hearty to stand up to it all. Don't you think so? And I've had a terrible cross-country journey from Wales. Are you Mrs Davis? But how delightful!' Molly's hand was seized in a quick, bony clasp. 'Not at all as I'd imagined you. I'd pictured you, you know, as an Indian army general's widow. Terrifically grim and *memsahibish*—and Benares *whatnot*—a real Victorian *whatnot*. Heavenly, simply heavenly—Have you got any wax flowers? Or birds of paradise? Oh, but I'm simply going to *love* this place. I was afraid, you know, it would be very Olde Worlde—very, very Manor House—failing the Benares brass, I mean. Instead, it's marvelous—real Victorian bedrock respectability. Tell me, have you got one of those beautiful sideboards—mahogany—purple-plummy mahogany with great carved fruits?'

'As a matter of fact,' said Molly, rather breathless under this torrent of words, 'we have.'

'No! Can I see it? At once. In here?'

His quickness was almost disconcerting. He had turned the handle of the dining-room door, and clicked on the light. Molly followed him in, conscious of Giles's disapproving profile on her left.

Mr Wren passed his long bony fingers over the rich carving of the massive sideboard with little cries of appreciation. Then he turned a reproachful glance upon his hostess.

'No big mahogany dining table? All these little tables dotted about instead?'

'We thought people would prefer it that way,' said Molly.

'Darling, of course you're *quite* right. I was being carried away by my feeling for period. Of course, if you had the table, you'd have to have the right family round it. Stern, handsome father with a beard—prolific, faded mother, eleven children, a grim governess, and somebody called "poor Harriet"—the poor relation who acts as general helper and is very, very grateful for being given a good home. Look at that grate—think of the flames leaping up the chimney and blistering poor Harriet's back.'

'I'll take your suitcase upstairs,' said Giles. 'East room?'

'Yes,' said Molly.

Mr Wren skipped out into the hall again as Giles went upstairs.

'Has it got a four-poster with little chintz roses?' he asked.

'No, it hasn't,' said Giles and disappeared round the bend of the staircase.

'I don't believe your husband is going to like me,' said Mr Wren. 'What's he been in? The navy?'

'Yes.'

'I thought so. They're much less tolerant than the army and the air force. How long have you been married? Are you very much in love with him?'

'Perhaps you'd like to come up and see your room.'

'Yes, of course that was impertinent. But I did really want to know. I mean, it's interesting, don't you think, to know all about people? What they feel and think, I mean, not just who they are and what they do.'

'I suppose,' said Molly in a demure voice, 'you are Mr Wren?'

The young man stopped short, clutched his hair in both hands and tugged at it.

'But how frightful—I never put first things first. Yes, I'm Christopher Wren—now, don't laugh. My parents were a romantic couple. They hoped I'd be an architect. So they thought it a splendid idea to christen me Christopher—halfway home, as it were.'

'And are you an architect?' asked Molly, unable to help smiling.

'Yes, I am,' said Mr Wren triumphantly. 'At least I'm nearly one. I'm not fully qualified yet. But it's really a remarkable example of wishful thinking coming off for once. Mind you, actually the name will be a handicap. I shall never be *the* Christopher Wren. However, Chris Wren's Pre-Fab Nests may achieve fame.'

Giles came down the stairs again, and Molly said, 'I'll show you your room now, Mr Wren.'

When she came down a few minutes later, Giles said, 'Well, did he like the pretty oak furniture?'

'He was very anxious to have a four-poster, so I gave him the rose room instead.'

Giles grunted and murmured something that ended, '. . . young twerp.'

'Now, look here, Giles,' Molly assumed a severe demeanor. 'This isn't a house party of guests we're entertaining. This is business. Whether you like Christopher Wren or not—'

'I don't,' Giles interjected.

'—has nothing whatever to do with it. He's paying seven guineas a week, and that's all that matters.'

'If he pays it, yes.'

'He's agreed to pay it. We've got his letter.'

'Did you transfer that suitcase of his to the rose room?'

'He carried it, of course.'

'Very gallant. But it wouldn't have strained you. There's certainly no question of stones wrapped up in newspaper. It's so light that there seems to me there's probably nothing in it.'

'*Ssh,* here he comes,' said Molly warningly.

Christopher Wren was conducted to the library which looked, Molly thought, very nice, indeed, with its big chairs and its log fire. Dinner, she told him, would be in half an hour's time. In reply to a question, she explained that there were no other guests at the moment. In that case, Christopher said, how would it be if he came into the kitchen and helped?

'I can cook you an omelette if you like,' he said engagingly.

The subsequent proceedings took place in the kitchen, and Christopher helped with the washing up.

Somehow, Molly felt, it was not quite the right start for a conventional guesthouse—and Giles had not liked it at all. Oh, well, thought Molly, as she fell asleep, tomorrow when the others came it would be different.

The morning came with dark skies and snow. Giles looked grave, and Molly's heart fell. The weather was going to make everything very difficult.

Mrs Boyle arrived in the local taxi with chains on the wheels, and the driver brought pessimistic reports of the state of the road.

'Drifts afore nightfall,' he prophesied.

Mrs Boyle herself did not lighten the prevailing gloom. She was a large, forbidding-looking woman with a resonant voice and a masterful manner. Her natural aggressiveness had been heightened by a war career of persistent and militant usefulness.

'If I had not believed this was a *running* concern, I should never have come,' she said. 'I naturally thought it was a well-established guesthouse, properly run on scientific lines.'

'There is no obligation for you to remain if you are not satisfied, Mrs Boyle,' said Giles.

'No, indeed, and I shall not think of doing so.'

'Perhaps, Mrs Boyle,' said Giles, 'you would like to ring up for a taxi. The roads are not yet blocked. If there has been any misapprehension it would, perhaps, be better if you went elsewhere.' He added, 'We have had so many applications for rooms that we shall be able to fill your place quite easily—indeed, in future we are charging a higher rate for our rooms.'

Mrs Boyle threw him a sharp glance. 'I am certainly not going to leave before I have tried what the place is like. Perhaps you would let me have a rather large bath towel, Mrs Davis. I am not accustomed to drying myself on a pocket handkerchief.'

Giles grinned at Molly behind Mrs Boyle's retreating back.

'Darling, you were wonderful,' said Molly. 'The way you stood up to her.'

'Bullies soon climb down when they get their own medicine,' said Giles.

'Oh, dear,' said Molly. 'I wonder how she'll get on with Christopher Wren.'

'She won't,' said Giles.

And, indeed, that very afternoon, Mrs Boyle remarked to Molly, 'That's a very peculiar young man,' with distinct disfavour in her voice.

The baker arrived looking like an Arctic explorer and delivered the bread with the warning that his next call, due in two days' time, might not materialize.

'Holdups everywhere,' he announced. 'Got plenty of stores in, I hope?'

'Oh, yes,' said Molly. 'We've got lots of tins. I'd better take extra flour, though.'

She thought vaguely that there was something the Irish made called soda bread. If the worst came to the worst she could probably make that.

The baker had also brought the papers, and she spread them out on the hall table. Foreign affairs had receded in importance. The weather and the murder of Mrs Lyon occupied the front page.

She was staring at the blurred reproduction of the dead woman's features when Christopher Wren's voice behind her said, 'Rather a *sordid* murder, don't you think? Such a *drab*-looking woman and such a *drab* street. One can't feel, can one, that there is any story behind it?'

'I've no doubt,' said Mrs Boyle with a snort, 'that the creature got no more than she deserved.'

'Oh.' Mr Wren turned to her with engaging eagerness. 'So you think it's definitely a *sex* crime, do you?'

'I suggested nothing of the kind, Mr Wren.'

'But she *was* strangled, wasn't she? I wonder—' he held out his long white hands—'what it would feel like to strangle anyone.'

'Really, Mr Wren!'

Christopher moved nearer to her, lowering his voice. 'Have you considered, Mrs Boyle, just what it would feel like to be strangled?'

Mrs Boyle said again, even more indignantly, 'Really, Mr Wren!'

Molly read hurriedly out, "The man the police are anxious to interview was wearing a dark overcoat and a light Homburg hat, was of medium height, and wore a woolen scarf." '

'In fact,' said Christopher Wren, 'he looked just like everybody else.' He laughed.

'Yes,' said Molly. 'Just like everybody else.'

In his room at Scotland Yard, Inspector Parminter said to Detective Sergeant Kane, 'I'll see those two workmen now.'

'Yes, sir.'

'What are they like?'

'Decent class workingmen. Rather slow reactions. Dependable.'

'Right.' Inspector Parminter nodded.

Presently two embarrassed-looking men in their best clothes were shown into his room. Parminter summed them up with a quick eye. He was an adept at setting people at their ease.

'So you think you've some information that might be useful to us on the Lyon case,' he said. 'Good of you to come along. Sit down. Smoke?'

He waited while they accepted cigarettes and lit up.

'Pretty awful weather outside.'

'It is that, sir.'

'Well, now, then—let's have it.'

The two men looked at each other, embarrassed now that it came to the difficulties of narration.

'Go ahead, Joe,' said the bigger of the two.

Joe went ahead. 'It was like this, see. We 'adn't got a match.'

'Where was this?'

'Jarman Street—we was working on the road there—gas mains.'

Inspector Parminter nodded. Later he would get down to exact details of time and place. Jarman Street, he knew was in the close vicinity of Culver Street where the tragedy had taken place.

'You hadn't got a match,' he repeated encouragingly.

'No. Finished my box, I 'ad, and Bill's lighter wouldn't work, and so I spoke to a bloke as was passing. 'Can you give us a match, mister?' I says. Didn't think nothing particular, I didn't, not then. He was just passing—like lots of others—I just 'appened to arsk 'im.'

Again Parminter nodded.

'Well, he give us a match, 'e did. Didn't say nothing. "Cruel cold," Bill said to 'im, and he just answered, whispering-like, "Yes, it is." Got a cold on his chest, I thought. He was all wrapped up, anyway. "Thanks mister," I says and gives him back his matches, and he moves off quick, so quick that when I sees 'e'd dropped something, it's almost too late to call 'im back. It was a little notebook as he must 'ave pulled out of 'is pocket when he got the matches out. "Hi, mister," I calls after 'im, "you've dropped something." But he didn't seem to hear—he just quickens up and bolts round the corner, didn't 'e, Bill?'

'That's right,' agreed Bill. 'Like a scurrying rabbit.'

'Into the Harrow Road, that was, and it didn't seem as we'd catch up with him there, not the rate 'e was going, and, anyway, by then it was a bit late—it was only a little book, not a wallet or anything like that—maybe it wasn't important. "Funny bloke," I says. "His hat pulled down over his eyes, and all buttoned up—like a crook on the pictures," I says to Bill, didn't I, Bill?'

'That's what you said,' agreed Bill.

'Funny I should have said that, not that I thought anything at the time. Just in a hurry to get home, that's what I thought, and I didn't blame 'im. Not 'arf cold, it was!'

'Not 'arf,' agreed Bill.

'So I says to Bill, "Let's 'ave a look at this little book and see if it's important." Well, sir, I took a look. "Only a couple of addresses," I says to Bill. Seventy-Four Culver Street and some blinking manor 'ouse.'

'Ritzy,' said Bill with a snort of disapproval.

Joe continued his tale with a certain gusto now that he had got wound up.

'"Seventy-Four Culver Street," I says to Bill. "That's

just round the corner from 'ere. When we knock off, we'll take it round"—and then I sees something written across the top of the page. "What's this?" I says to Bill. And he takes it and reads it out. ' "Three blind mice"—must be off 'is knocker,' he says—and just at that very moment—yes, it was that very moment, sir, we 'ears some woman yelling, "Murder!" a couple of streets away!'

Joe paused at this artistic climax.

'Didn't half yell, did she?' he resumed. "Here," I says to Bill, "you nip along." And by and by he comes back and says there's a big crowd and the police are there and some woman's had her throat cut or been strangled and that was the landlady who found her, yelling for the police. "Where was it?" I says to him. "In Culver Street," he says. "What number?" I asks, and he says he didn't rightly notice.'

Bill coughed and shuffled his feet with the sheepish air of one who has not done himself justice.

'So I says, "We'll nip around and make sure," and when we finds it's number seventy-four we talk it over, and "Maybe," Bill says, "the address in the notebook's got nothing to do with it," and I says as maybe it *has,* and, anyway, after we've talked it over and heard the police want to interview a man who left the 'ouse about that time, well, we come along 'ere and ask if we can see the gentleman who's handling the case, and I'm sure I 'ope as we aren't wasting your time.'

'You acted very properly,' said Parminter approvingly. 'You've brought the notebook with you? Thank you. Now—'

His questions became brisk and professional. He got places, times, dates—the only thing he did not get was a description of the man who had dropped the notebook. Instead he got the same description as he had already got from a hysterical landlady, the description of a hat pulled down over the eyes, a buttoned-up coat, a muffler swathed round the lower part of a face, a voice that was only a whisper, gloved hands.

When the men had gone he remained staring down at the little book lying open on his table. Presently it would go to the appropriate department to see what evidence, if any, of fingerprints it might reveal. But now his attention was held by the two addresses and by the line of small handwriting along the top of the page.

He turned his head as Sergeant Kane came into the room.

'Come here, Kane. Look at this.'

Kane stood behind him and let out a low whistle as he read out, '"Three Blind Mice!" Well, I'm dashed!'

'Yes.' Parminter opened a drawer and took out a half sheet of notepaper which he laid beside the notebook on his desk. It had been found pinned carefully to the murdered woman.

On it was written, *This is the first.* Below was a childish drawing of three mice and a bar of music.

Kane whistled the tune softly. *Three Blind Mice, See how they run—*

'That's it, all right. That's the signature tune.'

'Crazy, isn't it, sir?'

'Yes.' Parminter frowned. 'The identification of the woman is quite certain?'

'Yes, sir. Here's the report from the fingerprints department. Mrs Lyon, as she called herself, was really Maureen Gregg. She was released from Holloway two months ago on completion of her sentence.'

Parminter said thoughtfully, 'She went to Seventy-Four Culver Street calling herself Maureen Lyon. She occasionally drank a bit and she had been known to bring a man home with her once or twice. She displayed no fear of anything or anyone. There's no reason to believe she thought herself in any danger. This man rings the bell, asks for her, and is told by the landlady to go up to the second floor. She can't describe him, says only that he was of medium height and seemed to have a bad cold and lost his voice. She went back again to the basement and heard nothing of a suspicious nature. She did not hear the man go out. Ten minutes or so later she took tea to her lodger and discovered her strangled.

'This wasn't a casual murder, Kane. It was carefully planned.' He paused and then added abruptly, 'I wonder how many houses there are in England called Monkswell Manor?'

'There might be only one, sir.'

'That would probably be too much luck. But get on with it. There's no time to lose.'

The sergeant's eye rested appreciatively on two entries in the notebook—*74 Culver Street; Monkswell Manor.*

He said, 'So you think—'

Parminter said swiftly, 'Yes. Don't you?'

'Could be. Monkswell Manor—now where—Do you know, sir, I could swear I've seen that name quite lately.'

'Where?'

'That's what I'm trying to remember. Wait a minute—Newspaper—*Times*. Back page. Wait a minute—Hotels and boardinghouses—Half a sec, sir—it's an old one. I was doing the crossword.'

He hurried out of the room and returned in triumph, 'Here you are, sir, look.'

The inspector followed the pointing finger.

'Monkswell Manor, Harpleden, Berks.' He drew the

telephone towards him. 'Get me the Berkshire County police.'

With the arrival of Major Metcalf, Monkswell Manor settled into its routine as a going concern. Major Metcalf was neither formidable like Mrs Boyle, nor erratic like Christopher Wren. He was a stolid, middle-aged man of spruce military appearance, who had done most of his service in India. He appeared satisfied with his room and its furniture, and while he and Mrs Boyle did not actually find mutual friends, he had known cousins of friends of hers—'the Yorkshire branch,' out in Poonah. His luggage, however, two heavy pigskin cases, satisfied even Giles's suspicious nature.

Truth to tell, Molly and Giles did not have much time for speculating about their guests. Between them, dinner was cooked, served, eaten, and washed up satisfactorily. Major Metcalf praised the coffee, and Giles and Molly retired to bed, tired but triumphant—to be roused about two in the morning by the persistent ringing of a bell.

'Damn,' said Giles. 'It's the front door. What on earth—'

'Hurry up,' said Molly. 'Go and see.'

Casting a reproachful glance at her, Giles wrapped his dressing gown round him and descended the stairs. Molly heard the bolts being drawn back and a murmur of voices in the hall. Presently, driven by curiosity, she crept out of bed and went to peep from the top of the stairs. In the hall below, Giles was assisting a bearded stranger out of a snow-covered overcoat. Fragments of conversation floated up to her.

'Brrr.' It was an explosive foreign sound. 'My fingers are so cold I cannot feel them. And my feet—' A stamping sound was heard.

'Come in here.' Giles threw open the library door. 'It's warm. You'd better wait here while I get a room ready.'

'I am indeed fortunate,' said the stranger politely.

Molly peered inquisitively through the banisters. She saw an elderly man with a small black beard and Mephistophelean eyebrows. A man who moved with a young and jaunty step in spite of the gray at his temples.

Giles shut the library door on him and came quickly up the stairs. Molly rose from her crouching position.

'Who is it?' she demanded.

Giles grinned. 'Another guest for the guesthouse. Car overturned in a snowdrift. He got himself out and was making his way as best he could—it's a howling blizzard still, listen to it—along the road when he saw our board. He said it was like an answer to prayer.'

'You think he's—all right?'

'Darling, this isn't the sort of night for a housebreaker to be doing his rounds.'

'He's a foreigner, isn't he?'

'Yes. His name's Paravicini. I saw his wallet—I rather think he showed it on purpose—simply crammed with notes. Which room shall we give him?'

'The green room. It's all tidy and ready. We'll just have to make up the bed.'

'I suppose I'll have to lend him pajamas. All his things are in the car. He said he had to climb out through the window.'

Molly fetched sheets, pillowcases, and towels.

As they hurriedly made the bed up, Giles said, 'It's coming down thick. We're going to be snowed up, Molly, completely cut off. Rather exciting in a way, isn't it?'

'I don't know,' said Molly doubtfully. 'Do you think I can make soda bread, Giles?'

'Of course you can. You can make anything,' said her loyal husband.

'I've never tried to make bread. It's the sort of thing one takes for granted. It may be new or it may be stale but it's just something the baker brings. But if we're snowed up there won't be a baker.'

'Nor a butcher, nor a postman. No newspapers. And probably no telephone.'

'Just the wireless telling us what to do?'

'At any rate we make our own electric light.'

'You must run the engine again tomorrow. And we must keep the central heating well stoked.'

'I suppose our next lot of coke won't come in now. We're very low.'

'Oh, bother. Giles, I feel we are in for a simply frightful time. Hurry up and get Para—whatever his name is. I'll go back to bed.'

Morning brought confirmation of Giles's forebodings. Snow was piled five feet high, drifting up against the doors and windows. Outside it was still snowing. The world was white, silent, and—in some subtle way—menacing.

Mrs Boyle sat at breakfast. There was no one else in the dining room. At the adjoining table, Major Metcalf's place had been cleared away. Mr Wren's table was still laid for breakfast. One early riser, presumably, and one late one. Mrs Boyle herself knew definitely that there was only one proper time for breakfast, nine o'clock.

Mrs Boyle had finished her excellent omelette and was champing toast between her strong white teeth. She was in a grudging and undecided mood. Monkswell

Manor was not at all what she had imagined it would be. She had hoped for bridge, for faded spinsters whom she could impress with her social position and connections, and to whom she could hint at the importance and secrecy of her war service.

The end of the war had left Mrs Boyle marooned, as it were, on a desert shore. She had always been a busy woman, talking fluently of efficiency and organization. Her vigor and drive had prevented people asking whether she was, indeed, a good or efficient organizer. War activities had suited her down to the ground. She had bossed people and bullied people and worried heads of departments and, to give her her due, had at no time spared herself. Subservient women had run to and fro, terrified of her slightest frown. And now all that exciting hustling life was over. She was back in private life, and her former private life had vanished. Her house, which had been requisitioned by the army, needed thorough repairing and redecorating before she could return to it, and the difficulties of domestic help made a return to it impracticable in any case. Her friends were largely scattered and dispersed. Presently, no doubt, she would find her niche, but at the moment it was a case of marking time. A hotel or a boardinghouse seemed the answer. And she had chosen to come to Monkswell Manor.

She looked round her disparagingly.

Most dishonest, she said to herself, *not to have told me they were only just starting.*

She pushed her plate farther away from her. The fact that her breakfast had been excellently cooked and served, with good coffee and homemade marmalade, in a curious way annoyed her still more. It had deprived her of a legitimate cause of complaint. Her bed, too, had been comfortable, with embroidered sheets and a soft pillow. Mrs Boyle liked comfort, but she also liked to find fault. The latter was, perhaps, the stronger passion of the two.

Rising majestically, Mrs Boyle left the dining room, passing in the doorway that very extraordinary young man with the red hair. He was wearing this morning a checked tie of virulent green—a woolen tie.

Preposterous, said Mrs Boyle to herself. *Quite preposterous.*

The way he looked at her, too, sideways out of those pale eyes of his—she didn't like it. There was something upsetting—unusual—about that faintly mocking glance.

Unbalanced mentally, I shouldn't wonder, said Mrs Boyle to herself.

She acknowledged his flamboyant bow with a slight inclination of her head and marched into the big drawing room. Comfortable chairs here, particularly the large rose-colored one. She had better make it clear that that was to be *her* chair. She deposited her knitting on it as a precaution and walked over and laid a hand on the radiators. As she had suspected, they were only warm, not hot. Mrs Boyle's eye gleamed militantly. She could have something to say about *that.*

She glanced out of the window. Dreadful weather—quite dreadful. Well, she wouldn't stay here long—not unless more people came and made the place amusing.

Some snow slid off the roof with a soft whooshing sound. Mrs Boyle jumped. 'No,' she said out loud. 'I shan't stay here long.'

Somebody laughed—a faint, high chuckle. She turned her head sharply. Young Wren was standing in the doorway looking at her with that curious expression of his.

'No,' he said. 'I don't suppose you will.'

* * *

Major Metcalf was helping Giles to shovel away snow from the back door. He was a good worker, and Giles was quite vociferous in his expressions of gratitude.

'Good exercise,' said Major Metcalf. 'Must get exercise every day. Got to keep fit, you know.'

So the major was an exercise fiend. Giles had feared as much. It went with his demand for breakfast at half past seven.

As though reading Giles's thoughts, the major said, 'Very good of your missus to cook me an early breakfast. Nice to get a new-laid egg, too.'

Giles had risen himself before seven, owing to the exigencies of hotelkeeping. He and Molly had had boiled eggs and tea and had set to on the sitting rooms. Everything was spick-and-span. Giles could not help thinking that if he had been a guest in his own establishment, nothing would have dragged him out of bed on a morning such as this until the last possible moment.

The major, however, had been up and breakfasted, and roamed about the house, apparently full of energy seeking an outlet.

Well, thought Giles, *there's plenty of snow to shovel.*

He threw a sideways glance at his companion. Not an easy man to place, really. Hard-bitten, well over middle age, something queerly watchful about the eyes. A man who was giving nothing away. Giles wondered why he had come to Monkswell Manor. Demobilized, probably, and no job to go to.

Mr Paravicini came down late. He had coffee and a piece of toast—a frugal Continental breakfast.

He somewhat disconcerted Molly when she brought it to him by rising to his feet, bowing in an exaggerated manner, and exclaiming, 'My charming hostess? I am right, am I not?'

Molly admitted rather shortly that he was right. She was in no mood for compliments at this hour.

'And why,' she said, as she piled crockery recklessly in the sink, 'everybody has to have their breakfast at a different time—It's a bit hard.'

She slung the plates into the rack and hurried upstairs to deal with the beds. She could expect no assistance from Giles this morning. He had to clear a way to the boiler house and to the hen-house.

Molly did the beds at top speed and admittedly in the most slovenly manner, smoothing sheets and pulling them up as fast as she could.

She was at work on the baths when the telephone rang.

Molly first cursed at being interrupted, then felt a slight feeling of relief that the telephone at least was still in action, as she ran down to answer it.

She arrived in the library a little breathless and lifted the receiver.

'Yes?'

A hearty voice with a slight but pleasant country burr asked, 'Is that Monkswell Manor?'

'Monkswell Manor Guest House.'

'Can I speak to Commander David, please?'

'I'm afraid he can't come to the telephone just now,' said Molly. 'This is Mrs Davis. Who is speaking, please?'

'Superintendent Hogben, Berkshire Police.'

Molly gave a slight gasp. She said, 'Oh, yes—er—yes?'

'Mrs Davis, rather an urgent matter has arisen. I don't wish to say very much over the telephone, but I have sent Detective Sergeant Trotter out to you, and he should be there any minute now.'

'But he won't get here. We're snowed up—completely snowed up. The roads are impassable.'

There was no break in the confidence of the voice at the other end.

'Trotter will get to you, all right,' it said. 'And please impress upon your husband, Mrs Davis, to listen very carefully to what Trotter has to tell you, and to follow his instructions implicitly. That's all.'

'But, Superintendent Hogben, what—'

But there was a decisive click. Hogben had clearly said all he had to say and rung off. Molly waggled the telephone rest once or twice, then gave up. She turned as the door opened.

'Oh, Giles darling, there you are.'

Giles had snow on his hair and a good deal of coal grime on his face. He looked hot.

'What is it, sweetheart? I've filled the coal scuttles and brought in the wood. I'll do the hens next and then have a look at the boiler. Is that right? What's the matter, Molly? You looked scared.'

'Giles, it was the *police*.'

'The police?' Giles sounded incredulous.

'Yes, they're sending out an inspector or a sergeant or something.'

'But why? What have we done?'

'I don't know. Do you think it could be that two pounds of butter we had from Ireland?'

Giles was frowning. 'I did remember to get the wireless license, didn't I?'

'Yes, it's in the desk. Giles, old Mrs Bidlock gave me five of her coupons for that old tweed coat of mine. I suppose that's wrong—but *I* think it's perfectly fair.

I'm a coat less so why shouldn't I have the coupons? Oh, dear, what else is there we've done?'

'I had a near shave with the car the other day. But it was definitely the other fellow's fault. Definitely.'

'We must have done *something,*' wailed Molly.

'The trouble is that practically everything one does nowadays is illegal,' said Giles gloomily. 'That's why one has a permanent feeling of guilt. Actually I expect it's something to do with running this place. Running a guesthouse is probably chockfull of snags we've never heard of.'

'I thought drink was the only thing that mattered. We haven't given anyone anything to drink. Otherwise, why shouldn't we run our own house any way we please?'

'I know. It sounds all right. But as I say, everything's more or less forbidden nowadays.'

'Oh, dear,' sighed Molly. 'I wish we'd never started. We're going to be snowed up for days, and everybody will be cross and they'll eat all our reserves of tins—'

'Cheer up, sweetheart,' said Giles. 'We're having a bad break at the moment, but it will pan out all right.'

He kissed the top of her head rather absentmindedly and, releasing her, said in a different voice, 'You know, Molly, come to think of it, it must be something pretty serious to send a police sergeant trekking out here in all this.' He waved a hand towards the snow outside. He said, 'It must be something really *urgent*—'

As they stared at each other, the door opened, and Mrs Boyle came in.

'Ah, here you are, Mr Davis,' said Mrs Boyle. 'Do you know the central heating in the drawing room is practically stone-cold?'

'I'm sorry, Mrs Boyle. We're rather short of coke and—'

Mrs Boyle cut in ruthlessly. 'I am paying seven guineas a week here—*seven* guineas. And I do *not* expect to freeze.'

Giles flushed. He said shortly, 'I'll go and stoke it up.'

He went out of the room, and Mrs Boyle turned to Molly.

'If you don't mind my saying so, Mrs Davis, that is a very extraordinary young man you have staying here. His manners—and his ties—And does he never brush his hair?'

'He's an extremely brilliant young architect,' said Molly.

'I beg your pardon?'

'Christopher Wren is an architect and—'

'My dear young woman,' snapped Mrs Boyle, 'I have naturally heard of Sir Christopher Wren. Of course he was an architect. He built St. Paul's. You young people seem to think that education came in with the Education Act.'

'I meant this Wren. His name is Christopher. His parents called him that because they hoped he'd be an architect. And he is—or nearly—one, so it turned out all right.'

'Humph,' Mrs Boyle snorted. 'It sounds a very fishy story to me. I should make some inquiries about him if I were you. What do you know about him?'

'Just as much as I know about you, Mrs Boyle—which is that both you and he are paying us seven guineas a week. That's really all that I need to know, isn't it? And all that concerns me. It doesn't matter to me whether I like my guests, or whether—' Molly looked very steadily at Mrs Boyle—'or whether I don't.'

Mrs Boyle flushed angrily. 'You are young and inexperienced and should welcome advice from someone more knowledgeable than yourself. And what about this queer foreigner? When did *he* arrive?'

'In the middle of the night.'

'Indeed. Most peculiar. Not a very conventional hour.'

'To turn away bona fide travelers would be against the law, Mrs Boyle.' Molly added sweetly. 'You may not be aware of that.'

'All I can say is that this Paravicini, or whatever he calls himself, seems to me—'

'Beware, beware, dear lady. You talk of the devil and then—'

Mrs Boyle jumped as though it had been indeed the devil who addressed her. Mr Paravicini, who had crept quietly in without either of the two women noticing him, laughed and rubbed his hands together with a kind of elderly satanic glee.

'You startled me,' said Mrs Boyle. 'I did not hear you come in.'

'I come in on tiptoe, so,' said Mr Paravicini, 'nobody ever hears me come and go. That I find very amusing. Sometimes I over-hear things. That, too, amuses me.' He added softly, 'But I do not forget what I hear.'

Mrs Boyle said rather feebly, 'Indeed? I must get my knitting—I left it in the drawing room.'

She went out hurriedly. Molly stood looking at Mr Paravicini with a puzzled expression. He approached her with a kind of hop and skip.

'My charming hostess looks upset.' Before she could prevent it, he picked up her hand and kissed it. 'What is it, dear lady?'

Molly drew back a step. She was not sure that she

liked Mr Paravicini much. He was leering at her like an elderly satyr.

'Everything is rather difficult this morning,' she said lightly. 'Because of the snow.'

'Yes.' Mr Paravicini turned his head round to look out of the window. 'Snow makes everything very difficult, does it not? Or else it makes things very easy.'

'I don't know what you mean.'

'No,' he said thoughtfully. 'There is quite a lot that you do not know. I think, for one thing, that you do not know very much about running a guesthouse.'

Molly's chin went up belligerently. 'I daresay we don't. But we mean to make a go of it.'

'Bravo, bravo.'

'After all,' Molly's voice betrayed slight anxiety, 'I'm not such a very bad cook—'

'You are, without doubt, an enchanting cook,' said Mr Paravicini.

What a nuisance foreigners were, thought Molly.

Perhaps Mr Paravicini read her thoughts. At all events his manner changed. He spoke quietly and quite seriously.

'May I give you a little word of warning, Mrs Davis? You and your husband must not be too trusting, you know. Have you references with these guests of yours?'

'Is that usual?' Molly looked troubled. 'I thought people just—just came.'

'It is advisable always to know a little about the people who sleep under your roof.' He leaned forward and tapped her on the shoulder in a minatory kind of way. 'Take myself, for example. I turn up in the middle of the night. My car, I say, is overturned in a snowdrift. What do you know of me? Nothing at all. Perhaps you know nothing, either, of your other guests.'

'Mrs Boyle—' began Molly, but stopped as that lady herself re-entered the room, knitting in hand.

'The drawing room is too cold. I shall sit in here.' She marched towards the fireplace.

Mr Paravicini pirouetted swiftly ahead of her. 'Allow me to poke the fire for you.'

Molly was struck, as she had been the night before, by the youthful jauntiness of his step. She noticed that he always seemed careful to keep his back to the light, and now, as he knelt, poking the fire, she thought she saw the reason for it. Mr Paravicini's face was cleverly but decidedly 'made up.'

So the old idiot tried to make himself look younger than he was, did he? Well, he didn't succeed. He looked all his age and more. Only the youthful walk was incongruous. Perhaps that, too, had been carefully counterfeited.

She was brought back from speculation to the disagreeable realities by the brisk entrance of Major Metcalf.

'Mrs Davis. I'm afraid the pipes of the—er—' he lowered his voice modestly, 'downstairs cloakroom are frozen.'

'Oh, dear,' groaned Molly. 'What an awful day. First the police and then the pipes.'

Mr Paravicini dropped the poker into the grate with a clatter. Mrs Boyle stopped knitting. Molly, looking at Major Metcalf, was puzzled by his sudden stiff immobility and by the indescribable expression on his face. It was an expression she could not place. It was as though all emotion had been drained out of it, leaving something carved out of wood behind.

He said in a short, staccato voice, '*Police,* did you say?'

She was conscious that behind the stiff immobility of his demeanor, some violent emotion was at work. It might have been fear or alertness or excitement—but there was *something. This man,* she said to herself, *could be dangerous.*

He said again, and this time his voice was just mildly curious, 'What's that about the police?'

'They rang up,' said Molly. 'Just now. To say they're sending a sergeant out here.' She looked towards the window. 'But I shouldn't think he'll ever get here,' she said hopefully.

'Why are they sending the police here?' He took a step nearer to her, but before she could reply the door opened, and Giles came in.

'This ruddy coke's more than half stones,' he said angrily. Then he added sharply, 'Is anything the matter?'

Major Metcalf turned to him. 'I hear the police are coming out here,' he said. 'Why?'

'Oh, that's all right,' said Giles. 'No one can ever get through in this. Why, the drifts are five feet deep. The road's all banked up. Nobody will get here today.'

And at that moment there came distinctly three loud taps on the window.

It startled them all. For a moment or two they did not locate the sound. It came with the emphasis and menace of a ghostly warning. And then, with a cry, Molly pointed to the French window. A man was standing there tapping on the pane, and the mystery of his arrival was explained by the fact that he wore skis.

With an exclamation, Giles crossed the room, fumbled with the catch, and threw open the French window.

'Thank you, sir,' said the new arrival. He had a slightly common, cheerful voice and a well-bronzed face.

'Detective Sergeant Trotter,' he announced himself.

Mrs Boyle peered at him over her knitting with disfavour.

'You can't be a sergeant,' she said disapprovingly.

'You're too young.'

The young man, who was indeed very young, looked affronted at this criticism and said in a slightly annoyed tone, 'I'm not quite as young as I look, madam.'

His eye roved over the group and picked out Giles.

'Are you Mr Davis? Can I get these skis off and stow them somewhere?'

'Of course, come with me.'

Mrs Boyle said acidly as the door to the hall closed behind them, 'I suppose that's what we pay our police force for nowadays, to go round enjoying themselves at winter sports.'

Paravicini had come close to Molly. There was quite a hiss in his voice as he said in a quick, low voice, 'Why did you send for the police, Mrs Davis?'

She recoiled a little before the steady malignity of his glance. This was a new Mr Paravicini. For a moment she felt afraid. She said helplessly, 'But I didn't. I didn't.'

And then Christopher Wren came excitedly through the door, saying in a high penetrating whisper, 'Who's that man in the hall? Where did he come from? So terribly hearty and all over snow.'

Mrs Boyle's voice boomed out over the click of her knitting needles. 'You may believe it or not, but that man is a policeman. A policeman—skiing!'

The final disruption of the lower classes had come, so her manner seemed to say.

Major Metcalf murmured to Molly, 'Excuse me, Mrs Davis, but may I use your telephone?'

'Of course, Major Metcalf.'

He went over to the instrument, just as Christopher Wren said shrilly, 'He's very handsome, don't you think so? I always think policemen are terribly attractive.'

'Hullo, hullo—' Major Metcalf was rattling the telephone irritably. He turned to Molly. 'Mrs Davis, this telephone is dead, quite dead.'

'It was all right just now. I—'

She was interrupted. Christopher Wren was laughing, a high, shrill, almost hysterical laugh. 'So we're quite cut off now. Quite cut off. That's funny, isn't it?'

'I don't see anything to laugh at,' said Major Metcalf stiffly.

'No, indeed,' said Mrs Boyle.

Christopher was still in fits of laughter. 'It's a private joke of my own,' he said. '*Hsh,*' he put his finger to his lips, 'the sleuth is coming.'

Giles came in with Sergeant Trotter. The latter had got rid of his skis and brushed off the snow and was holding in his hand a large notebook and pencil. He brought an atmosphere of unhurried judicial procedure with him.

'Molly,' said Giles, 'Sergeant Trotter wants a word with us alone.'

Molly followed them both out of the room.

'We'll go in the study,' Giles said.

They went into the small room at the back of the hall which was dignified by that name. Sergeant Trotter closed the door carefully behind him.

'What have we done, Sergeant?' Molly demanded plaintively.

'Done?' Sergeant Trotter stared at her. Then he smiled broadly. 'Oh,' he said. 'It's nothing of that kind, madam. I'm sorry if there's been a misapprehension of any kind. No, Mrs Davis, it's something quite different. It's more a matter of police protection, if you understand me.'

Not understanding him in the least, they both looked at him inquiringly.

Sergeant Trotter went on fluently, 'It relates to the death of Mrs Lyon, Mrs Maureen Lyon, who was murdered in London two days ago. You may have read about the case.'

'Yes,' said Molly.

'The first thing I want to know is if you were acquainted with this Mrs Lyon?'

'Never heard of her,' said Giles, and Molly murmured concurrence.

'Well, that's rather what we expected. But as a matter of fact Lyon wasn't the murdered woman's real name. She had a police record, and her fingerprints were on file, so we were able to identify her without any difficulty. Her real name was Gregg; Maureen Gregg. Her late husband, John Gregg, was a farmer who resided at Longridge Farm not very far from here. You may have heard of the Longridge Farm case.'

The room was very still. Only one sound broke the stillness, a soft, unexpected *plop* as snow slithered off the roof and fell to the ground outside. It was a secret, almost sinister sound.

Trotter went on. 'Three evacuee children were billeted on the Greggs at Longridge Farm in 1940. One of those children subsequently died as the result of criminal neglect and ill-treatment. The case made quite a sensation, and the Greggs were both sentenced to terms of imprisonment. Gregg escaped on his way to prison, he stole a car and had a crash while trying to evade the police. He was killed outright. Mrs Gregg served her sentence and was released two months ago.'

'And now she's been murdered,' said Giles. 'Who do they think did it?'

But Sergeant Trotter was not to be hurried. 'You remember the case, sir?' he asked.

Giles shook his head. 'In 1940 I was a midshipman serving in the Mediterranean.'

'I—I do remember hearing about it, I think,' said Molly rather breathlessly. 'But why do you come to us? What have we to do with it?'

'It's a question of your being in danger, Mrs Davis!'

'Danger?' Giles spoke increduously.

'It's like this, sir. A notebook was picked up near the scene of the crime. In it were written two addresses. The first was Seventy-Four Culver Street.'

'Where the woman was murdered?' Molly put in.

'Yes, Mrs Davis. The other address was Monkswell Manor.'

'What?' Molly's tone was incredulous. 'But how extraordinary.'

'Yes. That's why Superintendent Hogben thought it imperative to find out if you knew of any connection between you, or between this house, and the Longridge Farm case.'

'There's nothing—absolutely nothing,' said Giles. 'It must be some coincidence.'

Sergeant Trotter said gently, 'Superintendent Hogben doesn't think it is a coincidence. He'd have come himself if it had been at all possible. Under the weather conditions, and as I'm an expert skier, he sent me with instructions to get full particulars of everyone in this house, to report back to him by phone, and to take all measures I thought expedient for the safety of the household.'

Giles said sharply, 'Safety? Good Lord, man, you don't think somebody is going to be killed *here?*'

Trotter said apologetically, 'I didn't want to upset the lady, but yes, that is just what Superintendent Hogben does think.'

'But what earthly reason could there be—'

Giles broke off, and Trotter said, 'That's just what I'm here to find out.'

'But the whole thing's *crazy*.'

'Yes, sir, but it's because it's crazy that it's dangerous.'

Molly said, 'There's something more you haven't told us yet, isn't there, Sergeant?'

'Yes, madam. At the top of the page in the notebook was written, "Three Blind Mice." Pinned to the dead woman's body was a paper with "This is the first" written on it. And below it a drawing of *three mice* and a bar of music. The music was the tune of the nursery rhyme "Three Blind Mice." '

Molly sang softly:

"Three Blind Mice,
See how they run.
They all ran after the farmer's wife!
She—"

She broke off. 'Oh, it's horrible—*horrible*. There were three children, weren't there?'

'Yes, Mrs Davis. A boy of fifteen, a girl of fourteen, and the boy of twelve who died.'

'What happened to the others?'

'The girl was, I believe, adopted by someone. We haven't been able to trace her. The boy would be just on twenty-three now. We've lost track of him. He was said to have always been a bit—queer. He joined up in the army at eighteen. Later he deserted. Since then he's disappeared. The army psychiatrist says definitely that he's not well.'

'You think that it was he who killed Mrs Lyon?' Giles asked. 'And that he's a homicidal maniac and may turn up here for some unknown reason?'

'We think that there must be a connection between someone here and the Longridge Farm business. Once we can establish what that connection is, we will be forearmed. Now you state, sir, that you yourself have no connection with that case. The same goes for you, Mrs Davis?'

'I—oh, yes—yes.'

'Perhaps you will tell me exactly who else there is in the house?'

They gave him the names. Mrs Boyle. Major Metcalf. Mr Christopher Wren. Mr Paravicini. He wrote them down in his notebook.

'Servants?'

'We haven't any servants,' said Molly. 'And that reminds me, I must go and put the potatoes on.'

She left the study abruptly.

Trotter turned to Giles. 'What do you know about these people, sir?'

'I—We—' Giles paused. Then he said quietly, 'Really, we don't know anything about them, Sergeant Trotter. Mrs Boyle wrote from a Bournemouth hotel. Major Metcalf from Leamington. Mr Wren from a private hotel in South Kensington. Mr Paravicini just turned up out of the blue—or rather out of the white—his car overturned in a snowdrift near here. Still, I suppose they'll have identity cards, ration books, that sort of thing?'

'I shall go into all that, of course.'

'In a way it's lucky that the weather is so awful,' said

Giles. 'The murderer can't very well turn up in this, can he?'

'Perhaps he doesn't need to, Mr Davis.'

'What do you mean?'

Sergeant Trotter hesitated for a moment and then he said, 'You've got to consider, sir, that *he may be here already.*'

Giles stared at him.

'What do you mean?'

'Mrs Gregg was killed two days ago. *All your visitors here have arrived since then, Mr Davis.*'

'Yes, but they'd booked beforehand—some time beforehand—except for Paravicini.'

Sergeant Trotter sighed. His voice sounded tired. 'These crimes were planned in advance.'

'Crimes? But only one crime has happened yet. Why are you sure that there will be another?'

'That it will happen—no. I hope to prevent that. That it will be attempted, yes.'

'But then—if you're right,' Giles spoke excitedly, 'there's only one person it could be. There's only one person who's the right age. *Christopher Wren!* "

Sergeant Trotter had joined Molly in the kitchen.

'I'd be glad, Mrs Davis, if you would come with me to the library. I want to make a general statement to everyone. Mr Davis has kindly gone to prepare the way—'

'All right—just let me finish these potatoes. Sometimes I wish Sir Walter Raleigh had never discovered the beastly things.'

Sergeant Trotter preserved a disapproving silence. Molly said apologetically, 'I can't really believe it, you see—It's so fantastic—'

'It isn't fantastic, Mrs Davis—It's just plain *facts.*'

'You have a description of the man?' Molly asked curiously.

'Medium height, slight build, wore a dark overcoat and a light hat, spoke in a whisper, his face was hidden by a muffler. You see—that might be anybody.' He paused and added, 'There are three dark overcoats and light hats hanging up in your hall here, Mrs Davis.'

'I don't think any of these people came from London.'

'Didn't they, Mrs Davis?' With a swift movement Sergeant Trotter moved to the dresser and picked up a newspaper.

'The *Evening Standard* of February 19th. Two days ago. *Someone* brought that paper here, Mrs Davis.'

'But how extraordinary.' Molly stared, some faint chord of memory stirred. 'Where can that paper have come from?'

'You mustn't take people always at their face value, Mrs Davis. You don't really know anything about these people you have admitted to your house.' He added, 'I take it you and Mr Davis are new to the guesthouse business?'

'Yes, we are,' Molly admitted. She felt suddenly young, foolish, and childish.

'You haven't been married long, perhaps, either?'

'Just a year.' She blushed slightly. 'It was all rather sudden.'

'Love at first sight,' said Sergeant Trotter sympathetically.

Molly felt quite unable to snub him. 'Yes,' she said, and added in a burst of confidence, 'we'd only known each other a fortnight.'

Her thoughts went back over those fourteen days of whirlwind courtship. There hadn't been any doubts—they had both known. In a worrying, nerve-racked world, they had found the miracle of each other. A little smile came to her lips.

She came back to the present to find Sergeant Trotter eying her indulgently.

'Your husband doesn't come from these parts, does he?'

'No,' said Molly vaguely. 'He comes from Lincolnshire.'

She knew very little of Giles's childhood and upbringing. His parents were dead, and he always avoided talking about his early days. He had had, she fancied, an unhappy childhood.

'You're both very young, if I may say so, to run a place of this kind,' said Sergeant Trotter.

'Oh, I don't know. I'm twenty-two and—'

She broke off as the door opened and Giles came in.

'Everything's all set. I've given them a rough outline,' he said. 'I hope that's all right, Sergeant?'

'Saves time,' said Trotter. 'Are you ready, Mrs Davis?'

Four voices spoke at once as Sergeant Trotter entered the library.

Highest and shrillest was that of Christopher Wren declaring that this was too, too thrilling and he wasn't going to sleep a wink tonight, and please, *please* could we have all the gory details?

A kind of double-bass accompaniment came from Mrs Boyle. 'Absolute outrage—sheer incompetence—police have no business to let murderers go roaming about the countryside.'

Mr Paravicini was eloquent chiefly with his hands. His gesticulations were more eloquent than his words, which were drowned by Mrs Boyle's double bass. Major Metcalf could be heard in an occasional short staccato bark. He was asking for facts.

Trotter waited a moment or two, then he held up an authoritative hand and, rather surprisingly, there was silence.

'Thank you,' he said. 'Now, Mr Davis has given you an outline of why I'm here. I want to know one thing, and one thing only, and I want to know it quick. *Which of you has some connection with the Longridge Farm case?'*

The silence was unbroken. Four blank faces looked at Sergeant Trotter. The emotions of a few moments back—excitement, indignation, hysteria, inquiry, were wiped away as a sponge wipes out the chalk marks on a slate.

Sergeant Trotter spoke again, more urgently. 'Please understand me. One of you, we have reason to believe, is in danger—deadly danger. *I have got to know which one of you it is!'*

And still no one spoke or moved.

Something like anger came into Trotter's voice. 'Very well—I'll ask you one by one. Mr Paravicini?'

A very faint smile flickered across Mr Paravicini's face. He raised his hands in a protesting foreign gesture.

'But I am a stranger in these parts, Inspector. I know nothing, but nothing, of these local affairs of bygone years.'

Trotter wasted no time. He snapped out, 'Mrs Boyle?'

'Really I don't see why—I mean—why should *I* have anything to do with such a distressing business?'

'Mr Wren?'

Christopher said shrilly, 'I was a mere child at the time. I don't remember even *hearing* about it.'

'Major Metcalf?'

The Major said abruptly, 'Read about it in the papers. I was stationed at Edinburgh at the time.'

'That's all you have to say—any of you?'

Silence again.

Trotter gave an exasperated sigh. 'If one of you gets murdered,' he said, 'you'll only have yourself to blame.' He turned abruptly and went out of the room.

'My dears,' said Christopher. 'How *melodramatic!*' He added, 'He's very handsome, isn't he? I do admire the police. So stern and hard-boiled. Quite a thrill, this whole business. "Three Blind Mice." How does the tune go?'

He whistled the air softly, and Molly cried out involuntarily, *'Don't!'*

He whirled round on her and laughed. 'But, darling,' he said, 'it's my *signature* tune. I've never been taken for a murderer before and I'm getting a tremendous kick out of it!'

'Melodramatic rubbish,' said Mrs Boyle. 'I don't believe a word of it.'

Christopher's light eyes danced with an impish mischief. 'But just wait, Mrs Boyle,' he lowered his voice, 'till I creep up behind you and you feel my hands round your throat.'

Molly flinched.

Giles said angrily, 'You're upsetting my wife, Wren. It's a damned poor joke, anyway.'

'It's no joking matter,' said Metcalf.

'Oh, but it is,' said Christopher. 'That's just what it is—a madman's joke. That's what makes it so deliciously *macabre.*'

He looked round at them and laughed again. 'If you could just see your faces,' he said.

Then he went swiftly out of the room.

Mrs Boyle recovered first. 'A singularly ill-mannered and neurotic young man,' she said. 'Probably a conscientious objector.'

'He tells me he was buried during an air raid for forty-eight hours before being dug out,' said Major Metcalf. 'That accounts for a good deal, I daresay.'

'People have so many excuses for giving way to nerves,' said Mrs Boyle acidly. 'I'm sure I went through as much as anybody in the war, and *my* nerves are all right.'

'Perhaps that's just as well for you, Mrs Boyle,' said Metcalf.

'What do you mean?'

Major Metcalf said quietly, 'I think you were actually the billeting officer for this district in 1940, Mrs Boyle.' He looked at Molly who gave a grave nod. 'That is so, isn't it?'

An angry flush appeared on Mrs Boyle's face. 'What of it?' she demanded.

Metcalf said gravely, '*You* were responsible for sending three children to Longridge Farm.'

'Really, Major Metcalf, I don't see how I can be held responsible for what happened. The Farm people seemed very nice and were most anxious to have the children. I don't see that I was to blame in any way—or that I can be held responsible—' Her voice trailed off.

Giles said sharply, 'Why didn't you tell Sergeant Trotter this?'

'No business of the police,' snapped Mrs Boyle. 'I can look after myself.'

Major Metcalf said quietly, 'You'd better watch out.'

Then he, too, left the room.

Molly murmured, 'Of course, you *were* the billeting officer. I remember.'

'Molly, did you know?' Giles stared at her.

'You had the big house on the common, didn't you?'

'Requisitioned,' said Mrs Boyle. 'And completely ruined,' she added bitterly. '*Devastated*. Iniquitous.'

Then, very softly, Mr Paravicini began to laugh. He threw his head back and laughed without restraint.

'You must forgive me,' he gasped. 'But, indeed, I find all this most amusing. I enjoy myself—yes, I enjoy myself greatly.'

Sergeant Trotter re-entered the room at that moment. He threw a glance of disapproval at Mr Paravicini. 'I'm glad,' he said acidly, 'that everyone finds this so funny.'

'I apologize, my dear Inspector. I do apologize. I am spoiling the effect of your solemn warning.'

Sergeant Trotter shrugged his shoulders. 'I've done my best to make the position clear,' he said. 'And I'm not an inspector. I'm only a sergeant. I'd like to use the telephone, please, Mrs Davis.'

'I abase myself,' said Mr Paravicini. 'I creep away.'

Far from creeping, he left the room with that jaunty and youthful step that Molly had noticed before.

'He's an odd fish,' said Giles.

'Criminal type,' said Trotter. 'Wouldn't trust him a yard.'

'Oh,' said Molly. 'You think *he*—but he's far too old—Or is he old at all? He uses makeup—quite a lot of it. And his walk is young. Perhaps, he's made up to *look* old. Sergeant Trotter, do you think—'

Sergeant Trotter snubbed her severely. 'We shan't get anywhere with unprofitable speculation, Mrs Davis,' he said. 'I must report to Superintendent Hogben.'

He crossed to the telephone.

'But you can't,' said Molly. 'The telephone's dead.'

'What?' Trotter swung round.

The sharp alarm in his voice impressed them all. 'Dead? Since when?'

'Major Metcalf tried it just before you came.'

'But it was all right before that. You got Superintendent Hogben's message?'

'Yes. I suppose—since ten—the line's down—with the snow.'

But Trotter's face remained grave. 'I wonder,' he said. 'It may have been—cut.'

Molly stared. 'You think so?'

'I'm going to make sure.'

He hurried out of the room. Giles hesitated, then went after him.

Molly exclaimed, 'Good heavens! Nearly lunchtime, I must get on—or we'll have nothing to eat.'

As she rushed from the room, Mrs Boyle muttered, 'Incompetent chit! What a place. *I* shan't pay seven guineas for *this* kind of thing.'

Sergeant Trotter bent down, following the wires. He asked Giles, 'Is there an extension?'

'Yes, in our bedroom upstairs. Shall I go up and see there?'

'If you please.'

Trotter opened the window and leaned out, brushing snow from the sill. Giles hurried up the stairs.

Mr Paravicini was in the big drawing room. He went across to the grand piano and opened it. Sitting on the music stool, he picked out a tune softly with one finger.

Three Blind Mice,
See how they run. . . .

Christopher Wren was in his bedroom. He moved about it, whistling briskly. Suddenly the whistle wavered and died. He sat down on the edge of the bed. He buried his face in his hands and began to sob. He murmured childishly, 'I can't go on.'

Then his mood changed. He stood up, squared his shoulders. 'I've got to go on,' he said. 'I've got to go through with it.'

Giles stood by the telephone in his and Molly's room. He bent down towards the skirting. One of Molly's gloves lay there. He picked it up. A pink bus ticket dropped out of it. Giles stood looking down at it as it fluttered to the ground. Watching it, his face changed. It might have been a different man who walked slowly, as though in a dream, to the door, opened it, and stood a moment peering along the corridor towards the head of the stairs.

Molly finished the potatoes, threw them into the pot, and set the pot on the fire. She glanced into the oven. Everything was all set, going according to plan.

On the kitchen table was the two-day-old copy of the *Evening Standard.* She frowned as she looked at it. If she could only just *remember*—

Suddenly her hands went to her eyes. 'Oh, no,' said Molly. 'Oh, *no!*'

Slowly she took her hands away. She looked round the kitchen like someone looking at a strange place. So warm and comfortable and spacious, with its faint savory smell of cooking.

'Oh, *no,*' she said again under her breath.

She moved slowly, like a sleepwalker, towards the door into the hall. She opened it. The house was silent except for someone whistling.

That tune—

Molly shivered and retreated. She waited a minute or two, glancing once more round the familiar kitchen. Yes, everything was in order and progressing. She went once more towards the kitchen door.

Major Metcalf came quietly down the back stairs. He waited a moment or two in the hall, then he opened the big cupboard under the stairs and peered in. Everything seemed quiet. Nobody about. As good a time as any to do what he had set out to do—

Mrs Boyle, in the library, turned the knobs of the radio with some irritation.

Her first attempt had brought her into the middle of a talk on the origin and significance of nursery rhymes. The last thing she wanted to hear. Twirling impatiently, she was informed by a cultured voice: 'The psychology of fear must be thoroughly understood. Say you are alone in a room. A door opens softly behind you—'

A door did open.

Mrs Boyle, with a violent start, turned sharply. 'Oh, it's you,' she said with relief. 'Idiotic programs they have on this thing. I can't find anything worth listening to!'

'I shouldn't bother to listen, Mrs Boyle.'

Mrs Boyle snorted. 'What else is there for me to do?' she demanded. 'Shut up in a house with a possible murderer—not that I believe *that* melodramatic story for a moment—'

'Don't you, Mrs Boyle?'

'Why—what do you mean—'

The belt of the raincoat was slipped round her neck so quickly that she hardly realized its significance. The knob of the radio amplifier was turned higher. The lecturer on the psychology of fear shouted his learned remarks into the room and drowned what incidental noises there were attendant on Mrs Boyle's demise.

But there wasn't much noise.

The killer was too expert for that.

They were all huddled in the kitchen. On the gas cooker the potatoes bubbled merrily. The savory smell from the oven of steak and kidney pie was stronger than ever.

Four shaken people stared at each other, the fifth, Molly, white and shivering, sipped at the glass of whisky that the sixth, Sergeant Trotter, had forced her to drink.

Sergeant Trotter himself, his face set and angry, looked round at the assembled people. Just five minutes had elapsed since Molly's terrified screams had brought him and the others racing to the library.

'She'd only just been killed when you got to her, Mrs Davis,' he said. 'Are you sure you didn't see or hear anybody as you came across the hall?'

'Whistling,' said Molly faintly. 'But that was earlier. I think—I'm not sure—I think I heard a door shut—softly, somewhere—just as I—as I—went into the library.'

'Which door?'

'I don't know.'

'Think, Mrs Davis—try and *think*—upstairs—downstairs—right, left?'

'I don't *know,* I tell you,' cried Molly. 'I'm not even sure I heard anything.'

'Can't you stop bullying her?' said Giles angrily. 'Can't you see she's all in?'

'I'm investigating a murder, Mr Davis—I beg your pardon—*Commander* Davis.'

'I don't use my war rank, Sergeant.'

'Quite so, sir.' Trotter paused, as though he had made some subtle point. 'As I say, I'm investigating a murder.

Up to now nobody has taken this thing seriously. Mrs Boyle didn't. She held out on me with information. You all held out on me. Well, Mrs Boyle is dead. Unless we get to the bottom of this—and quickly, mind, there may be another death.'

'Another? Nonsense. Why?'

'Because,' said Sergeant Trotter gravely, 'there were three little blind mice.'

Giles said incredulously, 'A death for each of them? But there would have to be a connection—I mean another connection with the case.'

'Yes, there would have to be that.'

'But why another death *here?*'

'Because there were only two addresses in the note-book. There was only one possible victim at Seventy-Four Culver Street. She's dead. But at Monkswell Manor there is a wider field.'

'Nonsense, Trotter. It would be a most unlikely coincidence that there should be *two* people brought here by chance, both of them with a share in the Longridge Farm case.'

'Given certain circumstances, it wouldn't be so much of a coincidence. Think it out, Mr Davis.' He turned towards the others. 'I've had your accounts of where you all were when Mrs Boyle was killed. I'll check them over. You were in your room, Mr Wren, when you heard Mrs Davis scream?'

'Yes, Sergeant.'

'Mr Davis, you were upstairs in your bedroom examining the telephone extension there?'

'Yes,' said Giles.

'Mr Paravicini was in the drawing room playing tunes on the piano. Nobody heard you, by the way, Mr Paravicini?'

'I was playing very, very softly, Sergeant, just with one finger.'

'What tune was it?'

'"Three Blind Mice," Sergeant.' He smiled. 'The same tune that Mr Wren was whistling upstairs. The tune that's running through everybody's head.'

'It's a horrid tune,' said Molly.

'How about the telephone wire?' asked Metcalf. 'Was it deliberately cut?'

'Yes, Major Metcalf. A section had been cut out just outside the dining room window—I had just located the break when Mrs Davis screamed.'

'But it's crazy. How can he hope to get away with it?' demanded Christopher shrilly.

The sergeant measured him carefully with his eye.

'Perhaps he doesn't very much care about that,' he said. 'Or again, he may be quite sure he's too clever for us. Murderers get like that.' He added, 'We take a psychology course, you know, in our training. A schizophrenic's mentality is very interesting.'

'Shall we cut out the long words?' said Giles.

'Certainly, Mr Davis. Two six-letter words are all that concern us at the moment. One's "murder" and the other's "danger." That's what we've got to concentrate upon. Now, Major Metcalf, let me be quite clear about your movements. You say you were in the *cellar*— Why?'

'Looking around,' said the major. 'I looked in that cupboard place under the stairs and then I noticed a door there and I opened it and saw a flight of steps, so I went down there. Nice cellar you've got,' he said to Giles. 'Crypt of an old monastery, I should say.'

'We're not engaged in antiquarian research, Major Metcalf. We're investigating a murder. Will you listen a moment, Mrs Davis? I'll leave the kitchen door open.' He went out; a door shut with a faint creak. 'Is that what you heard, Mrs Davis?' he asked as he reappeared in the open doorway.

'I—it does sound like it.'

'That was the cupboard under the stairs. It could be, you know, that after killing Mrs Boyle, the murderer, retreating across the hall, heard you coming out of the kitchen, and slipped into the cupboard, pulling the door to after him.'

'Then his fingerprints will be on the inside of the cupboard,' cried Christopher.

'Mine are there already,' said Major Metcalf.

'Quite so,' said Sergeant Trotter. 'But we've a satisfactory explanation for those, haven't we?' he added smoothly.

'Look here, Sergeant,' said Giles, 'admittedly you're in charge of this affair. But this is my house, and in a certain degree I feel responsible for the people staying in it. Oughtn't we to take precautionary measures?'

'Such as, Mr Davis?'

'Well, to be frank, putting under restraint the person who seems pretty clearly indicated as the chief suspect.'

He looked straight at Christopher Wren.

Christopher Wren sprang forward, his voice rose, shrill and hysterical. 'It's not true! It's not *true!* You're all against me. Everyone's always against me. You're going to frame me for this. It's persecution—persecution—'

'Steady on, lad,' said Major Metcalf.

'It's all right, Chris.' Molly came forward. She put her hand on his arm. 'Nobody's against you. Tell him it's all right,' she said to Sergeant Trotter.

'We don't frame people,' said Sergeant Trotter.

'Tell him you're not going to arrest him.'

'I'm not going to arrest anyone. To do that, I need evidence. There's no evidence—at present.'

Giles cried out, 'I think you're crazy, Molly. And you, too, Sergeant. There's only one person who fits the bill, and—'

'Wait, Giles, wait—' Molly broke in. 'Oh, do be quiet. Sergeant Trotter, can I—can I speak to you a minute?'

'I'm staying,' said Giles.

'No, Giles, you, too, please.'

Giles's face grew as dark as thunder. He said, 'I don't know what's come over you, Molly.'

He followed the others out of the room, banging the door behind him.

'Yes, Mrs Davis, what is it?'

'Sergeant Trotter, when you told us about the Longridge Farm case, you seemed to think that it must be the eldest boy who is—responsible for all this. But you don't *know* that?'

'That's perfectly true, Mrs Davis. But the probabilities lie that way—mental instability, desertion from the army, psychiatrist's report.'

'Oh, I know, and therefore it all seems to point to Christopher. But I don't believe it *is* Christopher. There must be other—possibilities. Hadn't those three children any relations—parents, for instance?'

'Yes. The mother was dead. But the father was serving abroad.'

'Well, what about him? Where is *he* now?'

'We've no information. He obtained his demobilization papers last year.'

'And if the son was mentally unstable, the father may have been, too.'

'That is so.'

'So the murderer may be middle-aged or old. Major Metcalf, remember, was frightfully upset when I told him the police had rung up. He really *was*.'

Sergeant Trotter said quietly, 'Please believe me, Mrs Davis, I've had all the possibilities in mind since the beginning. The boy, Jim—the father—even the sister. It *could* have been a woman, you know. I haven't overlooked anything. I may be pretty sure in my own mind—but I don't *know*—yet. It's very hard really to know about anything or anyone—especially in these days. You'd be surprised what we see in the police force. With marriages, especially. Hasty marriages—war marriages. There's no background, you see. No families or relations to meet. People accept each other's word. Fellow says he's a fighter pilot or an army major—the girl believes him implicitly. Sometimes she doesn't find out for a year or two that he's an absconding bank clerk with a wife and family, or an army deserter.'

He paused and went on.

'I know quite well what's in your mind, Mrs Davis. There's just one thing I'd like to say to you. *The murderer's enjoying himself.* That's the one thing I'm quite sure of.'

He went towards the door.

Molly stood very straight and still, a red flush burning in her cheeks. After standing rigid for a moment or two, she moved slowly towards the stove, knelt down, and opened the oven door. A savory, familiar smell came towards her. Her heart lightened. It was as though suddenly she had been wafted back into the dear, familiar world of everyday things. Cooking, housework, home-making, ordinary prosaic living.

So, from time immemorial women had cooked food for their men. The world of danger—of madness, receded. Woman, in her kitchen, was safe—eternally safe.

The kitchen door opened. She turned her head as Christopher Wren entered. He was a little breathless.

'My dear,' he said. '*Such* ructions! Somebody's stolen the sergeant's skis!'

'The sergeant's skis? But why should anyone want to do that?'

'I really can't imagine. I mean, if the sergeant decided to go away and leave us, I should imagine that the murderer would be only too pleased. I mean, it really doesn't make *sense,* does it?'

'Giles put them in the cupboard under the stairs.'

'Well, they're not there now. Intriguing, isn't it?' He laughed gleefully. 'The sergeant's awfully angry about it. Snapping like a turtle. He's been pitching into poor Major Metcalf. The old boy sticks to it that he didn't notice whether they were there or not when he looked into the cupboard just before Mrs Boyle was murdered. Trotter says he *must* have noticed. If you ask me,' Christopher lowered his voice and leaned forward, 'this business is beginning to get Trotter down.'

'It's getting us all down,' said Molly.

'Not me. I find it most stimulating. It's all so delightfully unreal.'

Molly said sharply, 'You wouldn't say that if—if you'd been the one to find her. Mrs Boyle, I mean. I keep thinking of it—I can't forget it. Her face—all swollen and purple—'

She shivered. Christopher came across to her. He put a hand on her shoulder.

'I know. I'm an idiot. I'm sorry. I didn't think.'

A dry sob rose in Molly's throat. 'It seemed all right just now—cooking—the kitchen,' she spoke confusedly, incoherently. 'And then suddenly—it was all back again—like a nightmare.'

There was a curious expression on Christopher Wren's face as he stood there looking down on her bent head.

'I see,' he said. 'I see.' He moved away. 'Well, I'd better clear out and—not interrupt you.'

Molly cried, 'Don't go!' just as his hand was on the door handle.

He turned round, looking at her questioningly. Then he came slowly back.

'Do you really mean that?'

'Mean what?'

'You definitely don't want to—go?'

'No, I tell you. I don't want to be alone. I'm afraid to be alone.'

Christopher sat down by the table. Molly bent to the oven, lifted the pie to a higher shelf, shut the oven door, and came and joined him.

'That's very interesting,' said Christopher in a level voice.

'What is?'

'That you're not afraid to be—alone with me. You're not, are you?'

She shook her head. 'No, I'm not.'

'Why aren't you afraid, Molly?'

'I don't know—I'm not.'

'And yet I'm the only person who—fits the bill. One murderer as per schedule.'

'No,' said Molly. 'There are—other possibilities, I've been talking to Sergeant Trotter about them.'

'Did he agree with you?'

'He didn't disagree,' said Molly slowly.

Certain words sounded over and over again in her

head. Especially that last phrase: *I know exactly what's in your mind, Mrs Davis.* But did he? Could he possibly know? He had said, too, that the murderer was enjoying himself. Was that true?

She said to Christopher, '*You're* not exactly enjoying yourself, are you? In spite of what you said just now.'

'Good God, no,' said Christopher, staring. 'What a very odd thing to say.'

'Oh, I didn't say it. Sergeant Trotter did. I hate that man! He—he puts things into your head—things that aren't true—that can't possibly be true.'

She put her hands to her head, covering her eyes with them. Very gently Christopher took those hands away.

'Look here, Molly,' he said, 'what is all this?'

She let him force her gently into a chair by the kitchen table. His manner was no longer hysterical or childish.

'What's the matter, Molly?' he said.

Molly looked at him—a long appraising glance. She asked irrelevantly, 'How long have I known you, Christopher? Two days?'

'Just about. You're thinking, aren't you, that though it's such a short time, we seem to know each other rather well.'

'Yes—it's odd, isn't it?'

'Oh, I don't know. There's a kind of sympathy between us. Possibly because we've both—been up against it.'

It was not a question. It was a statement. Molly let it pass. She said very quietly, and again it was a statement rather than a question, 'Your name isn't really Christopher Wren, is it.'

'No.'

'Why did you—'

'Choose that? Oh, it seemed rather a pleasant whimsy.

They used to jeer at me and call me Christopher Robin at school. Robin—Wren—association of ideas, I suppose.'

'What's your real name?'

Christopher said quietly, 'I don't think we'll go into that. It wouldn't mean anything to you. I'm not an architect. Actually, I'm a deserter from the army.'

Just for a moment swift alarm leaped into Molly's eyes.

Christopher saw it. 'Yes,' he said. 'Just like our unknown murderer. I told you I was the only one the specification fitted.'

'Don't be stupid,' said Molly. 'I told you I didn't believe you were the murderer. Go on—tell me about yourself. What made you desert—nerves?'

'Being afraid, you mean? No, curiously enough, I wasn't afraid—not more than anyone else, that is to say. Actually I got a reputation for being rather cool under fire. No, it was something quite different. It was—my mother.'

'Your mother?'

'Yes—you see, she was killed—in an air raid. Buried. They—they had to dig her out. I don't know what happened to me when I heard about it—I suppose I went a little mad. I thought, you see, it happened to *me*. I felt I had to get home quickly and—and dig myself out—I can't explain—it was all confused.' He lowered his head to his hands and spoke in a muffled voice. 'I wandered about a long time, looking for her—or for myself—I don't know which. And then, when my mind cleared up, I was afraid to go back—or to report—I knew I could never explain. Since then, I've just been—nothing.'

He stared at her, his young face hollow with despair.

'You mustn't feel like that,' said Molly gently. 'You can start again.'

'Can one ever do that?'

'Of course—you're quite young.'

'Yes, but you see—I've come to the end.'

'No,' said Molly. 'You haven't come to the end, you only think you have. I believe everyone has that feeling once, at least, in their lives—that it's the end, that they can't go on.'

'You've had it, haven't you, Molly? You must have—to be able to speak like that.'

'Yes.'

'What was yours?'

'Mine was just what happened to a lot of people. I was engaged to a young fighter pilot—and he was killed.'

'Wasn't there more to it than that?'

'I suppose there was. I'd had a nasty shock when I was younger. I came up against something that was rather cruel and beastly. It predisposed me to think that life was always—horrible. When Jack was killed it just confirmed my belief that the whole of life was cruel and treacherous.'

'I know. And then, I suppose,' said Christopher, watching her, 'Giles came along.'

'Yes.' He saw the smile, tender, almost shy, that trembled on her mouth. 'Giles came—everything felt right and safe and happy—Giles!'

The smile fled from her lips. Her face was suddenly stricken. She shivered as though with cold.

'What's the matter, Molly? What's frightening you? You *are* frightened, aren't you?'

She nodded.

'And it's something to do with Giles? Something he's said or done?'

'It's not Giles, really. It's that horrible man!'

'What horrible man?' Christopher was surprised. 'Paravicini?'

'No, *no*. Sergeant Trotter.'

'Sergeant Trotter?'

'Suggesting things—hinting things—putting horrible thoughts into my mind about Giles—thoughts that I didn't know were there. Oh, I hate him—I hate him.'

Christopher's eyebrows rose in slow surprise. 'Giles? *Giles!* Yes, of course, he and I are much of an age. He seems to me much older than I am—but I suppose he isn't, really. Yes, Giles might fit the bill equally well. But look here, Molly, that's all nonsense. Giles was down here with you the day that woman was killed in London.'

Molly did not answer.

Christopher looked at her sharply. 'Wasn't he here?'

Molly spoke breathlessly, the words coming out in an incoherent jumble. 'He was out all day—in the car—he went over to the other side of the county about some wire netting in a sale there—at least that's what he said—that's what I thought—until—until—'

'Until what?'

Slowly Molly's hand reached out and traced the date of the *Evening Standard* that covered a portion of the kitchen table.

Christopher looked at it and said, 'London edition, two days ago.'

'It was in Giles's pocket when he came back. He—he must have been in London.'

Christopher stared. He stared at the paper and he stared at Molly. He pursed up his lips and began to whistle, then checked himself abruptly. It wouldn't do to whistle that tune just now.

Choosing his words very carefully, and avoiding her

eye, he said, 'How much do you actually—know about Giles?'

'Don't,' cried Molly. 'Don't! That's just what that beast Trotter said—or hinted. That women often didn't know anything about the men that they married—especially in wartime. They—they just took the man's own account of himself.'

'That's true enough, I suppose.'

'Don't *you* say it, too! I can't bear it. It's just because we're all in such a state, so worked up. We'd—we'd believe *any* fantastic suggestion—It's not true! I—'

She stopped. The kitchen door had opened.

Giles came in. There was rather a grim look on his face. 'Am I interrupting anything?' he asked.

Christopher slipped from the table. 'I'm just taking a few cookery lessons,' he said.

'Indeed? Well, look here, Wren, tête-à-têtes aren't very healthy things at the present time. You keep out of the kitchen, do you hear?'

'Oh, but surely—'

'You keep away from my wife, Wren. She's not going to be the next victim.'

'That,' said Christopher, 'is just what I'm worrying about.'

If there was significance in the words, Giles did not apparently notice them. He merely turned a rather darker shade of brick red. 'I'll do the worrying,' he said. 'I can look after my own wife. Get the hell out of here.'

Molly said in a clear voice, 'Please go, Christopher. Yes—really.'

Christopher moved slowly towards the door. 'I shan't go very far,' he said, and the words were addressed to Molly and held a very definite meaning.

'*Will* you get out of here?'

Christopher gave a high childish giggle. 'Aye, aye, Commander,' he said.

The door shut behind him. Giles turned on Molly.

'For God's sake, Molly, haven't you got *any* sense? Shut in here alone with a dangerous homicidal maniac!'

'He isn't the—' she changed her phrase quickly—'he isn't dangerous. Anyway, I'm on my guard. I can—look after myself.'

Giles laughed unpleasantly. 'So could Mrs Boyle.'

'Oh, Giles, *don't*.'

'Sorry, my dear. But I'm het up. That wretched boy. What you see in him I can't imagine.'

Molly said slowly, 'I'm sorry for him.'

'Sorry for a homicidal lunatic?'

Molly gave him a curious glance. 'I could be sorry for a homicidal lunatic,' she said.

'Calling him Christopher, too. Since when have you been on Christian-name terms?'

'Oh Giles, don't be ridiculous. Everyone always uses Christian names nowadays. You know they do.'

'Even after a couple of days? But perhaps it's more than that. Perhaps you knew Mr Christopher Wren, the phony architect, before he came here? Perhaps you suggested to him that he *should* come here? Perhaps you cooked it all up between you?'

Molly stared at him. 'Giles, have you gone out of your mind? What on earth are you suggesting?'

'I'm suggesting that Christopher Wren is an old friend, that you're on rather closer terms with him than you'd like me to know.'

'Giles, you must be crazy!'

'I suppose you'll stick to it that you never saw him until he walked in here. Rather odd that he should come and stay in an out-of-the-way place like this, isn't it?'

'Is it any odder than that Major Metcalf and—and Mrs Boyle should?'

'Yes—I think it is. I've always read that these lunatics had a peculiar fascination for women. Looks as though it were true. How did you get to know him? How long has this been going on?'

'You're being absolutely absurd, Giles. I never saw Christopher Wren until he arrived here.'

'You didn't go up to London to meet him two days ago and fix up to meet here as strangers?'

'You know perfectly well, Giles, I haven't been up to London for weeks.'

'Haven't you? That's interesting.' He fished a fur-lined glove out of his pocket and held it out. 'That's one of the gloves you were wearing day before yesterday, isn't it? The day I was over at Sailham getting the netting.'

'The day *you* were over at Sailham getting the netting,' said Molly, eying him steadily. 'Yes, I wore those gloves when I went out.'

'You went to the village, you said. If you only went to the village, what is this doing inside that glove?'

Accusingly, he held out a pink bus ticket.

There was a moment's silence.

'You went to London,' said Giles.

'All right,' said Molly. Her chin shot up. 'I went to London.'

'To meet this chap Christopher Wren.'

'No, not to meet Christopher.'

'Then why did you go?'

'Just at the moment, Giles,' said Molly, 'I'm not going to tell you.'

'Meaning you'll give yourself time to think up a good story!'

'I think,' said Molly, 'that I hate you!'

'I don't hate you,' said Giles slowly. 'But I almost wish I did. I simply feel that—I don't know you any more—I don't know anything about you.'

'I feel the same,' said Molly. 'You—you're just a stranger. A man who lies to me—'

'When have I ever lied to you?'

Molly laughed. 'Do you think I believed that story of yours about the wire netting? *You* were in London, too, that day.'

'I suppose you saw me there,' said Giles. 'And you didn't trust me enough—'

'Trust you? I'll never trust anyone—ever—again.'

Neither of them had noticed the soft opening of the kitchen door. Mr Paravicini gave a little cough.

'So embarrassing,' he murmured. 'I do hope you young people are not both saying just a little more than you mean. One is so apt to in these lovers' quarrels.'

'Lovers' quarrels,' said Giles derisively. 'That's good.'

'Quite so, quite so,' said Mr Paravicini. 'I know just how you feel. I have been through all this myself when I was a younger man. But what I came to say was that the inspector person is simply insisting that we should all come into the drawing room. It appears that he has an idea.' Mr Paravicini sniggered gently. 'The police have a clue—yes, one hears that frequently. But an *idea?* I very much doubt it. A zealous and painstaking officer, no doubt, our Sergeant Trotter, but not, I think, over endowed with brains.'

'Go on, Giles,' said Molly. 'I've got the cooking to see to. Sergeant Trotter can do without me.'

'Talking of cooking,' said Mr Paravicini, skipping

nimbly across the kitchen to Molly's side, 'have you ever tried chicken livers served on toast that has been thickly spread with *foie gras* and a very thin rasher of bacon smeared with French mustard?'

'One doesn't see much *foie gras* nowadays,' said Giles, 'Come on, Paravicini.'

'Shall I stay and assist you, dear lady?'

'You come along to the drawing room, Paravicini,' said Giles.

Mr Paravicini laughed softly.

'Your husband is afraid for you. Quite natural. He doesn't fancy the idea of leaving you alone with *me.* It is my sadistic tendencies he fears—not my dishonorable ones. I yield to force.' He bowed gracefully and kissed the tips of his fingers.

Molly said uncomfortably, 'Oh, Mr Paravicini, I'm sure—'

Mr Paravicini shook his head. He said to Giles, 'You're very wise, young man. *Take no chances.* Can I prove to you—or to the inspector for that matter—that I am not a homicidal maniac? No, I cannot. Negatives are such difficult things to prove.'

He hummed cheerfully.

Molly flinched. 'Please Mr Paravicini—not that horrible tune.'

'"Three Blind Mice"—so it was! The tune has got into my head. Now I come to think of it, it is a gruesome little rhyme. Not a nice little rhyme at all. But children like gruesome things. You may have noticed that? That rhyme is very English—the bucolic, cruel English countryside. 'She cut off their tails with a carving knife.' Of course a child would love that—I could tell you things about children—'

'Please don't,' said Molly faintly, 'I think you're

cruel, too.' Her voice rose hysterically. 'You laugh and smile—you're like a cat playing with a mouse—playing—'

She began to laugh.

'Steady, Molly,' said Giles. 'Come along, we'll all go into the drawing room together. Trotter will be getting impatient. Never mind the cooking. Murder is more important than food.'

'I'm not sure that I agree with you,' said Mr Paravicini as he followed them with little skipping steps. 'The condemned man ate a hearty breakfast—that's what they always say.'

Christopher Wren joined them in the hall and received a scowl from Giles. He looked at Molly with a quick, anxious glance, but Molly, her head held high, walked looking straight ahead of her. They marched almost like a procession to the drawing room door. Mr Paravicini brought up the rear with his little skipping steps.

Sergeant Trotter and Major Metcalf were standing waiting in the drawing room. The major was looking sulky. Sergeant Trotter was looking flushed and energetic.

'That's right,' he said, as they entered. 'I wanted you all together. I want to make a certain experiment—and for that I shall require your cooperation.'

'Will it take long?' Molly asked. 'I'm rather busy in the kitchen. After all, we've got to have a meal sometime.'

'Yes,' said Trotter. 'I appreciate that, Mrs Davis. But, if you'll excuse me, there are more important things than meals! Mrs Boyle, for instance, won't need another meal.'

'Really, Sergeant,' said Major Metcalf, 'that's an extraordinarily tactless way of putting things.'

'I'm sorry, Major Metcalf, but I want everyone to cooperate in this.'

'Have you found your skis, Sergeant Trotter?' asked Molly.

The young man reddened. 'No, I have not, Mrs Davis. But I may say I have a very shrewd suspicion who took them. And of why they were taken. I won't say any more at present.'

'Please don't,' begged Mr Paravicini. 'I always think explanations should be kept to the very end—that exciting last chapter, you know.'

'This isn't a game, sir.'

'Isn't it? Now there I think you're wrong. I think it *is* a game—to somebody.'

'The *murderer* is enjoying himself,' murmured Molly softly. The others looked at her in astonishment. She flushed.

'I'm only quoting what Sergeant Trotter said to me.'

Sergeant Trotter did not look too pleased. 'It's all very well, Mr Paravicini, mentioning last chapters and speaking as though this was a mystery thriller,' he said. 'This is real. This is happening.'

'So long,' said Christopher Wren, fingering his neck gingerly, 'as it doesn't happen to me.'

'Now, then,' said Major Metcalf. 'None of that, young fellow. The sergeant here is going to tell us just what he wants us to do.'

Sergeant Trotter cleared his throat. His voice became official.

'I took certain statements from you all a short time ago,' he said. 'Those statements related to your positions at the time when the murder of Mrs Boyle occurred. Mr Wren and Mr Davis were in their separate bedrooms. Mrs Davis was in the kitchen. Major Metcalf was in the cellar. Mr Paravicini was here in this room—'

He paused and then went on.

'Those are the statements you made. I have no means of checking those statements. They may be true—they may not. To put it quite clearly—four of those statements are true—but *one of them is false.* Which one?'

He looked from face to face. Nobody spoke.

'Four of you are speaking the truth—one is lying. I have a plan that may help me to discover the liar. And if I discover that one of you lied to me—then I know who the murderer is.'

Giles said sharply, 'Not necessarily. Someone might have lied—for some other reason.'

'I rather doubt that, Mr Davis.'

'But what's the idea, man? You've just said you've no means of checking these statements?'

'No, but supposing everyone was to go through these movements a second time.'

'Bah,' said Major Metcalf disparagingly. 'Reconstruction of the crime. Foreign idea.'

'Not a reconstruction of the *crime,* Major Metcalf. A reconstruction of the movements of apparently innocent persons.'

'And what do you expect to learn from that?'

'You will forgive me if I don't make that clear just at the moment.'

'You want,' asked Molly, 'a repeat performance?'

'More or less, Mrs Davis.'

There was a silence. It was, somehow, an uneasy silence.

It's a trap, thought Molly. *It's a trap—but I don't see how—*

You might have thought that there were five guilty people in the room, instead of one guilty and four innocent ones. One and all cast doubtful sideways glances at the assured, smiling young man who proposed this innocent-sounding maneuver.

Christopher burst out shrilly, 'But I don't see—I simply can't see—what you can possibly hope to find out—just by making people do the same thing they did before. It seems to me just nonsense!'

'Does it, Mr Wren?'

'Of course,' said Giles slowly, 'what you say goes, Sergeant. We'll co-operate. Are we all to do exactly what we did before?'

'The same actions will be performed, yes.'

A faint ambiguity in the phrase made Major Metcalf look up sharply. Sergeant Trotter went on.

'Mr Paravicini has told us that he sat at the piano and played a certain tune. Perhaps, Mr Paravicini, you would kindly show us exactly what you did do?'

'But certainly, my dear Sergeant.'

Mr Paravicini skipped nimbly across the room to the grand piano and settled himself on the music stool.

'The maestro at the piano will play the signature tune to a murder,' he said with a flourish.

He grinned, and with elaborate mannerisms he picked out with one finger the tune of "Three Blind Mice."

He's enjoying himself, thought Molly. *He's enjoying himself.*

In the big room the soft, muted notes had an almost eerie effect.

'Thank you, Mr Paravicini,' said Sergeant Trotter. 'That, I take it, is exactly how you played the tune on the—former occasion?'

'Yes, Sergeant, it is. I repeated it three times.'

Sergeant Trotter turned to Molly. 'Do you play the piano, Mrs Davis?'

'Yes, Sergeant Trotter.'

'Could you pick out the tune, as Mr Paravicini has done, playing it in exactly the same manner?'

'Certainly I could.'

'Then will you go and sit at the piano and be ready to do so when I give the signal?'

Molly looked slightly bewildered. Then she crossed slowly to the piano.

Mr Paravicini rose from the piano stool with a shrill protest. 'But, Sergeant, I understood that we were each to repeat our former roles. *I* was at the piano here.'

'The same actions will be performed as on the former occasion—*but they will not necessarily be performed by the same people.*'

'I—don't see the point of that,' said Giles.

'There *is* a point, Mr Davis. It is a means of checking up on the original statements—and I may say of *one* statement in particular. Now, then, please. I will assign you your various stations. Mrs Davis will be here—at the piano. Mr Wren, will you kindly go to the kitchen? Just keep an eye on Mrs Davis's dinner. Mr Paravicini, will you go to Mr Wren's bedroom? There you can exercise your musical talents by whistling "Three Blind Mice" just as he did. Major Metcalf, will you go up to Mr Davis's bedroom and examine the telephone there? And you, Mr Davis, will you look into the cupboard in the hall and then go down to the cellar?'

There was a moment's silence. Then four people moved slowly towards the door. Trotter followed them. He looked over his shoulder.

'Count up to fifty and then begin to play, Mrs Davis,' he said.

He followed the others out. Before the door closed Molly heard Mr Paravicini's voice say shrilly, 'I never knew the police were so fond of parlor games.'

'Forty-eight, forty-nine, fifty.'

Obediently, the counting finished, Molly began to play. Again the soft cruel little tune crept out into the big, echoing room.

Three Blind Mice
See how they run. . . .

Molly felt her heart beating faster and faster. As Paravicini had said, it was a strangely haunting and gruesome little rhyme. It had that childish incomprehension of pity which is so terrifying if met with in an adult.

Very faintly, from upstairs, she could hear the same tune being whistled in the bedroom above—Paravicini enacting the part of Christopher Wren.

Suddenly, next door, the wireless went on in the library. Sergeant Trotter must have set that going. He himself, then, was playing the part of Mrs Boyle.

But why? What was the point of it all? Where was the trap? For there was a trap, of that she was certain.

A draft of cold air blew across the back of her neck. She turned her head sharply. Surely the door had opened. Someone had come into the room—No, the room was empty. But suddenly she felt nervous—afraid. If someone *should* come in. Supposing Mr Paravicini should skip round the door, should come skipping over to the piano, his long fingers twitching and twisting—

'So you are playing your own funeral march, dear lady, a happy thought—' *Nonsense—don't be stupid—don't*

imagine things. Besides, you can hear him whistling over your head, just as he can hear you.

She almost took her fingers off the piano as the idea came to her! Nobody *had* heard Mr Paravicini playing. Was that the trap? Was it, perhaps, possible that Mr Paravicini hadn't been playing at all? That he had been, not in the drawing room, but in the library. In the library, strangling Mrs Boyle?

He had been annoyed, very annoyed, when Trotter had arranged for her to play. He had laid stress on the softness with which he had picked out the tune. Of course, he had emphasized the softness in the hopes that it would be too soft to be heard outside the room. Because if anyone heard it this time who hadn't heard it last time—why then, Trotter would have got what he wanted—*the person who had lied*.

The door of the drawing room opened. Molly, strung up to expect Paravicini, nearly screamed. But it was only Sergeant Trotter who entered, just as she finished the third repetition of the tune.

'Thank you, Mrs Davis,' he said.

He was looking extremely pleased with himself, and his manner was brisk and confident.

Molly took her hands from the keys. 'Have you got what you wanted?' she asked.

'Yes, indeed.' His voice was exultant. 'I've got exactly what I wanted.'

'Which? Who?'

'Don't you know, Mrs Davis? Come, now—it's not so difficult. By the way, you've been, if I may say so, extraordinarily foolish. You've left me hunting about for the third victim. As a result, you've been in serious danger.'

'Me? I don't know what you mean.'

'I mean that you haven't been honest with me, Mrs Davis. You held out on me—just as Mrs Boyle held out on me.'

'I don't understand.'

'Oh, yes, you do. Why, when I first mentioned the Longridge Farm case, *you knew all about it.* Oh, yes, you did. You were upset. And it was you who confirmed that Mrs Boyle was the billeting officer for this part of the country. Both you and she came from these parts. So when I began to speculate who the third victim was likely to be, I plumped at once for you. You'd shown firsthand knowledge of the Longridge Farm business. We policemen aren't so dumb as we look, you know.'

Molly said in a low voice, 'You don't understand. I didn't want to remember.'

'I can understand that.' His voice changed a little. 'Your maiden name was Wainwright, wasn't it?'

'Yes.'

'And you're just a little older than you pretend to be. In 1940, when this thing happened, you were the schoolteacher at Abbeyvale school.'

'No!'

'Oh, yes, you were, Mrs Davis.'

'I wasn't, I tell you.'

'The child who died managed to get a letter posted to you. He stole a stamp. The letter begged for help—help from his kind teacher. It's a teacher's business to find out why a child doesn't come to school. You didn't find out. You ignored the poor little devil's letter.'

'Stop.' Molly's cheeks were flaming. 'It's my sister you are talking about. She was the schoolmistress. And she didn't ignore his letter. She was ill—with pneumonia. She never saw the letter until after the child was dead. It upset her dreadfully—dreadfully—she was a terribly sensitive person. But it wasn't her fault. It's because she took it to heart so dreadfully that I've never been able to bear being reminded of it. It's been a nightmare to me, always.'

Molly's hands went to her eyes, covering them. When she took them away, Trotter was staring at her.

He said softly, 'So it was your sister. Well, after all—' He gave a sudden queer smile. 'It doesn't much matter, does it? Your sister—*my* brother—' He took something out of his pocket. He was smiling now, happily.

Molly stared at the object he held. 'I always thought the police didn't carry revolvers,' she said.

'The police don't,' said the young man. He went on, 'But you see, Mrs Davis, *I'm not a policeman.* I'm Jim. I'm Georgie's brother. You thought I was a policeman because I rang up from the call box in the village and said that Sergeant Trotter was on his way. Then I cut the telephone wires outside the house when I got here, so that you shouldn't be able to ring back to the police station.'

Molly stared at him. The revolver was pointing at her now.

'Don't move, Mrs Davis—and don't scream—or I pull the trigger at once.'

He was still smiling. It was, Molly realized with horror, a child's smile. And his voice, when he spoke, was becoming a child's voice.

'Yes,' he said, 'I'm Georgie's brother. Georgie died at Longridge Farm. That nasty woman sent us there, and the farmer's wife was cruel to us, and you wouldn't help us—three little blind mice. I said then I'd kill you all when I grew up. I meant it. I've thought of it ever since.' He frowned suddenly. 'They bothered me a lot in the army—that doctor kept asking me questions—I had to get away. I was afraid they'd stop me doing what I wanted to do. But I'm grown up now. Grown-ups can do what they like.'

Molly pulled herself together. *Talk to him,* she said to herself. *Distract his mind.*

'But, Jim, listen,' she said. 'You'll never get safely away.'

His face clouded over. 'Somebody's hidden my skis. I can't find them.' He laughed. 'But I daresay it will be all right. It's your husband's revolver. I took it out of his drawer. I daresay they'll think *he* shot you. Anyway—I don't much care. It's been such fun—all of it. Pretending! That woman in London, her face when she recognized me. That stupid woman this morning!'

He nodded his head.

Clearly, with eerie effect, came a whistle. Someone whistling the tune of 'Three Blind Mice.'

Trotter started, the revolver wavered—a voice shouted, 'Down, Mrs Davis.'

Molly dropped to the floor as Major Metcalf, rising from behind the concealment of the sofa by the door flung himself upon Trotter. The revolver went off—and the bullet lodged in one of the somewhat mediocre oil paintings dear to the heart of the late Miss Emory.

A moment later, all was pandemonium—Giles rushed in, followed by Christopher and Mr Paravicini.

Major Metcalf, retaining his grasp of Trotter, spoke in short explosive sentences.

'Came in while you were playing—slipped behind the sofa—I've been on to him from the beginning—that's to say, I knew he wasn't a police officer. *I'm* a police officer—Inspector Tanner. We arranged with Metcalf I should take his place. Scotland Yard thought it advisable to have someone on the spot. Now, my lad—'

He spoke quite gently to the now docile Trotter. 'You come with me. No one will hurt you. You'll be all right. We'll look after you.'

In a piteous child's voice the bronzed young man asked, 'Georgie won't be angry with me?'

Metcalf said, 'No. Georgie won't be angry.'

He murmured to Giles as he passed him, 'Mad as a hatter, poor devil.'

They went out together. Mr Paravicini touched Christopher Wren on the arm.

'You, also, my friend,' he said, 'come with me.'

Giles and Molly, left alone, looked at each other. In another moment they were in each other's arms.

'Darling,' said Giles, 'you're sure he didn't hurt you?'

'No, no, I'm quite all right. Giles, I've been so terribly mixed up. I almost thought you—why did you go to London that day?'

'Darling, I wanted to get you an anniversary present, for tomorrow. I didn't want you to know.'

'How extraordinary! *I* went to London to get *you* a present and I didn't want you to know.'

'I was insanely jealous of that neurotic ass. I must have been mad. Forgive me, darling.'

The door opened, and Mr Paravicini skipped in in his goatlike way. He was beaming.

'Interrupting the reconciliation—Such a charming scene—But, alas, I must bid you adieu. A police jeep has managed to get through. I shall persuade them to take me with them.' He bent and whispered mysteriously in Molly's ear, 'I may have a few embarrassments in the near future—but I am confident I can arrange matters, and if you should receive a case—with a goose, say, a turkey, some tins of *foie gras,* a ham—some nylon stockings, yes? Well, you understand, it will be with my compliments to a very charming lady. Mr Davis, my check is on the hall table.'

He kissed Molly's hand and skipped to the door.

'Nylons?' murmured Molly, '*Foie gras?* Who is Mr Paravicini? Santa Claus?'

'Black-market style, I suspect,' said Giles.

Christopher Wren poked a diffident head in. 'My dears,' he said, 'I hope I'm not intruding, but there's a terrible smell of burning from the kitchen. Ought I to *do* something about it?'

With an anguished cry of '*My pie!*' Molly fled from the room.

The Chocolate Box

It was a wild night. Outside, the wind howled malevolently, and the rain beat against the windows in great gusts.

Poirot and I sat facing the hearth, our legs stretched out to the cheerful blaze. Between us was a small table. On my side of it stood some carefully brewed hot toddy; on Poirot's was a cup of thick, rich chocolate which I would not have drunk for a hundred pounds! Poirot sipped the thick brown mess in the pink china cup, and sighed with contentment.

'*Quelle belle vie*!' he murmured.

'Yes, it's a good old world,' I agreed. 'Here am I with a job, and a good job too! And here are you, famous—'

'Oh, *mon ami*!' protested Poirot.

'But you are. And rightly so! When I think back on your long line of successes, I am positively amazed. I don't believe you know what failure is!'

'He would be a droll kind of original who could say that!'

'No, but seriously, *have* you ever failed?'

'Innumerable times, my friend. What would you? *La bonne chance*, it cannot always be on your side. I have been called in too late. Very often another, working towards the same goal, has arrived there first. Twice have I been stricken down with illness just as I was on the point of success. One must take the downs with the ups, my friend.'

'I didn't quite mean that,' I said. 'I meant, had you ever been completely down and out over a case through your own fault?'

'Ah, I comprehend! You ask if I have ever made the complete prize ass of myself, as you say over here? Once, my friend—' A slow, reflective smile hovered over his face. 'Yes, once I made a fool of myself.'

He sat up suddenly in his chair.

'See here, my friend, you have, I know, kept a record of my little successes. You shall add one more story to the collection, the story of a failure!'

He leaned forward and placed a log on the fire. Then, after carefully wiping his hands on a little duster that hung on a nail by the fireplace, he leaned back and commenced his story.

That of which I tell you (said M. Poirot) took place in Belgium many years ago. It was at the time of the terrible struggle in France between church and state. M. Paul Déroulard was a French deputy of note. It was an open secret that the portfolio of a Minister awaited him. He was among the bitterest of the anti-Catholic party, and it was certain that on his accession to power, he would have to face violent enmity. He was in many ways a peculiar man. Though he neither drank nor smoked, he was nevertheless not so scrupulous in other ways. You comprehend, Hastings, *c'était des femmes—toujours des femmes*!

He had married some years earlier a young lady from Brussels who had brought him a substantial *dot*. Undoubtedly the money was useful to him in his career, as his family was not rich, though on the other hand he was entitled to call himself M. le Baron if he chose.

There were no children of the marriage, and his wife died after two years—the result of a fall downstairs. Among the property which she bequeathed to him was a house on the Avenue Louise in Brussels.

It was in this house that his sudden death took place, the event coinciding with the resignation of the Minister whose portfolio he was to inherit. All the papers printed long notices of his career. His death, which had taken place quite suddenly in the evening after dinner, was attributed to heart-failure.

At that time, *mon ami*, I was, as you know, a member of the Belgian detective force. The death of M. Paul Déroulard was not particularly interesting to me. I am, as you also know, *bon catholique*, and his demise seemed to me fortunate.

It was some three days afterwards, when my vacation had just begun, that I received a visitor at my own apartments—a lady, heavily veiled, but evidently quite young; and I perceived at once that she was a *jeune fille tout à fait comme il faut.*

'You are Monsieur Hercule Poirot?' she asked in a low sweet voice.

I bowed.

'Of the detective service?'

Again I bowed. 'Be seated, I pray of you, mademoiselle,' I said.

She accepted a chair and drew aside her veil. Her face was charming, though marred with tears, and haunted as though with some poignant anxiety.

'Monsieur,' she said, 'I understand that you are now taking a vacation. Therefore you will be free to take up a private case. You understand that I do not wish to call in the police.'

I shook my head. 'I fear what you ask is impossible,

mademoiselle. Even though on vacation, I am still of the police.'

She leaned forward. '*Ecoutez, monsieur.* All that I ask of you is to investigate. The result of your investigations you are at perfect liberty to report to the police. If what I believe to be true *is* true, we shall need all the machinery of the law.'

That placed a somewhat different complexion on the matter, and I placed myself at her service without more ado.

A slight colour rose in her cheeks. 'I thank you, monsieur. It is the death of M. Paul Déroulard that I ask you to investigate.'

'*Comment*?' I exclaimed, surprised.

'Monsieur, I have nothing to go upon—nothing but my woman's instinct, but I am convinced—*convinced*, I tell you—that M. Déroulard did not die a natural death!'

'But surely the doctors—'

'Doctors may be mistaken. He was so robust, so strong. Ah, Monsieur Poirot, I beseech of you to help me—'

The poor child was almost beside herself. She would have knelt to me. I soothed her as best I could.

'I will help you, mademoiselle. I feel almost sure that your fears are unfounded, but we will see. First, I will ask you to describe to me the inmates of the house.'

'There are the domestics, of course, Jeannette, Félice, and Denise the cook. She has been there many years; the others are simple country girls. Also there is François, but he too is an old servant. Then there is Monsieur Déroulard's mother who lived with him, and myself. My name is Virginie Mesnard. I am a poor cousin of the late Madame Déroulard, M. Paul's wife, and I have been a member of their ménage for over three years. I have now described to you the household. There were also two guests staying in the house.'

'And they were?'

'M. de Saint Alard, a neighbour of M. Déroulard's in France. Also an English friend, Mr John Wilson.'

'Are they still with you?'

'Mr Wilson, yes, but M. de Saint Alard departed yesterday.'

'And what is your plan, Mademoiselle Mesnard?'

'If you will present yourself at the house in half an hour's time, I will have arranged some story to account for your presence. I had better represent you to be connected with journalism in some way. I shall say you have come from Paris, and that you have brought a card of introduction from M. de Saint Alard. Madame Déroulard is very feeble in health, and will pay little attention to details.'

On mademoiselle's ingenious pretext I was admitted to the house, and after a brief interview with the dead deputy's mother, who was a wonderfully imposing and aristocratic figure though obviously in failing health, I was made free of the premises.

I wonder, my friend (continued Poirot), whether you can possibly figure to yourself the difficulties of my task? Here was a man whose death had taken place three days previously. If there *had* been foul play, only one possibility was admittable—*poison*! And I had no chance of seeing the body, and there was no possibility of examining, or analysing, any medium in which the poison could have been administered. There were no clues, false or otherwise, to consider. Had the man been poisoned? Had he died a natural death? I, Hercule Poirot, with nothing to help me, had to decide.

First, I interviewed the domestics, and with their aid, I recapitulated the evening. I paid especial notice to the food at dinner, and the method of serving it. The soup had been served by M. Déroulard himself from a tureen. Next a dish of cutlets, then a chicken. Finally, a compote of fruits. And all placed on the table, and served by Monsieur himself. The coffee was brought in a big pot to the dinner-table. Nothing there, *mon ami*—impossible to poison one without poisoning all!

After dinner Madame Déroulard had retired to her own apartments and Mademoiselle Virginie had accompanied her. The three men had adjourned to M. Déroulard's study. Here they had chatted amicably for some time, when suddenly, without any warning, the deputy had fallen heavily to the ground. M. de Saint Alard had rushed out and told François to fetch the doctor immediately. He said it was without doubt an apoplexy, explained the man. But when the doctor arrived, the patient was past help.

Mr John Wilson, to whom I was presented by Mademoiselle Virginie, was what was known in those days as a regular John Bull Englishman, middle-aged and burly. His account, delivered in very British French, was substantially the same.

'Déroulard went very red in the face, and down he fell.'

There was nothing further to be found out there. Next I went to the scene of the tragedy, the study, and was left alone there at my own request. So far there was nothing to support Mademoiselle Mesnard's theory. I could not but believe that it was a delusion on her part. Evidently she had entertained a romantic passion for the dead man which had not permitted her to take a normal view of the case. Nevertheless, I searched the study with meticulous care. It was just possible that a hypodermic needle might have been introduced into the dead man's chair in such a way as to allow of a fatal injection. The minute puncture it would cause was likely to remain unnoticed. But I could discover no sign to support the theory. I flung myself down in the chair with a gesture of despair.

'*Enfin*, I abandon it!' I said aloud. 'There is not a clue anywhere! Everything is perfectly normal.'

As I said the words, my eyes fell on a large box of chocolates standing on a table near by, and my heart gave a leap. It might not be a clue to M. Déroulard's death, but here at least was something that was *not* normal. I lifted the lid. The box was full, untouched; not a chocolate was missing—but that only made the peculiarity that had caught my eye more striking. For, see you, Hastings, while the box itself was pink, the lid was *blue*. Now, one often sees a blue ribbon on a pink box, and vice versa, but a box of one colour, and a lid of another—no, decidedly—*ça ne se voit jamais*!

I did not as yet see that this little incident was of any use to me, yet I determined to investigate it as being out of the ordinary. I rang the bell for François, and asked him if his late master had been fond of sweets. A faint melancholy smile came to his lips.

'Passionately fond of them, monsieur. He would always have a box of chocolates in the house. He did not drink wine of any kind, you see.'

'Yet this box has not been touched?' I lifted the lid to show him.

'Pardon, monsieur, but that was a new box purchased on the day of his death, the other being nearly finished.'

'Then the other box was finished on the day of his death,' I said slowly.

'Yes, monsieur, I found it empty in the morning and threw it away.'

'Did M. Déroulard eat sweets at all hours of the day?'

'Usually after dinner, monsieur.'

I began to see light.

'François,' I said, 'you can be discreet?'

'If there is need, monsieur.'

'*Bon*! Know, then, that I am of the police. Can you find me that other box?'

'Without doubt, monsieur. It will be in the dustbin.'

He departed, and returned in a few minutes with a dust-covered object. It was the duplicate of the box I held, save for the fact that this time the box was *blue* and the lid was *pink*. I thanked François, recommended him once more to be discreet, and left the house in the Avenue Louise without more ado.

Next I called upon the doctor who had attended M. Déroulard. With him I had a difficult task. He entrenched himself prettily behind a wall of learned phraseology, but I fancied that he was not quite as sure about the case as he would like to be.

'There have been many curious occurrences of the kind,' he observed, when I had managed to disarm him somewhat. 'A sudden fit of anger, a violent emotion—after a heavy dinner, *c'est entendu*—then, with an access of rage, the blood flies to the head, and *pst*!—there you are!'

'But M. Déroulard had had no violent emotion.'

'No? I made sure that he had been having a stormy altercation with M. de Saint Alard.'

'Why should he?'

'*C'est évident*!' The doctor shrugged his shoulders. 'Was not M. de Saint Alard a Catholic of the most fanatical? Their friendship was being ruined by this question of church and state. Not a day passed without discussions. To M. de Saint Alard, Déroulard appeared almost as Antichrist.'

This was unexpected, and gave me food for thought.

'One more question, Doctor: would it be possible to introduce a fatal dose of poison into a chocolate?'

'It would be possible, I suppose,' said the doctor slowly. 'Pure prussic acid would meet the case if there were no chance of evaporation, and a tiny globule of anything might be swallowed unnoticed—but it does not seem a very likely supposition. A chocolate full of morphine or strychnine—' He made a wry face. 'You comprehend, M. Poirot—one bite would be enough! The unwary one would not stand upon ceremony.'

'Thank you, M. le Docteur.'

I withdrew. Next I made inquiries of the chemists, especially those in the neighbourhood of the Avenue Louise. It is good to be of the police. I got the information I wanted without any trouble. Only in one case could I hear of any poison having been supplied to the house in question. This was some eye drops of atropine sulphate for Madame Déroulard. Atropine is a potent poison, and for the moment I was elated, but the symptoms of atropine poisoning are closely allied to those of ptomaine, and bear no resemblance to those I was studying. Besides, the prescription was an old one. Madame Déroulard had suffered from cataract in both eyes for many years.

I was turning away discouraged when the chemist's voice called me back.

'*Un moment, M. Poirot*. I remember, the girl who brought that prescription, she said something about having to go on to the *English* chemist. You might try there.'

I did. Once more enforcing my official status, I got the information I wanted. On the day before M. Déroulard's death they had made up a prescription for Mr John Wilson. Not that there was any making up about it. They were simply little tablets of trinitrine. I asked if I might see some. He showed me them, and my heart beat faster—for the tiny tablets were of *chocolate*.

'Is it a poison?' I asked.

'No, monsieur.'

'Can you describe to me its effect?'

'It lowers the blood-pressure. It is given for some forms of heart trouble—angina pectoris for instance. It relieves the arterial tension. In arteriosclerosis—'

I interrupted him. '*Ma foi*! This rigmarole says nothing to me. Does it cause the face to flush?'

'Certainly it does.'

'And supposing I ate ten—twenty of your little tablets, what then?'

'I should not advise you to attempt it,' he replied drily.

'And yet you say it is not poison?'

'There are many things not called poison which can kill a man,' he replied as before.

I left the shop elated. At last, things had begun to march!

I now knew that John Wilson had the means for the crime—but what about the motive? He had come to Belgium on business, and had asked M. Déroulard, whom he knew slightly, to put him up. There was apparently no way in which Déroulard's death could benefit him. Moreover, I discovered by inquiries in England that he had suffered for some years from that painful form of heart disease known as angina. Therefore he had a genuine right to have those tablets in his possession. Nevertheless, I was convinced that someone had gone to the chocolate box, opening the full one first by mistake, and had abstracted the contents of the last chocolate, cramming in instead as many little trinitrine tablets as it would hold. The chocolates were large ones. Between twenty or thirty tablets, I felt sure, could have been inserted. But who had done this?

There were two guests in the house. John Wilson had the means. Saint Alard had the motive. Remember, he was a fanatic, and there is no fanatic like a religious fanatic. Could he, by any means, have got hold of John Wilson's trinitrine?

Another little idea came to me. Ah, you smile at my little ideas! Why had Wilson run out of trinitrine? Surely he would bring an adequate supply from England. I called once more at the house in the Avenue Louise. Wilson was out, but I saw the girl who did his room, Félicie. I demanded of her immediately whether it was not true that M. Wilson had lost a bottle from his washstand some little time ago. The girl responded eagerly. It was quite true. She, Félicie, had been blamed for it. The English gentleman had evidently thought that she had broken it, and did not like to say so. Whereas she had never even touched it. Without doubt it was Jeannette always nosing round where she had no business to be—

I calmed the flow of words, and took my leave. I knew now all that I wanted to know. It remained for me to prove my case. That, I felt, would not be easy. *I* might be sure that Saint Alard had removed the bottle of trinitrine from John Wilson's washstand, but to convince others, I would have to produce evidence. And I had none to produce!

Never mind. I *knew*—that was the great thing. You remember our difficulty in the Styles case, Hastings?

There again, I *knew*—but it took me a long time to find the last link which made my chain of evidence against the murderer complete.

I asked for an interview with Mademoiselle Mesnard. She came at once. I demanded of her the address of M. de Saint Alard. A look of trouble came over her face.

'Why do you want it, monsieur?'

'Mademoiselle, it is necessary.'

She seemed doubtful—troubled.

'He can tell you nothing. He is a man whose thoughts are not in this world. He hardly notices what goes on around him.'

'Possibly, mademoiselle. Nevertheless, he was an old friend of M. Déroulard's. There may be things he can tell me—things of the past—old grudges—old love-affairs.'

The girl flushed and bit her lip. 'As you please—but—but I feel sure now that I have been mistaken. It was good of you to accede to my demand, but I was upset—almost distraught at the time. I see now that there is no mystery to solve. Leave it, I beg of you, monsieur.'

I eyed her closely.

'Mademoiselle,' I said, 'it is sometimes difficult for a dog to find a scent, but once he *has* found it, nothing on earth will make him leave it! That is if he is a good dog! And I, mademoiselle, I, Hercule Poirot, am a very good dog.'

Without a word she turned away. A few minutes later she returned with the address written on a sheet of paper. I left the house. François was waiting for me outside. He looked at me anxiously.

'There is no news, monsieur?'

'None as yet, my friend.'

'Ah! *Pauvre* Monsieur Déroulard!' he sighed. 'I too was of his way of thinking. I do not care for priests. Not that I would say so in the house. The women are all devout—a good thing perhaps. *Madame est très pieuse—et Mademoiselle Virginie aussi.*'

Mademoiselle Virginie? Was she '*très pieuse*?' Thinking of the tear-stained passionate face I had seen that first day, I wondered.

Having obtained the address of M. de Saint Alard, I wasted no time. I arrived in the neighbourhood of his château in the Ardennes but it was some days before I could find a pretext for gaining admission to the house. In the end I did—how do you think—as a plumber, *mon ami*! It was the affair of a moment to arrange a neat little gas leak in his bedroom. I departed for my tools, and took care to return with them at an hour when I knew I should have the field pretty well to myself. What I was searching for, I hardly knew. The one thing needful, I could not believe there was any chance of finding. He would never have run the risk of keeping it.

Still when I found the little cupboard above the washstand locked, I could not resist the temptation of seeing what was inside it. The lock was quite a simple one to pick. The door swung open. It was full of old bottles. I took them up one by one with a trembling hand. Suddenly, I uttered a cry. Figure to yourself, my friend, I held in my hand a little phial with an English chemist's label. On it were the words: '*Trinitrine Tablets. One to be taken when required. Mr John Wilson.*'

I controlled my emotion, closed the cupboard, slipped the bottle into my pocket, and continued to repair the gas leak! One must be methodical. Then I left the château, and took train for my own country as soon as possible. I arrived in Brussels late that night. I was writing out a report for the préfet in the morning, when a note was brought to me. It was from old Madame Déroulard, and it summoned me to the house in the Avenue Louise without delay.

François opened the door to me.

'Madame la Baronne is awaiting you.'

He conducted me to her apartments. She sat in state in a large armchair. There was no sign of Mademoiselle Virginie.

'M. Poirot,' said the old lady, 'I have just learned that you are not what you pretend to be. You are a police officer.'

'That is so, madame.'

'You came here to inquire into the circumstances of my son's death?'

Again I replied: 'That is so, madame.'

'I should be glad if you would tell me what progress you have made.'

I hesitated.

'First I would like to know how you have learned all this, madame.'

'From one who is no longer of this world.'

Her words, and the brooding way she uttered them, sent a chill to my heart. I was incapable of speech.

'Therefore, monsieur, I would beg of you most urgently to tell me exactly what progress you have made in your investigation.'

'Madame, my investigation is finished.'

'My son?'

'Was killed deliberately.'

'You know by whom?'

'Yes, madame.'

'Who, then?'

'M. de Saint Alard.'

'You are wrong. M. de Saint Alard is incapable of such a crime.'

'The proofs are in my hands.'

'I beg of you once more to tell me all.'

This time I obeyed, going over each step that had led me to the discovery of the truth. She listened attentively. At the end she nodded her head.

'Yes, yes, it is all as you say, all but one thing. It was not M. de Saint Alard who killed my son. It was I, his mother.'

I stared at her. She continued to nod her head gently.

'It is well that I sent for you. It is the providence of the good God that Virginie told me before she departed for the convent, what she had done. Listen, M. Poirot! My son was an evil man. He persecuted the church. He led a life of mortal sin. He dragged down the other souls beside his own. But there was worse than that. As I came out of my room in this house one morning, I saw my daughter-in-law standing at the head of the stairs. She was reading a letter. I saw my son steal up behind her. One swift push, and she fell, striking her head on the marble steps. When they picked her up she was dead. My son was a murderer, and only I, his mother, knew it.'

She closed her eyes for a moment. 'You cannot conceive, monsieur, of my agony, my despair. What was I to do? Denounce him to the police? I could not bring myself to do it. It was my duty, but my flesh was weak. Besides, would they believe me? My eyesight had been failing for some time—they would say I was mistaken. I kept silence. But my conscience gave me no peace. By keeping silence I too was a murderer. My son inherited his wife's money. He flourished as the green bay tree. And now he was to have a Minister's portfolio. His persecution of the church would be redoubled. And there was Virginie. She, poor child, beautiful, naturally pious, was fascinated by him. He had a strange and terrible power over women. I saw it coming. I was powerless to prevent it. He had no intention of marrying her. The time came when she was ready to yield everything to him.

'Then I saw my path clear. He was my son. I had given him life. I was responsible for him. He had killed one woman's body, now he would kill another's soul! I went to Mr Wilson's room, and took the bottle of tablets. He had once said laughingly that there were enough in it to kill a man! I went into the study and opened the big box of chocolates that always stood on the table. I opened a new box by mistake. The other was on the table also. There was just one chocolate left in it. That simplified things. No one ate chocolates except my son and Virginie. I would keep her with me that night. All went as I had planned—'

She paused, closing her eyes a minute then opened them again.

'M. Poirot, I am in your hands. They tell me I have not many days to live. I am willing to answer for my action before the good God. Must I answer for it on earth also?'

I hesitated. 'But the empty bottle, madame,' I said to gain time. 'How came that into M. de Saint Alard's possession?'

'When he came to say goodbye to me, monsieur, I slipped it into his pocket. I did not know how to get rid of it. You see, I cannot move about much without help, and finding it empty in my rooms might have caused suspicion. You understand, monsieur—' she drew herself up to her full height—'it was with no idea of casting suspicion on M. de Saint Alard! I never dreamed of such a thing. I thought his valet would find an empty bottle and throw it away without question.'

I bowed my head. 'I comprehend, madame,' I said.

'And your decision, monsieur?'

Her voice was firm and unfaltering, her head held as high as ever.

I rose to my feet.

'Madame,' I said, 'I have the honour to wish you good day. I have made my investigations—and failed! The matter is closed.'

He was silent for a moment, then said quietly: 'She died just a week later. Mademoiselle Virginie passed through her novitiate, and duly took the veil. That, my friend, is the story. I must admit that I do not make a fine figure in it.'

'But that was hardly a failure,' I expostulated. 'What else could you have thought under the circumstances?'

'*Ah, sacré, mon ami*,' cried Poirot, becoming suddenly animated. 'Is it that you do not see? But I was thirty-six times an idiot! My grey cells, they functioned not at all. The whole time I had the clue in my hands.'

'What clue?'

'*The chocolate box*! Do you not see? Would anyone in possession of their full eyesight make such a mistake? I knew Madame Déroulard had cataract—the atropine drops told me that. There was only one person in the household whose eyesight was such that she could not see which lid to replace. It was the chocolate box that started me on the track, and yet up to the end I failed consistently to perceive its real significance!

'Also my psychology was at fault. Had M. de Saint Alard been the criminal, he would never have kept an incriminating bottle. Finding it was a proof of his innocence. I had learned already from Mademoiselle Virginie that he was absent-minded. Altogether it was a miserable affair that I have recounted to you there! Only to you have I told the story. You comprehend, I do not figure well in it! An old lady commits a crime in such a simple and clever fashion that I, Hercule Poirot, am completely deceived. *Sapristi*! It does not bear thinking of! Forget it. Or no—remember it, and if you think at any time that I am growing conceited—it is not likely, but it might arise.'

I concealed a smile.

'*Eh bien*, my friend, you shall say to me, 'Chocolate box''. Is it agreed?'

'It's a bargain!'

'After all,' said Poirot reflectively, 'it was an experience! I, who have undoubtedly the finest brain in Europe at present, can afford to be magnanimous!'

'Chocolate box,' I murmured gently.

'Pardon, mon ami?'

I looked at Poirot's innocent face, as he bent forward inquiringly, and my heart smote me. I had suffered often at his hands, but I, too, though not possessing the finest brain in Europe, could afford to be magnanimous!

'Nothing,' I lied, and lit another pipe, smiling to myself.

A Christmas Tragedy

'I have a complaint to make,' said Sir Henry Clithering. His eyes twinkled gently as he looked round at the assembled company. Colonel Bantry, his legs stretched out, was frowning at the mantelpiece as though it were a delinquent soldier on parade, his wife was surreptitiously glancing at a catalogue of bulbs which had come by the late post, Dr Lloyd was gazing with frank admiration at Jane Helier, and that beautiful young actress herself was thoughtfully regarding her pink polished nails. Only that elderly, spinster lady, Miss Marple, was sitting bolt upright, and her faded blue eyes met Sir Henry's with an answering twinkle.

'A complaint?' she murmured.

'A very serious complaint. We are a company of six, three representatives of each sex, and I protest on behalf of the downtrodden males. We have had three stories told tonight—and told by the three men! I protest that the ladies have not done their fair share.'

'Oh!' said Mrs Bantry with indignation. 'I'm sure we have. We've listened with the most intelligent appreciation. We've displayed the true womanly attitude—not wishing to thrust ourselves in the limelight!'

'It's an excellent excuse,' said Sir Henry; 'but it won't do. And there's a very good precedent in the Arabian Nights! So, forward, Scheherazade.'

'Meaning me?' said Mrs Bantry. 'But I don't know anything to tell. I've never been surrounded by blood or mystery.'

'I don't absolutely insist upon blood,' said Sir Henry. 'But I'm sure one of you three ladies has got a pet mystery. Come now, Miss Marple—the 'Curious Coincidence of the Charwoman" or the 'Mystery of the Mothers' Meeting". Don't disappoint me in St Mary Mead.'

Miss Marple shook her head.

'Nothing that would interest you, Sir Henry. We have our little mysteries, of course—there was that gill of picked shrimps that disappeared so incomprehensibly; but that wouldn't interest you because it all turned out to be so trivial, though throwing a considerable light on human nature.'

'You have taught me to dote on human nature,' said Sir Henry solemnly.

'What about you, Miss Helier?' asked Colonel Bantry. 'You must have had some interesting experiences.'

'Yes, indeed,' said Dr Lloyd.

'Me?' said Jane. 'You mean—you want me to tell you something that happened to me?'

'Or to one of your friends,' amended Sir Henry.

'Oh!' said Jane vaguely. 'I don't think anything has ever happened to me—I mean not that kind of thing. Flowers, of course, and queer messages—but that's just men, isn't it? I don't think'—she paused and appeared lost in thought.

'I see we shall have to have that epic of the shrimps,' said Sir Henry. 'Now then, Miss Marple.'

'You're so fond of your joke, Sir Henry. The shrimps are only nonsense; but now I come to think of it, I *do* remember one incident—at least not exactly an incident, something very much more serious—a tragedy. And I was, in a way, mixed up in it; and for what I did, I have never had any regrets—no, no regrets at all. But it didn't happen in St Mary Mead.'

'That disappoints me,' said Sir Henry. 'But I will endeavour to bear up. I knew we should not rely upon you in vain.'

He settled himself in the attitude of a listener. Miss Marple grew slightly pink.

'I hope I shall be able to tell it properly,' she said anxiously. 'I fear I am very inclined to become *rambling*. One wanders from the point—altogether without knowing that one is doing so. And it is so hard to remember each fact in its proper order. You must all bear with me if I tell my story badly. It happened a very long time ago now.

'As I say, it was not connected with St Mary Mead. As a matter of fact, it had to do with a Hydro—'

'Do you mean a seaplane?' asked Jane with wide eyes.

'You wouldn't know, dear,' said Mrs Bantry, and explained. Her husband added his quota:

'Beastly places—absolutely beastly! Got to get up early and drink filthy-tasting water. Lot of old women sitting about. Ill-natured tittle tattle. God, when I think—'

'Now, Arthur,' said Mrs Bantry placidly. 'You know it did you all the good in the world.'

'Lot of old women sitting round talking scandal,' grunted Colonel Bantry.

'That I am afraid is true,' said Miss Marple. 'I myself—'

'My dear Miss Marple,' cried the Colonel, horrified. 'I didn't mean for one moment—'

With pink cheeks and a little gesture of the hand, Miss Marple stopped him.

'But it is *true*, Colonel Bantry. Only I should just like to say this. Let me recollect my thoughts. Yes. Talking scandal, as you say—well, it *is* done a good deal. And people are very down on it—especially young people. My nephew, who writes books—and very clever ones, I believe—has said some most *scathing* things about taking people's characters away without any kind of proof—and how wicked it is, and all that. But what I say is that none of these young people ever stop to *think*. They really don't examine the facts. Surely the whole crux of the matter is this: *How often is tittle tattle*, as you call it, *true*! And I think if, as I say, they really examined the facts they would find that it was true nine times out of ten! That's really just what makes people so annoyed about it.'

'The inspired guess,' said Sir Henry.

'No, not that, not that at all! It's really a matter of practice and experience. An Egyptologist, so I've heard, if you show him one of those curious little beetles, can tell you by the look and the feel of the thing what date bc it is, or if it's a Birmingham imitation. And he can't always give a definite rule for doing so. He just *knows*. His life has been spent handling such things.

'And that's what I'm trying to say (very badly, I know). What my nephew calls 'superfluous women" have a lot of time on their hands, and their chief interest is usually *people*. And so, you see, they get to be what one might call *experts*. Now young people nowadays—they talk very freely about things that weren't mentioned in my young days, but on the other hand their minds are terribly innocent. They believe in everyone and everything. And if one tries to warn them, ever so gently, they tell one that one has a Victorian mind—and that, they say, is like a *sink*.'

'After all,' said Sir Henry, 'what is wrong with a *sink*?'

'Exactly,' said Miss Marple eagerly. 'It's the most necessary thing in any house; but, of course, not romantic. Now I must confess that I have my *feelings*, like everyone else, and I have sometimes been cruelly hurt by unthinking remarks. I know gentlemen are not interested in domestic matters, but I must just mention my maid Ethel—a very good-looking girl and obliging in every way. Now I realized as soon as I saw her that she was the same type as Annie Webb and poor Mrs Bruitt's girl. If the opportunity arose *mine* and *thine* would mean nothing to her. So I let her go at the month and I gave her a written reference saying she was honest and sober, but privately I warned old Mrs Edwards against taking her; and my nephew, Raymond, was exceedingly angry and said he had never heard of anything so wicked—yes, *wicked*. Well, she went to Lady Ashton, whom I felt no obligation to warn—and what happened? All the lace cut off her underclothes and two diamond brooches taken—and the girl departed in the middle of the night and never heard of since!'

Miss Marple paused, drew a long breath, and then went on.

'You'll be saying this has nothing to do with what went on at Keston Spa Hydro—but it has in a way. It explains why I felt no doubt in my mind the first moment I saw the Sanders together that he meant to do away with her.'

'Eh?' said Sir Henry, leaning forward.

Miss Marple turned a placid face to him.

'As I say, Sir Henry, I felt no doubt in my own mind. Mr Sanders was a big, good-looking, florid-faced man, very hearty in his manner and popular with all. And nobody could have been pleasanter to his wife than he was. But I knew! He meant to make away with her.'

'My dear Miss Marple—'

'Yes, I know. That's what my nephew, Raymond West, would say. He'd tell me I hadn't a shadow of proof. But I remember Walter Hones, who kept the Green Man. Walking home with his wife one night she fell into the river—and *he* collected the insurance money! And one or two other people that are walking about scot-free to this day—one indeed in our own class of life. Went to Switzerland for a summer holiday climbing with his wife. I warned her not to go—the poor dear didn't get angry with me as she might have done—she only laughed. It seemed to her funny that a queer old thing like me should say such things about her Harry. Well, well, there was an accident—and Harry is married to another woman now. But what could I *do*? I *knew*, but there was no proof.'

'Oh! Miss Marple,' cried Mrs Bantry. 'You don't really mean—'

'My dear, these things are very common—very common indeed. And gentlemen are especially tempted, being so much the stronger. So easy if a thing looks like an accident. As I say, I knew at once with the Sanders. It was on a tram. It was full inside and I had had to go on top. We all three got up to get off and Mr Sanders lost his balance and fell right against his wife, sending her headfirst down the stairs. Fortunately the conductor was a very strong young man and caught her.'

'But surely that must have been an accident.'

'Of course it was an accident—nothing could have looked more accidental! But Mr Sanders had been in the Merchant Service, so he told me, and a man who can keep his balance on a nasty tilting boat doesn't lose it on top of a tram if an old woman like me doesn't. Don't tell me!'

'At any rate we can take it that you made up your mind, Miss Marple,' said Sir Henry. 'Made it up then and there.'

The old lady nodded.

'I was sure enough, and another incident in crossing the street not long afterwards made me surer still. Now I ask you, what could I do, Sir Henry? Here was a nice contented happy little married woman shortly going to be murdered.'

'My dear lady, you take my breath away.'

'That's because, like most people nowadays, you won't face facts. You prefer to think such a thing couldn't be. But it was so, and I knew it. But one is so sadly handicapped! I couldn't, for instance, go to the police. And to warn the young woman would, I could see, be useless. She was devoted to the man. I just made it my business to find out as much as I could about them. One has a lot of opportunities doing one's needlework round the fire. Mrs Sanders (Gladys, her name was) was only too willing to talk. It seems they had not been married very long. Her husband had some property that was coming to him, but for the moment they were very badly off. In fact, they were living on her little income. One has heard that tale before. She bemoaned the fact that she could not touch the capital. It seems that somebody had had some sense somewhere! But the money was hers to will away—I found that out. And she and her husband had made wills in favour of each other directly after their marriage. Very touching. Of course, when Jack's affairs came right—That was the burden all day long, and in the meantime they were very hard up indeed—actually had a room on the top floor, all among the servants—and so dangerous in case of fire, though, as it happened, there was a fire escape just outside their window. I inquired carefully if there was a balcony—dangerous things, balconies. One push—you know!

'I made her promise not to go out on the balcony; I said I'd had a dream. That impressed her—one can do a lot with superstition sometimes. She was a fair girl, rather washed-out complexion, and an untidy roll of hair on her neck. Very credulous. She repeated what I had said to her husband, and I noticed him looking at me in a curious way once or twice. *He* wasn't credulous; and he knew I'd been on that tram.

'But I was very worried—terribly worried—because I couldn't see how to circumvent him. I could prevent anything happening at the Hydro, just by saying a few words to show him I suspected. But that only meant his putting off his plan till later. No, I began to believe that the only policy was a bold one—somehow or other to lay a trap for him. If I could induce him to attempt her life in a way of my own choosing—well, then he would be unmasked, and she would be forced to face the truth however much of a shock it was to her.'

'You take my breath away,' said Dr Lloyd. 'What conceivable plan could you adopt?'

'I'd have found one—never fear,' said Miss Marple. 'But the man was too clever for me. He didn't wait. He thought I might suspect, and so he struck before I could be sure. He knew I would suspect an accident. So he made it murder.'

A little gasp went round the circle. Miss Marple nodded and set her lips grimly together.

'I'm afraid I've put that rather abruptly. I must try and tell you exactly what occurred. I've always felt very bitterly about it—it seems to me that I ought, somehow, to have prevented it. But doubtless Providence knew best. I did what I could at all events.

'There was what I can only describe as a curiously eerie feeling in the air. There seemed to be something weighing on us all. A feeling of misfortune. To begin with, there was George, the hall porter. Had been there for years and knew everybody. Bronchitis and pneumonia, and passed away on the fourth day. Terribly sad. A real blow to everybody. And four days before Christmas too. And then one of the housemaids—such a nice girl—a septic finger, actually died in twenty-four hours.

'I was in the drawing-room with Miss Trollope and old Mrs Carpenter, and Mrs Carpenter was being positively ghoulish—relishing it all, you know.

''Mark my words,' she said. '*This isn't the end.* You know the saying? *Never two without three.* I've proved it true time and again. There'll be another death. Not a doubt of it. And we shan't have long to wait. *Never two without three.*'

'As she said the last words, nodding her head and clicking her knitting needles, I just chanced to look up and there was Mr Sanders standing in the doorway. Just for a minute he was off guard, and I saw the look in his face as plain as plain. I shall believe till my dying day that it was that ghoulish Mrs Carpenter's words that put the whole thing into his head. I saw his mind working.

'He came forward into the room smiling in his genial way.

''Any Christmas shopping I can do for you ladies?' he asked. 'I'm going down to Keston presently.'

'He stayed a minute or two, laughing and talking, and then went out. As I tell you, I was troubled, and I said straight away:

''Where's Mrs Sanders? Does anyone know?'

'Mrs Trollope said she'd gone out to some friends of hers, the Mortimers, to play bridge, and that eased my mind for the moment. But I was still very worried and most uncertain as to what to do. About half an hour later I went up to my room. I met Dr Coles, my doctor, there, coming down the stairs as I was going up, and as I happened to want to consult him about my rheumatism, I took him into my room with me then and there. He mentioned to me then (in confidence, he said) about the death of the poor girl Mary. The manager didn't want the news to get about, he said, so would I keep it to myself. Of course I didn't tell him that we'd all been discussing nothing else for the last hour—ever since the poor girl breathed her last. These things are always known at once, and a man of his experience should know that well enough; but Dr Coles always was a simple unsuspicious fellow who believed what he wanted to believe and that's just what alarmed me a minute later. He said as he was leaving that Sanders had asked him to have a look at his wife. It seemed she'd been seedy of late—indigestion, etc.

'*Now that very self-same day Gladys Sanders had said to me that she'd got a wonderful digestion and was thankful for it.*

'You see? All my suspicions of that man came back a hundredfold. He was preparing the way—for what? Dr Coles left before I could make up my mind whether to speak to him or not—though really if I had spoken I shouldn't have known what to say. As I came out of my room, the man himself—Sanders—came down the stairs from the floor above. He was dressed to go out and he asked me again if he could do anything for me in the town. It was all I could do to be civil to the man! I went straight into the lounge and ordered tea. It was just on half past five, I remember.

'Now I'm very anxious to put clearly what happened next. I was still in the lounge at a quarter to seven when

Mr Sanders came in. There were two gentlemen with him and all three of them were inclined to be a little on the lively side. Mr Sanders left his two friends and came right over to where I was sitting with Miss Trollope. He explained that he wanted our advice about a Christmas present he was giving his wife. It was an evening bag.

''And you see, ladies,' he said. 'I'm only a rough sailorman. What do I know about such things? I've had three sent to me on approval and I want an expert opinion on them.'

'We said, of course, that we would be delighted to help him, and he asked if we'd mind coming upstairs, as his wife might come in any minute if he brought the things down. So we went up with him. I shall never forget what happened next—I can feel my little fingers tingling now.

'Mr Sanders opened the door of the bedroom and switched on the light. I don't know which of us saw it first . . .

'*Mrs Sanders was lying on the floor, face downwards—dead.*

'I got to her first. I knelt down and took her hand and felt for the pulse, but it was useless, the arm itself was cold and stiff. Just by her head was a stocking filled with sand—the weapon she had been struck down with. Miss Trollope, silly creature, was moaning and moaning by the door and holding her head. Sanders gave a great cry of 'My wife, my wife,' and rushed to her. I stopped him touching her. You see, I was sure at the moment he had done it, and there might have been something that he wanted to take away or hide.

''Nothing must be touched,' I said. 'Pull yourself together, Mr Sanders. Miss Trollope, please go down and fetch the manager.'

'I stayed there, kneeling by the body. I wasn't going to leave Sanders alone with it. And yet I was forced to admit that if the man was acting, he was acting marvellously. He looked dazed and bewildered and scared out of his wits.

'The manager was with us in no time. He made a quick inspection of the room then turned us all out and locked the door, the key of which he took. Then he went off and telephoned to the police. It seemed a positive age before they came (we learnt afterwards that the line was out of order). The manager had to send a messenger to the police station, and the Hydro is right out of the town, up on the edge of the moor; and Mrs Carpenter tried us all very severely. She was so pleased at her prophecy of 'Never two without three" coming true so quickly. Sanders, I hear, wandered out into the grounds, clutching his head and groaning and displaying every sign of grief.

'However, the police came at last. They went upstairs with the manager and Mr Sanders. Later they sent down for me. I went up. The Inspector was there, sitting at a table writing. He was an intelligent-looking man and I liked him.

''Miss Jane Marple?' he said.

''Yes.'

''I understand, Madam, that you were present when the body of the deceased was found?'

'I said I was and I described exactly what had occurred. I think it was a relief to the poor man to find someone who could answer his questions coherently, having previously had to deal with Sanders and Emily Trollope, who, I gather, was completely demoralized—she would be, the silly creature! I remember my dear mother teaching me that a gentlewoman should always be able to control herself in public, however much she may give way in private.'

'An admirable maxim,' said Sir Henry gravely.

'When I had finished the Inspector said:

''Thank you, Madam. Now I'm afraid I must ask you just to look at the body once more. Is that exactly the position in which it was lying when you entered the room? It hasn't been moved in any way?'

'I explained that I had prevented Mr Sanders from doing so, and the Inspector nodded approval.

''The gentleman seems terribly upset,' he remarked.

''He seems so—yes,' I replied.

'I don't think I put any special emphasis on the 'seems'', but the Inspector looked at me rather keenly.

''So we can take it that the body is exactly as it was when found?' he said.

''Except for the hat, yes,' I replied.

'The Inspector looked up sharply.

''What do you mean—the hat?'

'I explained that the hat had been on poor Gladys's head, whereas now it was lying beside her. I thought, of course, that the police had done this. The Inspector, however, denied it emphatically. Nothing had, as yet, been moved or touched. He stood looking down at that poor prone figure with a puzzled frown. Gladys was dressed in her outdoor clothes—a big dark-red tweed coat with a grey fur collar. The hat, a cheap affair of red felt, lay just by her head.

'The Inspector stood for some minutes in silence, frowning to himself. Then an idea struck him.

''Can you, by any chance, remember, Madam, whether there were earrings in the ears, or whether the deceased habitually wore earrings?'

'Now fortunately I am in the habit of observing

closely. I remembered that there had been a glint of pearls just below the hat brim, though I had paid no particular notice to it at the time. I was able to answer his first question in the affirmative.

''Then that settles it. The lady's jewel case was rifled—not that she had anything much of value, I understand—and the rings were taken from her fingers. The murderer must have forgotten the earrings, and come back for them after the murder was discovered. A cool customer! Or perhaps—' He stared round the room and said slowly, 'He may have been concealed here in this room—all the time.'

'But I negatived that idea. I myself, I explained, had looked under the bed. And the manager had opened the doors of the wardrobe. There was nowhere else where a man could hide. It is true the hat cupboard was locked in the middle of the wardrobe, but as that was only a shallow affair with shelves, no one could have been concealed there.

'The Inspector nodded his head slowly whilst I explained all this.

''I'll take your word for it, Madam,' he said. 'In that case, as I said before, he must have come back. A very cool customer.'

''But the manager locked the door and took the key!'

''That's nothing. The balcony and the fire escape—that's the way the thief came. Why, as likely as not, you actually disturbed him at work. He slips out of the window, and when you've all gone, back he comes and goes on with his business.'

''You are sure,' I said, 'that there *was* a thief?'

'He said drily:

''Well, it looks like it, doesn't it?'

'But something in his tone satisfied me. I felt that he

wouldn't take Mr Sanders in the rôle of the bereaved widower too seriously.

'You see, I admit it frankly. I was absolutely under the opinion of what I believe our neighbours, the French, call the *idée fixe*. I knew that that man, Sanders, intended his wife to die. What I didn't allow for was that strange and fantastic thing, coincidence. My views about Mr Sanders were—I was sure of it—absolutely right and *true*. The man was a scoundrel. But although his hypocritical assumptions of grief didn't deceive me for a minute, I do remember feeling at the time that his *surprise* and *bewilderment* were marvellously well done. They seemed absolutely *natural*—if you know what I mean. I must admit that after my conversation with the Inspector, a curious feeling of doubt crept over me. Because if Sanders had done this dreadful thing, I couldn't imagine any conceivable reason why he should creep back by means of the fire escape and take the earrings from his wife's ears. It wouldn't have been a *sensible* thing to do, and Sanders was such a very sensible man—that's just why I always felt he was so dangerous.'

Miss Marple looked round at her audience.

'You see, perhaps, what I am coming to? It is, so often, the unexpected that happens in this world. I was so *sure*, and that, I think, was what blinded me. The result came as a shock to me. *For it was proved, beyond any possible doubt, that Mr Sanders could not possibly have committed the crime . . .*'

A surprised gasp came from Mrs Bantry. Miss Marple turned to her.

'I know, my dear, that isn't what you expected when I began this story. It wasn't what I expected either. But facts are facts, and if one is proved to be wrong, one must just be humble about it and start again. That Mr

Sanders was a murderer at heart I knew—and nothing ever occurred to upset that firm conviction of mine.

'And now, I expect, you would like to hear the actual facts themselves. Mrs Sanders, as you know, spent the afternoon playing bridge with some friends, the Mortimers. She left them at about a quarter past six. From her friends' house to the Hydro was about a quarter of an hour's walk—less if one hurried. She must have come in then about six-thirty. No one saw her come in, so she must have entered by the side door and hurried straight up to her room. There she changed (the fawn coat and skirt she wore to the bridge party were hanging up in the cupboard) and was evidently preparing to go out again, when the blow fell. Quite possibly, they say, she never even knew who struck her. The sandbag, I understand, is a very efficient weapon. That looks as though the attackers were concealed in the room, possibly in one of the big wardrobe cupboards—the one she didn't open.

'Now as to the movements of Mr Sanders. He went out, as I have said, at about five-thirty—or a little after. He did some shopping at a couple of shops and at about six o'clock he entered the Grand Spa Hotel where he encountered two friends—the same with whom he returned to the Hydro later. They played billiards and, I gather, had a good many whiskies and sodas together. These two men (Hitchcock and Spender, their names were) were actually with him the whole time from six o'clock onwards. They walked back to the Hydro with him and he only left them to come across to me and Miss Trollope. That, as I told you, was about a quarter to seven—at which time his wife must have been already dead.

'I must tell you that I talked myself to these two friends of his. I did not like them. They were neither pleasant nor gentlemanly men, but I was quite certain of one thing, that they were speaking the absolute truth when they said that Sanders had been the whole time in their company.

'There was just one other little point that came up. It seems that while bridge was going on Mrs Sanders was called to the telephone. A Mr Littleworth wanted to speak to her. She seemed both excited and pleased about something—and incidentally made one or two bad mistakes. She left rather earlier than they had expected her to do.

'Mr Sanders was asked whether he knew the name of Littleworth as being one of his wife's friends, but he declared he had never heard of anyone of that name. And to me that seems borne out by his wife's attitude—she too, did not seem to know the name of Littleworth. Nevertheless she came back from the telephone smiling and blushing, so it looks as though whoever it was did not give his real name, and that in itself has a suspicious aspect, does it not?

'Anyway, that is the problem that was left. The burglar story, which seems unlikely—or the alternative theory that Mrs Sanders was preparing to go out and meet somebody. Did that somebody come to her room by means of the fire escape? Was there a quarrel? Or did he treacherously attack her?'

Miss Marple stopped.

'Well?' said Sir Henry. 'What is the answer?'

'I wondered if any of you could guess.'

'I'm never good at guessing,' said Mrs Bantry. 'It seems a pity that Sanders had such a wonderful alibi; but if it satisfied you it must have been all right.'

Jane Helier moved her beautiful head and asked a question.

'Why,' she said, 'was the hat cupboard locked?'

'How very clever of you, my dear,' said Miss Marple, beaming. 'That's just what I wondered myself. Though the explanation was quite simple. In it were a pair of embroidered slippers and some pocket handkerchiefs that the poor girl was embroidering for her husband for Christmas. That's why she locked the cupboard. The key was found in her handbag.'

'Oh!' said Jane. 'Then it isn't very interesting after all.'

'Oh! but it is,' said Miss Marple. 'It's just the one really interesting thing—the thing that made all the murderer's plans go wrong.'

Everyone stared at the old lady.

'I didn't see it myself for two days,' said Miss Marple. 'I puzzled and puzzled—and then suddenly there it was, all clear. I went to the Inspector and asked him to try something and he did.'

'What did you ask him to try?'

'*I asked him to fit that hat on the poor girl's head*—and of course he couldn't. It wouldn't go on. *It wasn't her hat, you see.*'

Mrs Bantry stared.

'But it was on her head to begin with?'

'Not on *her* head—'

Miss Marple stopped a moment to let her words sink in, and then went on.

'We took it for granted that it was poor Gladys's body there; but we never looked at the face. She was face downwards, remember, and the hat hid everything.'

'But she *was* killed?'

'Yes, later. At the moment that we were telephoning to the police, Gladys Sanders was alive and well.'

'You mean it was someone pretending to be her? But surely when you touched her—'

'It was a dead body, right enough,' said Miss Marple gravely.

'But, dash it all,' said Colonel Bantry, 'you can't get hold of dead bodies right and left. What did they do with the—the first corpse afterwards?'

'He put it back,' said Miss Marple. 'It was a wicked idea—but a very clever one. It was our talk in the drawing-room that put it into his head. The body of poor Mary, the housemaid—why not use it? Remember, the Sanders' room was up amongst the servants' quarters. Mary's room was two doors off. The undertakers wouldn't come till after dark—he counted on that. He carried the body along the balcony (it was dark at five), dressed it in one of his wife's dresses and her big red coat. And then he found the hat cupboard locked! There was only one thing to be done, he fetched one of the poor girl's own hats. No one would notice. He put the sandbag down beside her. Then he went off to establish his alibi.

'He telephoned to his wife—calling himself Mr Littleworth. I don't know what he said to her—she was a credulous girl, as I said just now. But he got her to leave the bridge party early and not to go back to the Hydro, and arranged with her to meet him in the grounds of the Hydro near the fire escape at seven o'clock. He probably told her he had some surprise for her.

'He returns to the Hydro with his friends and arranges that Miss Trollope and I shall discover the crime with him. He even pretends to turn the body over—and I stop him! Then the police are sent for, and he staggers out into the grounds.

'Nobody asked him for an alibi *after* the crime. He meets his wife, takes her up the fire escape, they enter their room. Perhaps he has already told her some story about the body. She stoops over it, and he picks up his sandbag and strikes . . . Oh, dear! It makes me sick to think of, even now! Then quickly he strips off her coat and skirt, hangs them up, and dresses her in the clothes from the other body.

'*But the hat won't go on.* Mary's head is shingled—Gladys Sanders, as I say, had a great bun of hair. He is forced to leave it beside the body and hope no one will notice. Then he carries poor Mary's body back to her own room and arranges it decorously once more.'

'It seems incredible,' said Dr Lloyd. 'The risks he took. The police might have arrived too soon.'

'You remember the line was out of order,' said Miss Marple. 'That was a piece of *his* work. He couldn't afford to have the police on the spot too soon. When they did come, they spent some time in the manager's office before going up to the bedroom. That was the weakest point—the chance that someone might notice the difference between a body that had been dead two hours and one that had been dead just over half an hour; but he counted on the fact that the people who first discovered the crime would have no expert knowledge.'

Dr Lloyd nodded.

'The crime would be supposed to have been committed about a quarter to seven or thereabouts, I suppose,' he said. 'It was actually committed at seven or a few minutes after. When the police surgeon examined the body it would be about half past seven at the earliest. He couldn't possibly tell.'

'I am the person who should have known,' said Miss Marple. 'I felt the poor girl's hand and it was icy cold. Yet a short time later the Inspector spoke as though the murder must have been committed just before we arrived—and I saw nothing!'

'I think you saw a good deal, Miss Marple,' said Sir Henry. 'The case was before my time. I don't even remember hearing of it. What happened?'

'Sanders was hanged,' said Miss Marple crisply. 'And a good job too. I have never regretted my part in bringing that man to justice. I've no patience with modern humanitarian scruples about capital punishment.'

Her stern face softened.

'But I have often reproached myself bitterly with failing to save the life of that poor girl. But who would have listened to an old woman jumping to conclusions? Well, well—who knows? Perhaps it was better for her to die while life was still happy than it would have been for her to live on, unhappy and disillusioned, in a world that would have seemed suddenly horrible. She loved that scoundrel and trusted him. She never found him out.'

'Well, then,' said Jane Helier, 'she was all right. Quite all right. I wish—' she stopped.

Miss Marple looked at the famous, the beautiful, the successful Jane Helier and nodded her head gently.

'I see, my dear,' she said very gently. 'I see.'

The Coming of Mr Quin

It was New Year's Eve.

The elder members of the house party at Royston were assembled in the big hall.

Mr Satterthwaite was glad that the young people had gone to bed. He was not fond of young people in herds. He thought them uninteresting and crude. They lacked subtlety and as life went on he had become increasingly fond of subtleties.

Mr Satterthwaite was sixty-two—a little bent, dried-up man with a peering face oddly elflike, and an intense and inordinate interest in other people's lives. All his life, so to speak, he had sat in the front row of the stalls watching various dramas of human nature unfold before him. His role had always been that of the onlooker. Only now, with old age holding him in its clutch, he found himself increasingly critical of the drama submitted to him. He demanded now something a little out of the common.

There was no doubt that he had a flair for these things. He knew instinctively when the elements of drama were at hand. Like a war horse, he sniffed the scent. Since his arrival at Royston this afternoon, that strange inner sense of his had stirred and bid him be ready. Something interesting was happening or going to happen.

The house party was not a large one. There was Tom Evesham, their genial good-humoured host, and his serious political wife who had been before her marriage Lady Laura Keene. There was Sir Richard Conway, soldier, traveller and sportsman, there were six or seven young people whose names Mr Satterthwaite had not grasped and there were the Portals.

It was the Portals who interested Mr Satterthwaite.

He had never met Alex Portal before, but he knew all about him. Had known his father and his grandfather. Alex Portal ran pretty true to type. He was a man of close on forty, fair-haired, and blue-eyed like all the Portals, fond of sport, good at games, devoid of imagination. Nothing unusual about Alex Portal. The usual good sound English stock.

But his wife was different. She was, Mr Satterthwaite knew, an Australian. Portal had been out in Australia two years ago, had met her out there and had married her and brought her home. She had never been to England previous to her marriage. All the same, she wasn't at all like any other Australian woman Mr Satterthwaite had met.

He observed her now, covertly. Interesting woman—very. So still, and yet so—alive. Alive! That was just it! Not exactly beautiful—no, you wouldn't call her beautiful, but there was a kind of calamitous magic about her that you couldn't miss—that no man could miss. The masculine side of Mr Satterthwaite spoke there, but the feminine side (for Mr Satterthwaite had a large share of femininity) was equally interested in another question. *Why did Mrs Portal dye her hair?*

No other man would probably have known that she dyed her hair, but Mr Satterthwaite knew. He knew all those things. And it puzzled him. Many dark women dye their hair blonde; he had never before come across a fair woman who dyed her hair black.

Everything about her intrigued him. In a queer intuitive way, he felt certain that she was either very happy or very unhappy—but he didn't know which, and it annoyed him not to know. Furthermore there was the curious effect she had upon her husband.

'He adores her,' said Mr Satterthwaite to himself, 'but sometimes he's—yes, afraid of her! That's very interesting. That's uncommonly interesting.'

Portal drank too much. That was certain. And he had a curious way of watching his wife when she wasn't looking.

'Nerves,' said Mr Satterthwaite. 'The fellow's all nerves. She knows it too, but she won't do anything about it.'

He felt very curious about the pair of them. Something was going on that he couldn't fathom.

He was roused from his meditations on the subject by the solemn chiming of the big clock in the corner.

'Twelve o'clock,' said Evesham. 'New Year's Day. Happy New Year—everybody. As a matter of fact that clock's five minutes fast ... I don't know why the children wouldn't wait up and see the New Year in?'

'I don't suppose for a minute they've really gone to bed,' said his wife placidly. 'They're probably putting hairbrushes or something in our beds. That sort of thing does so amuse them. I can't think why. We should never have been allowed to do such a thing in my young days.'

'*Autre temps, autres moeurs*,' said Conway, smiling.

He was a tall soldierly-looking man. Both he and Evesham were much of the same type—honest upright kindly men with no great pretensions to brains.

'In my young days we all joined hands in a circle and

sang 'Auld Lang Syne",' continued Lady Laura. "Should auld acquaintance be forgot"—so touching, I always think the words are.'

Evesham moved uneasily.

'Oh! drop it, Laura,' he muttered. '*Not here.*'

He strode across the wide hall where they were sitting, and switched on an extra light.

'Very stupid of me,' said Lady Laura, *sotto voce.* 'Reminds him of poor Mr Capel, of course. My dear, is the fire too hot for you?'

Eleanor Portal made a brusque movement.

'Thank you. I'll move my chair back a little.'

What a lovely voice she had—one of those low murmuring echoing voices that stay in your memory, thought Mr Satterthwaite. Her face was in shadow now. What a pity.

From her place in the shadow she spoke again.

'Mr—Capel?'

'Yes. The man who originally owned this house. He shot himself you know—oh! very well, Tom dear, I won't speak of it unless you like. It was a great shock for Tom, of course, because he was here when it happened. So were you, weren't you, Sir Richard?'

'Yes, Lady Laura.'

An old grandfather clock in the corner groaned, wheezed, snorted asthmatically, and then struck twelve.

'Happy New Year, Tom,' grunted Evesham perfunctorily.

Lady Laura wound up her knitting with some deliberation.

'Well, we've seen the New Year in,' she observed, and added, looking towards Mrs Portal, 'What do you think, my dear?'

Eleanor Portal rose quickly to her feet.

'Bed, by all means,' she said lightly.

'She's very pale,' thought Mr Satterthwaite, as he too rose, and began busying himself with candlesticks. 'She's not usually as pale as that.'

He lighted her candle and handed it to her with a funny little old-fashioned bow. She took it from him with a word of acknowledgment and went slowly up the stairs.

Suddenly a very odd impulse swept over Mr Satterthwaite. He wanted to go after her—to reassure her—he had the strangest feeling that she was in danger of some kind. The impulse died down, and he felt ashamed. *He* was getting nervy too.

She hadn't looked at her husband as she went up the stairs, but now she turned her head over her shoulder and gave him a long searching glance which had a queer intensity in it. It affected Mr Satterthwaite very oddly.

He found himself saying goodnight to his hostess in quite a flustered manner.

'I'm sure I hope it *will* be a happy New Year,' Lady Laura was saying. 'But the political situation seems to me to be fraught with grave uncertainty.'

'I'm sure it is,' said Mr Satterthwaite earnestly. 'I'm sure it is.'

'I only hope,' continued Lady Laura, without the least change of manner, 'that it will be a dark man who first crosses the threshold. You know that superstition, I suppose, Mr Satterthwaite? No? You surprise me. To bring luck to the house it must be a dark man who first steps over the door step on New Year's Day. Dear me, I hope I shan't find anything *very* unpleasant in my bed. I never trust the children. They have such very high spirits.'

Shaking her head in sad foreboding, Lady Laura moved majestically up the staircase.

With the departure of the women, chairs were pulled in closer round the blazing logs on the big open hearth.

'Say when,' said Evesham, hospitably, as he held up the whisky decanter.

When everybody had said when, the talk reverted to the subject which had been tabooed before.

'You knew Derek Capel, didn't you, Satterthwaite?' asked Conway.

'Slightly—yes.'

'And you, Portal?'

'No, I never met him.'

So fiercely and defensively did he say it, that Mr Satterthwaite looked up in surprise.

'I always hate it when Laura brings up the subject,' said Evesham slowly. 'After the tragedy, you know, this place was sold to a big manufacturer fellow. He cleared out after a year—didn't suit him or something. A lot of tommy rot was talked about the place being haunted of course, and it gave the house a bad name. Then, when Laura got me to stand for West Kidleby, of course it meant living up in these parts, and it wasn't so easy to find a suitable house. Royston was going cheap, and—well, in the end I bought it. Ghosts are all tommy rot, but all the same one doesn't exactly care to be reminded that you're living in a house where one of your own friends shot himself. Poor old Derek—we shall never know why he did it.'

'He won't be the first or the last fellow who's shot himself without being able to give a reason,' said Alex Portal heavily.

He rose and poured himself out another drink, splashing the whisky in with a liberal hand.

'There's something very wrong with him,' said Mr Satterthwaite, to himself. 'Very wrong indeed. I wish I knew what it was all about.'

'Gad!' said Conway. 'Listen to the wind. It's a wild night.'

'A good night for ghosts to walk,' said Portal with a reckless laugh. 'All the devils in Hell are abroad tonight.'

'According to Lady Laura, even the blackest of them would bring us luck,' observed Conway, with a laugh. 'Hark to that!'

The wind rose in another terrific wail, and as it died away there came three loud knocks on the big nailed doorway.

Everyone started.

'Who on earth can that be at this time of night?' cried Evesham.

They stared at each other.

'I will open it,' said Evesham. 'The servants have gone to bed.'

He strode across to the door, fumbled a little over the heavy bars, and finally flung it open. An icy blast of wind came sweeping into the hall.

Framed in the doorway stood a man's figure, tall and slender. To Mr Satterthwaite, watching, he appeared by some curious effect of the stained glass above the door, to be dressed in every colour of the rainbow. Then, as he stepped forward, he showed himself to be a thin dark man dressed in motoring clothes.

'I must really apologize for this intrusion,' said the stranger, in a pleasant level voice. 'But my car broke down. Nothing much, my chauffeur is putting it to rights, but it will take half an hour or so, and it is so confoundedly cold outside—'

He broke off, and Evesham took up the thread quickly.

'I should think it was. Come in and have a drink. We can't give you any assistance about the car, can we?'

'No, thanks. My man knows what to do. By the way, my name is Quin—Harley Quin.'

'Sit down, Mr Quin,' said Evesham. 'Sir Richard Conway, Mr Satterthwaite. My name is Evesham.'

Mr Quin acknowledged the introductions, and dropped into the chair that Evesham had hospitably pulled forward. As he sat, some effect of the firelight threw a bar of shadow across his face which gave almost the impression of a mask.

Evesham threw a couple more logs on the fire.

'A drink?'

'Thanks.'

Evesham brought it to him and asked as he did so:

'So you know this part of the world well, Mr Quin?'

'I passed through it some years ago.'

'Really?'

'Yes. This house belonged then to a man called Capel.'

'Ah! yes,' said Evesham. 'Poor Derek Capel. You knew him?'

'Yes, I knew him.'

Evesham's manner underwent a faint change, almost imperceptible to one who had not studied the English character. Before, it had contained a subtle reserve, now this was laid aside. Mr Quin had known Derek Capel. He was the friend of a friend, and, as such, was vouched for and fully accredited.

'Astounding affair, that,' he said confidentially. 'We were just talking about it. I can tell you, it went against the grain, buying this place. If there had been anything else suitable, but there wasn't you see. I was in the house the night he shot himself—so was Conway, and upon my word, I've always expected his ghost to walk.'

'A very inexplicable business,' said Mr Quin, slowly and deliberately, and he paused with the air of an actor who has just spoken an important cue.

'You may well say inexplicable,' burst in Conway. 'The thing's a black mystery—always will be.'

'I wonder,' said Mr Quin, non-committally. 'Yes, Sir Richard, you were saying?'

'Astounding—that's what it was. Here's a man in the prime of life, gay, light-hearted, without a care in the world. Five or six old pals staying with him. Top of his spirits at dinner, full of plans for the future. And from the dinner table he goes straight upstairs to his room, takes a revolver from a drawer and shoots himself. Why? Nobody ever knew. Nobody ever will know.'

'Isn't that rather a sweeping statement, Sir Richard?' asked Mr Quin, smiling.

Conway stared at him.

'What d'you mean? I don't understand.'

'A problem is not necessarily unsolvable because it has remained unsolved.'

'Oh! Come, man, if nothing came out at the time, it's not likely to come out now—ten years afterwards?'

Mr Quin shook his head gently.

'I disagree with you. The evidence of history is against you. The contemporary historian never writes such a true history as the historian of a later generation. It is a question of getting the true perspective, of seeing things in proportion. If you like to call it so, it is, like everything else, a question of relativity.'

Alex Portal leant forward, his face twitching painfully.

'You are right, Mr Quin,' he cried, 'you are right. Time does not dispose of a question—it only presents it anew in a different guise.'

Evesham was smiling tolerantly.

'Then you mean to say, Mr Quin, that if we were to hold, let us say, a Court of Inquiry tonight, into the circumstances of Derek Capel's death, we are as likely to arrive at the truth as we should have been at the time?'

'*More* likely, Mr Evesham. The personal equation has largely dropped out, and you will remember facts as facts without seeking to put your own interpretation upon them.'

Evesham frowned doubtfully.

'One must have a starting point, of course,' said Mr Quin in his quiet level voice. 'A starting point is usually a theory. One of you must have a theory, I am sure. How about you, Sir Richard?'

Conway frowned thoughtfully.

'Well, of course,' he said apologetically, 'we thought—naturally we all thought—that there must be a woman in it somewhere. It's usually either that or money, isn't it? And it certainly wasn't money. No trouble of that description. So—what else could it have been?'

Mr Satterthwaite started. He had leant forward to contribute a small remark of his own and in the act of doing so, he had caught sight of a woman's figure crouched against the balustrade of the gallery above. She was huddled down against it, invisible from everywhere but where he himself sat, and she was evidently listening with strained attention to what was going on below. So immovable was she that he hardly believed the evidence of his own eyes.

But he recognized the pattern of the dress easily enough—an old-world brocade. It was Eleanor Portal.

And suddenly all the events of the night seemed to fall into pattern—Mr Quin's arrival, no fortuitous chance, but the appearance of an actor when his cue was given. There was a drama being played in the big hall at Royston tonight—a drama none the less real in that one of the actors was dead. Oh! yes, Derek Capel had a part in the play. Mr Satterthwaite was sure of that.

And, again suddenly, a new illumination came to him. This was Mr Quin's doing. It was he who was staging the play—was giving the actors their cues. He was at the heart of the mystery pulling the strings, making the puppets work. He knew everything, even to the presence of the woman crouched against the woodwork upstairs. Yes, he knew.

Sitting well back in his chair, secure in his role of audience, Mr Satterthwaite watched the drama unfold before his eyes. Quietly and naturally, Mr Quin was pulling the strings, setting his puppets in motion.

'A woman—yes,' he murmured thoughtfully. 'There was no mention of any woman at dinner?'

'Why, of course,' cried Evesham. 'He announced his engagement. That's just what made it seem so absolutely mad. Very bucked about it he was. Said it wasn't to be announced just yet—but gave us the hint that he was in the running for the Benedick stakes.'

'Of course we all guessed who the lady was,' said Conway. 'Marjorie Dilke. Nice girl.'

It seemed to be Mr Quin's turn to speak, but he did not do so, and something about his silence seemed oddly provocative. It was as though he challenged the last statement. It had the effect of putting Conway in a defensive position.

'Who else could it have been? Eh, Evesham?'

'I don't know,' said Tom Evesham slowly. 'What did he say exactly now? Something about being in the running for the Benedick stakes—that he couldn't tell us the lady's name till he had her permission—it wasn't to be announced yet. He said, I remember, that he was a damned lucky fellow. That he wanted his two old friends to know that by that time next year he'd be a happy married man. Of course, we assumed it was Marjorie. They were great friends and he'd been about with her a lot.'

'The only thing—' began Conway and stopped.

'What were you going to say, Dick?'

'Well, I mean, it was odd in a way, if it were Marjorie, that the engagement shouldn't be announced at once. I mean, why the secrecy? Sounds more as though it were a married woman—you know, someone whose husband had just died, or who was divorcing him.'

'That's true,' said Evesham. 'If that were the case, of course, the engagement couldn't be announced at once. And you know, thinking back about it, I don't believe he had been seeing much of Marjorie. All that was the year before. I remember thinking things seemed to have cooled off between them.'

'Curious,' said Mr Quin.

'Yes—looked almost as though someone had come between them.'

'Another woman,' said Conway thoughtfully.

'By jove,' said Evesham. 'You know, there was something almost indecently hilarious about old Derek that night. He looked almost drunk with happiness. And yet—I can't quite explain what I mean—but he looked oddly defiant too.'

'Like a man defying Fate,' said Alex Portal heavily.

Was it of Derek Capel he was speaking—or was it of himself? Mr Satterthwaite, looking at him, inclined to the latter view. Yes, that was what Alex Portal represented—a man defying Fate.

His imagination, muddled by drink, responded

suddenly to that note in the story which recalled his own secret preoccupation.

Mr Satterthwaite looked up. She was still there. Watching, listening—still motionless, frozen—like a dead woman.

'Perfectly true,' said Conway. 'Capel *was* excited—curiously so. I'd describe him as a man who had staked heavily and won against well nigh overwhelming odds.'

'Getting up courage, perhaps, for what he's made up his mind to do?' suggested Portal.

And as though moved by an association of ideas, he got up and helped himself to another drink.

'Not a bit of it,' said Evesham sharply. 'I'd almost swear nothing of that kind was in his mind. Conway's right. A successful gambler who has brought off a long shot and can hardly believe in his own good fortune. That was the attitude.'

Conway gave a gesture of discouragement.

'And yet,' he said. 'Ten minutes later—'

They sat in silence. Evesham brought his hand down with a bang on the table.

'Something must have happened in that ten minutes,' he cried. 'It must! But what? Let's go over it carefully. We were all talking. In the middle of it Capel got up suddenly and left the room—'

'Why?' said Mr Quin.

The interruption seemed to disconcert Evesham.

'I beg your pardon?'

'I only said: Why?' said Mr Quin.

Evesham frowned in an effort of memory.

'It didn't seem vital—at the time—Oh! of course—the Post. Don't you remember that jangling bell, and how excited we were. We'd been snowed up for three days, remember. Biggest snowstorm for years and years.

All the roads were impassable. No newspapers, no letters. Capel went out to see if something had come through at last, and got a great pile of things. Newspapers and letters. He opened the paper to see if there was any news, and then went upstairs with his letters. Three minutes afterwards, we heard a shot . . . Inexplicable—absolutely inexplicable.'

'That's not inexplicable,' said Portal. 'Of course the fellow got some unexpected news in a letter. Obvious, I should have said.'

'Oh! Don't think we missed anything so obvious as that. It was one of the Coroner's first questions. *But Capel never opened one of his letters.* The whole pile lay unopened on his dressing-table.'

Portal looked crestfallen.

'You're sure he didn't open just one of them? He might have destroyed it after reading it?'

'No, I'm quite positive. Of course, that would have been the natural solution. No, every one of the letters was unopened. Nothing burnt—nothing torn up—There was no fire in the room.'

Portal shook his head.

'Extraordinary.'

'It was a ghastly business altogether,' said Evesham in a low voice. 'Conway and I went up when we heard the shot, and found him—It gave me a shock, I can tell you.'

'Nothing to be done but telephone for the police, I suppose?' said Mr Quin.

'Royston wasn't on the telephone then. I had it put in when I bought the place. No, luckily enough, the local constable happened to be in the kitchen at the time. One of the dogs—you remember poor old Rover, Conway?—had strayed the day before. A passing carter had found it half buried in a snowdrift and had taken it to the police station. They recognized it as Capel's, and a dog he was particularly fond of, and the constable came up with it. He'd just arrived a minute before the shot was fired. It saved us some trouble.'

'Gad, that was a snowstorm,' said Conway reminiscently. 'About this time of year, wasn't it? Early January.'

'February, I think. Let me see, we went abroad soon afterwards.'

'I'm pretty sure it was January. My hunter Ned—you remember Ned?—lamed himself the end of January. That was just after this business.'

'It must have been quite the end of January then. Funny how difficult it is to recall dates after a lapse of years.'

'One of the most difficult things in the world,' said Mr Quin, conversationally. 'Unless you can find a landmark in some big public event—an assassination of a crowned head, or a big murder trial.'

'Why, of course,' cried Conway, 'it was just before the Appleton case.'

'Just after, wasn't it?'

'No, no, don't you remember—Capel knew the Appletons—he'd stayed with the old man the previous Spring—just a week before he died. He was talking of him one night—what an old curmudgeon he was, and how awful it must have been for a young and beautiful woman like Mrs Appleton to be tied to him. There was no suspicion then that she had done away with him.'

'By jove, you're right. I remember reading the paragraph in the paper saying an exhumation order had been granted. It would have been that same day—I remember only seeing it with half my mind, you know, the other half wondering about poor old Derek lying dead upstairs.'

'A common, but very curious phenomenon, that,' observed Mr Quin. 'In moments of great stress, the mind focuses itself upon some quite unimportant matter which is remembered long afterwards with the utmost fidelity, driven in, as it were, by the mental stress of the moment. It may be some quite irrelevant detail, like the pattern of a wallpaper, but it will never be forgotten.'

'Rather extraordinary, your saying that, Mr Quin,' said Conway. 'Just as you were speaking, I suddenly felt myself back in Derek Capel's room—with Derek lying dead on the floor—I saw as plainly as possible the big tree outside the window, and the shadow it threw upon the snow outside. Yes, the moonlight, the snow, and the shadow of the tree—I can see them again this minute. By Gad, I believe I could draw them, and yet I never realized I was looking at them at the time.'

'His room was the big one over the porch, was it not?' asked Mr Quin.

'Yes, and the tree was the big beech, just at the angle of the drive.'

Mr Quin nodded, as though satisfied. Mr Satterthwaite was curiously thrilled. He was convinced that every word, every inflection of Mr Quin's voice, was pregnant with purpose. He was driving at something—exactly what Mr Satterthwaite did not know, but he was quite convinced as to whose was the master hand.

There was a momentary pause, and then Evesham reverted to the preceding topic.

'That Appleton case, I remember it very well now. What a sensation it made. She got off, didn't she? Pretty woman, very fair—remarkably fair.'

Almost against his will, Mr Satterthwaite's eyes sought the kneeling figure up above. Was it his fancy, or did he see it shrink a little as though at a blow. Did he see a hand slide upwards to the table cloth—and then pause.

There was a crash of falling glass. Alex Portal, helping himself to whisky, had let the decanter slip.

'I say—sir, damn' sorry. Can't think what came over me.'

Evesham cut short his apologies.

'Quite all right. Quite all right, my dear fellow. Curious—That smash reminded me. That's what she did, didn't she? Mrs Appleton? Smashed the port decanter?'

'Yes. Old Appleton had his glass of port—only one—each night. The day after his death, one of the servants saw her take the decanter out and smash it deliberately. That set them talking, of course. They all knew she had been perfectly wretched with him. Rumour grew and grew, and in the end, months later, some of his relatives applied for an exhumation order. And sure enough, the old fellow had been poisoned. Arsenic, wasn't it?'

'No—strychnine, I think. It doesn't much matter. Well, of course, there it was. Only one person was likely to have done it. Mrs Appleton stood her trial. She was acquitted more through lack of evidence against her than from any overwhelming proof of innocence. In other words, she was lucky. Yes, I don't suppose there's much doubt she did it right enough. What happened to her afterwards?'

'Went out to Canada, I believe. Or was it Australia? She had an uncle or something of the sort out there who offered her a home. Best thing she could do under the circumstances.'

Mr Satterthwaite was fascinated by Alex Portal's right hand as it clasped his glass. How tightly he was gripping it.

'You'll smash that in a minute or two, if you're not careful,' thought Mr Satterthwaite. 'Dear me, how interesting all this is.'

Evesham rose and helped himself to a drink.

'Well, we're not much nearer to knowing why poor Derek Capel shot himself,' he remarked. 'The Court of Inquiry hasn't been a great success, has it, Mr Quin?'

Mr Quin laughed . . .

It was a strange laugh, mocking—yet sad. It made everyone jump.

'I beg your pardon,' he said. 'You are still living in the past, Mr Evesham. You are still hampered by your preconceived notion. But I—the man from outside, the stranger passing by, see only—facts!'

'Facts?'

'Yes—facts.'

'What do you mean?' said Evesham.

'I see a clear sequence of facts, outlined by yourselves but of which you have not seen the significance. Let us go back ten years and look at what we see—untrammelled by ideas or sentiment.'

Mr Quin had risen. He looked very tall. The fire leaped fitfully behind him. He spoke in a low compelling voice.

'You are at dinner. Derek Capel announces his engagement. You think then it was to Marjorie Dilke. You are not so sure now. He has the restlessly excited manner of a man who has successfully defied Fate—who, in your own words, has pulled off a big coup against overwhelming odds. Then comes the clanging of the bell. He goes out to get the long overdue mail. He doesn't open his letters, but you mention yourselves that *he opened the paper to glance at the news*. It is ten years ago—so we cannot know what the news was that day—a far-off earthquake, a near at hand political crisis? The only thing we do know about the contents of that paper is that it contained one small paragraph—*a paragraph stating that the Home Office had given permission to exhume* the body of Mr Appleton three days ago.'

'What?'

Mr Quin went on.

'Derek Capel goes up to his room, and there he sees something out of the window. Sir Richard Conway has told us that the curtain was not drawn across it and further that it gave on to the drive. What did he see? What could he have seen that forced him to take his life?'

'What do you mean? What did he see?'

'I think,' said Mr Quin, 'that he saw a policeman. A policeman who had come about a dog—But Derek Capel didn't know that—he just saw—a policeman.'

There was a long silence—as though it took some time to drive the inference home.

'My God!' whispered Evesham at last. 'You can't mean that? Appleton? But he wasn't there at the time Appleton died. The old man was alone with his wife—'

'But he may have been there a week earlier. Strychnine is not very soluble unless it is in the form of hydrochloride. The greater part of it, put into the port, would be taken in the last glass, perhaps a week after he left.'

Portal sprung forward. His voice was hoarse, his eyes bloodshot.

'Why did she break the decanter?' he cried. 'Why did she break the decanter? Tell me that!'

For the first time that evening, Mr Quin addressed himself to Mr Satterthwaite.

'You have a wide experience of life, Mr Satterthwaite. Perhaps you can tell us that.'

Mr Satterthwaite's voice trembled a little. His cue had come at last. He was to speak some of the most important lines in the play. He was an actor now—not a looker-on.

'As I see it,' he murmured modestly, 'she—cared for Derek Capel. She was, I think, a good woman—and she had sent him away. When her husband—died, she suspected the truth. And so, to save the man she loved, she tried to destroy the evidence against him. Later, I think, he persuaded her that her suspicions were unfounded, and she consented to marry him. But even then, she hung back—women, I fancy, have a lot of instinct.'

Mr Sattherthwaite had spoken his part.

Suddenly a long trembling sigh filled the air.

'My God!' cried Evesham, starting, 'what was that?'

Mr Satterthwaite could have told him that it was Eleanor Portal in the gallery above, but he was too artistic to spoil a good effect.

Mr Quin was smiling.

'My car will be ready by now. Thank you for your hospitality, Mr Evesham. I have, I hope, done something for my friend.'

They stared at him in blank amazement.

'That aspect of the matter has not struck you? He loved this woman, you know. Loved her enough to commit murder for her sake. When retribution overtook him, as he mistakenly thought, he took his own life. But unwittingly, he left her to face the music.'

'She was acquitted,' muttered Evesham.

'Because the case against her could not be proved. I fancy—it may be only a fancy—that she is still—facing the music.'

Portal had sunk into a chair, his face buried in his hands.

Quin turned to Satterthwaite.

'Goodbye, Mr Satterthwaite. You are interested in the drama, are you not?'

Mr Satterthwaite nodded—surprised.

'I must recommend the Harlequinade to your attention. It is dying out nowadays—but it repays attention, I assure you. Its symbolism is a little difficult to follow—but the immortals are always immortal, you know. I wish you all goodnight.'

They saw him stride out into the dark. As before, the coloured glass gave the effect of motley . . .

Mr Satterthwaite went upstairs. He went to draw down his window, for the air was cold. The figure of Mr Quin moved down the drive, and from a side door came a woman's figure, running. For a moment they spoke together, then she retraced her steps to the house. She passed just below the window, and Mr Satterthwaite was struck anew by the vitality of her face. She moved now like a woman in a happy dream.

'Eleanor!'

Alex Portal had joined her.

'Eleanor, forgive me—forgive me—You told me the truth, but God forgive me—I did not quite believe . . .'

Mr Satterthwaite was intensely interested in other people's affairs, but he was also a gentleman. It was borne in upon him that he must shut the window. He did so.

But he shut it very slowly.

He heard her voice, exquisite and indescribable.

'I know—I know. You have been in hell. So was I once. Loving—yet alternately believing and suspecting—thrusting aside one's doubts and having them spring up again with leering faces ... I know, Alex, I know ... But there is a worse hell than that, the hell I have lived in with you. I have seen your doubt—your fear of me ... poisoning all our love. That man—that chance passer by, saved me. I could bear it no longer, you understand. Tonight—tonight I was going to kill myself ... Alex ... Alex ...'

The Clergyman's Daughter

'I wish,' said Tuppence, roaming moodily round the office, 'that we could befriend a clergyman's daughter.'

'Why?' asked Tommy.

'You may have forgotten the fact, but I was once a clergyman's daughter myself. I remember what it was like. Hence this altruistic urge—this spirit of thoughtful consideration for others—this—'

'You are getting ready to be Roger Sheringham, I see,' said Tommy. 'If you will allow me to make a criticism, you talk quite as much as he does, but not nearly so well.'

'On the contrary,' said Tuppence. 'There is a feminine subtlety about my conversation, a *je ne sais quoi* that no gross male could ever attain to. I have, moreover, powers unknown to my prototype—do I mean prototype? Words are such uncertain things, they so often sound well, but mean the opposite of what one thinks they do.'

'Go on,' said Tommy kindly.

'I was. I was only pausing to take breath. Touching these powers, it is my wish today to assist a clergyman's daughter. You will see, Tommy, the first person to enlist the aid of Blunt's Brilliant Detectives will be a clergyman's daughter.'

'I'll bet you it isn't,' said Tommy.

'Done,' said Tuppence. 'Hist! To your typewriters, Oh! Israel. One comes.'

Mr Blunt's office was humming with industry as Albert opened the door and announced:

'Miss Monica Deane.'

A slender, brown-haired girl, rather shabbily dressed, entered and stood hesitating. Tommy came forward.

'Good-morning, Miss Deane. Won't you sit down and tell us what we can do for you? By the way, let me introduce my confidential secretary, Miss Sheringham.'

'I am delighted to make your acquaintance, Miss Deane,' said Tuppence. 'Your father was in the Church, I think.'

'Yes, he was. But how *did* you know that?'

'Oh! we have our methods,' said Tuppence. 'You mustn't mind me rattling on. Mr Blunt likes to hear me talk. He always says it gives him ideas.'

The girl stared at her. She was a slender creature, not beautiful, but possessing a wistful prettiness. She had a quantity of soft mouse-coloured hair, and her eyes were dark blue and very lovely, though the dark shadows round them spoke of trouble and anxiety.

'Will you tell me your story, Miss Deane?' said Tommy.

The girl turned to him gratefully.

'It's such a long rambling story,' said the girl. 'My name is Monica Deane. My father was the rector of Little Hampsley in Suffolk. He died three years ago, and my mother and I were left very badly off. I went out as a governess, but my mother's physical condition deteriorated, and I had to come home to look after her. We were desperately poor, but one day we received a lawyer's letter telling us that an aunt of my father's had died and had left everything to me. I had often heard of this aunt, who had quarrelled with my father many years ago, and I knew that she was very well off, so it really seemed that our troubles were at an end. But matters did not turn out quite as well as we had hoped. I inherited the house she had lived in, but after paying one or two small legacies, there was no money left. I suppose she must have lost it during the war, or perhaps she had been living on her capital. Still, we had the house, and almost at once we had a chance of selling it at quite an advantageous price. But, foolishly perhaps, I refused the offer. We were in tiny, but expensive lodgings, and I thought it would be much nicer to live in the Red House, where my mother could have comfortable rooms and take in paying guests to cover our expenses.

'I adhered to this plan, notwithstanding a further tempting offer from the gentleman who wanted to buy. We moved in, and I advertised for paying guests. For a time, all went well, we had several answers to our advertisement; my aunt's old servant remained on with us, and she and I between us did the work of the house. And then these unaccountable things began to happen.'

'What things?'

'The queerest things. The whole place seemed bewitched. Pictures fell down, crockery flew across the room and broke; one morning we came down to find all the furniture moved round. At first we thought someone was playing a practical joke, but we had to give up that explanation. Sometimes when we were all sitting down to dinner, a terrific crash would be heard overhead. We would go up and find no one there, but a piece of furniture thrown violently to the ground.'

'A *poltergeist*,' cried Tuppence, much interested.

'Yes, that's what Dr O'Neill said—though I don't know what it means.'

'It's a sort of evil spirit that plays tricks,' explained Tuppence, who in reality knew very little about the subject, and was not even sure that she had got the word *poltergeist* right.

'Well, at any rate, the effect was disastrous. Our visitors were frightened to death, and left as soon as possible. We got new ones, and they too left hurriedly. I was in despair, and, to crown all, our own tiny income ceased suddenly—the Company in which it was invested failed.'

'You poor dear,' said Tuppence sympathetically. 'What a time you have had. Did you want Mr Blunt to investigate this 'haunting" business?'

'Not exactly. You see, three days ago, a gentleman called upon us. His name was Dr O'Neill. He told us that he was a member of the Society for Physical Research, and that he had heard about the curious manifestations that had taken place in our house and was much interested. So much so, that he was prepared to buy it from us, and conduct a series of experiments there.'

'Well?'

'Of course, at first, I was overcome with joy. It seemed the way out of all our difficulties. But—'

'Yes?'

'Perhaps you will think me fanciful. Perhaps I am. But—oh! I'm sure I haven't made a mistake. It was the same man!'

'What same man?'

'The same man who wanted to buy it before. Oh! I'm sure I'm right.'

'But why shouldn't it be?'

'You don't understand. The two men were quite different, different name and everything. The first man was quite young, a spruce, dark young man of thirty odd. Dr O'Neill is about fifty, he has a grey beard and wears glasses and stoops. But when he talked I saw a gold tooth one side of his mouth. It only shows when he laughs. The other man had a tooth in just the same position, and then I looked at his ears. I had noticed the other man's ears, because they were a peculiar shape with hardly any lobe. Dr O'Neill's were just the same. Both things couldn't be a coincidence, could they? I thought and thought and finally I wrote and said I would let him know in a week. I had noticed Mr Blunt's advertisement some time ago—as a matter of fact in an old paper that lined one of the kitchen drawers. I cut it out and came up to town.'

'You were quite right,' said Tuppence, nodding her head with vigour. 'This needs looking into.'

'A very interesting case, Miss Deane,' observed Tommy.

'We shall be pleased to look into this for you—eh, Miss Sheringham?'

'Rather,' said Tuppence, 'and we'll get to the bottom of it too.'

'I understand, Miss Deane,' went on Tommy, 'that the household consists of you and your mother and a servant. Can you give me any particulars about the servant?'

'Her name is Crockett. She was with my aunt about eight or ten years. She is an elderly woman, not very pleasant in manner, but a good servant. She is inclined to give herself airs because her sister married out of her station. Crockett has a nephew whom she is always telling us is 'quite the gentleman".'

'H'm,' said Tommy, rather at a loss how to proceed.

Tuppence had been eyeing Monica keenly, now she spoke with sudden decision.

'I think the best plan would be for Miss Deane to come out and lunch with me. It's just one o'clock. I can get full details from her.'

'Certainly, Miss Sheringham,' said Tommy. 'An excellent plan.'

'Look here,' said Tuppence, when they were comfortably ensconced at a little table in a neighbouring restaurant, 'I want to know: Is there any special reason why you want to find out about all this?'

Monica blushed.

'Well, you see—'

'Out with it,' said Tuppence encouragingly.

'Well—there are two men who—who—want to marry me.'

'The usual story, I suppose? One rich, one poor, and the poor one is the one you like!'

'I don't know how you know all these things,' murmured the girl.

'That's a sort of law of Nature,' explained Tuppence. 'It happens to everybody. It happened to me.'

'You see, even if I sell the house, it won't bring us in enough to live on. Gerald is a dear, but he's desperately poor—though he's a very clever engineer; and if only he had a little capital, his firm would take him into partnership. The other, Mr Partridge, is a very good man, I am sure—and well off, and if I married him, it would be an end to all our troubles. But—but—'

'I know,' said Tuppence sympathetically. 'It isn't the same thing at all. You can go on telling yourself how good and worthy he is, and adding up his qualities as though they were an addition sum—and it all has a simply refrigerating effect.'

Monica nodded.

'Well,' said Tuppence, 'I think it would be as well

if we went down to the neighbourhood and studied matters upon the spot. What is the address?'

'The Red House, Stourton-in-the-Marsh.'

Tuppence wrote down the address in her notebook.

'I didn't ask you,' Monica began—'about terms—' she ended, blushing a little.

'Our payments are strictly by results,' said Tuppence gravely. 'If the secret of the Red House is a profitable one, as seems possible from the anxiety displayed to acquire the property, we should expect a small percentage, otherwise—nothing!'

'Thank you very much,' said the girl gratefully.

'And now,' said Tuppence, 'don't worry. Everything's going to be all right. Let's enjoy lunch and talk of interesting things.'

The Red House

'Well,' said Tommy, looking out of the window of the Crown and Anchor, 'here we are at Toad in the Hole—or whatever this blasted village is called.'

'Let us review the case,' said Tuppence.

'By all means,' said Tommy. 'To begin with, getting my say in first, *I* suspect the disabled mother!'

'Why?'

'My dear Tuppence, grant that this *poltergeist* business is all a put-up job, got up in order to persuade the girl to sell the house, someone must have thrown the things about. Now the girl said everyone was at dinner—but if the mother is disabled, she'd be upstairs in her room.'

'If she was disabled she could hardly throw furniture about.'

'Ah! but she wouldn't really be disabled. She'd be shamming.'

'Why?'

'There you have me,' confessed her husband. 'I was really going on the well-known principle of suspecting the most unlikely person.'

'You always make fun of everything,' said Tuppence severely. 'There must be *something* that makes these people so anxious to get hold of the house. And if you don't care about getting to the bottom of this matter, I do. I like that girl. She's a dear.'

Tommy nodded seriously enough.

'I quite agree. But I never can resist ragging you, Tuppence. Of course, there's something queer about the house, and whatever it is, it's something that's difficult to get at. Otherwise a mere burglary would do the trick. But to be willing to buy the house means either that you've got to take up floors or pull down walls, or else that there's a coal mine under the back garden.'

'I don't want it to be a coal mine. Buried treasure is much more romantic.'

'H'm,' said Tommy. 'In that case I think that I shall pay a visit to the local Bank Manager, explain that I am staying here over Christmas and probably buying the Red House, and discuss the question of opening an account.'

'But why—?'

'Wait and see.'

Tommy returned at the end of half an hour. His eyes were twinkling.

'We advance, Tuppence. Our interview proceeded on the lines indicated. I then asked casually whether he had had much gold paid in, as is often the case nowadays in these small country banks—small farmers who hoarded it during the war, you understand. From that we proceeded quite naturally to the extraordinary vagaries of old ladies. I invented an aunt who on the outbreak of war drove to the Army and Navy Stores in a four-wheeler, and returned with sixteen hams. He immediately mentioned a client of his own, who had insisted on drawing out every penny of money she had—in gold as far as possible, and who also insisted on having her securities, bearer bonds and such things, given into her own custody. I exclaimed on such an act of folly, and he mentioned casually that she was the former owner of the Red House. You see, Tuppence? She drew out all this money, and she hid it somewhere. You remember that Monica Deane mentioned that they were astonished at the small amount of her estate? Yes, she hid it in the Red House, and someone knows about it. I can make a pretty good guess who that someone is too.'

'Who?'

'What about the faithful Crockett? She would know all about her mistress's peculiarities.'

'And that gold-toothed Dr O'Neill?'

'The gentlemanly nephew, of course! That's it. But whereabouts did she hide it. You know more about old ladies than I do, Tuppence. Where do they hide things?'

'Wrapped up in stockings and petticoats, under mattresses.'

Tommy nodded.

'I expect you're right. All the same, she can't have done that because it would have been found when her things were turned over. It worries me—you see, an old lady like that can't have taken up floors or dug holes in the garden. All the same it's there in the Red House somewhere. Crockett hasn't found it, but she knows it's there, and once they get the house to themselves, she and her precious nephew, they can turn it upside down until they find what they're after. We've got to get ahead of them. Come on, Tuppence. We'll go to the Red House.'

Monica Deane received them. To her mother and Crockett they were represented as would-be purchasers of the Red House, which would account for their being taken all over the house and grounds. Tommy did not tell Monica of the conclusions he had come to, but he asked her various searching questions. Of the garments and personal belongings of the dead woman, some had been given to Crockett and the others sent to various poor families. Everything had been gone through and turned out.

'Did your aunt leave any papers?'

'The desk was full, and there were some in a drawer in her bedroom, but there was nothing of importance amongst them.'

'Have they been thrown away?'

'No, my mother is always very loath to throw away old papers. There were some old-fashioned recipes among them which she intends to go through one day.'

'Good,' said Tommy approvingly. Then, indicating an old man who was at work upon one of the flower beds in the garden, he asked: 'Was that old man the gardener here in your aunt's time?'

'Yes, he used to come three days a week. He lives in the village. Poor old fellow, he is past doing any really useful work. We have him just once a week to keep things tidied up. We can't afford more.'

Tommy winked at Tuppence to indicate that she was to keep Monica with her, and he himself stepped across to where the gardener was working. He spoke a few pleasant words to the old man, asked him if he had been there in the old lady's time, and then said casually.

'You buried a box for her once, didn't you?'

'No, sir, I never buried naught for her. What should she want to bury a box for?'

Tommy shook his head. He strolled back to the house frowning. It was to be hoped that a study of the old lady's papers would yield some clue—otherwise the problem was a hard one to solve. The house itself was old fashioned, but not old enough to contain a secret room or passage.

Before leaving, Monica brought them down a big cardboard box tied with string.

'I've collected all the papers,' she whispered. 'And they're in here. I thought you could take it away with you, and then you'll have plenty of time to go over them—but I'm sure you won't find anything to throw light on the mysterious happenings in this house—'

Her words were interrupted by a terrific crash overhead. Tommy ran quickly up the stairs. A jug and a basin in one of the front rooms was lying on the ground broken to pieces. There was no one in the room.

'The ghost up to its tricks again,' he murmured with a grin.

He went downstairs again thoughtfully.

'I wonder, Miss Deane, if I might speak to the maid, Crockett, for a minute.'

'Certainly. I will ask her to come to you.'

Monica went off to the kitchen. She returned with the elderly maid who had opened the door to them earlier.

'We are thinking of buying this house,' said Tommy pleasantly, 'and my wife was wondering whether, in that case, you would care to remain on with us?'

Crockett's respectable face displayed no emotion of any kind.

'Thank you, sir,' she said. 'I should like to think it over if I may.'

Tommy turned to Monica.

'I am delighted with the house, Miss Deane. I understand that there is another buyer in the market. I know what he has offered for the house, and I will willingly give a hundred more. And mind you, that is a good price I am offering.'

Monica murmured something noncommittal, and the Beresfords took their leave.

'I was right,' said Tommy, as they went down the drive, 'Crockett's in it. Did you notice that she was out of breath? That was from running down the backstairs after smashing the jug and basin. Sometimes, very likely, she has admitted her nephew secretly, and he has done a little poltergeisting, or whatever you call it, whilst she has been innocently with the family. You'll see Dr O'Neill will make a further offer before the day is out.'

True enough, after dinner, a note was brought. It was from Monica.

'I have just heard from Dr O'Neill. He raises his previous offer by £150.'

'The nephew must be a man of means,' said Tommy thoughtfully. 'And I tell you what, Tuppence, the prize he's after must be well worth while.'

'Oh! Oh! Oh! if only we could find it!'

'Well, let's get on with the spade work.'

They were sorting through the big box of papers, a wearisome affair, as they were all jumbled up pell mell without any kind of order or method. Every few minutes they compared notes.

'What's the latest, Tuppence?'

'Two old receipted bills, three unimportant letters, a

recipe for preserving new potatoes and one for making lemon cheesecake. What's yours?'

'One bill, a poem on Spring, two newspaper cuttings: 'Why Women buy Pearls—a sound investment", and 'Man with Four Wives—Extraordinary Story", and a recipe for Jugged Hare.'

'It's heart-breaking,' said Tuppence, and they fell to once more. At last the box was empty. They looked at each other.

'I put this aside,' said Tommy, picking up a half sheet of notepaper, 'because it struck me as peculiar. But I don't suppose it's got anything to do with what we're looking for.'

'Let's see it. Oh! it's one of these funny things, what do they call them? Anagrams, charades or something.' She read it:

'My first you put on glowing coal
And into it you put my whole;
My second really is the first;
My third mislikes the winter blast.'

'H'm,' said Tommy critically. 'I don't think much of the poet's rhymes.'

'I don't see what you find peculiar about it, though,' said Tuppence. 'Everybody used to have a collection of these sort of things about fifty years ago. You saved them up for winter evenings round the fire.'

'I wasn't referring to the verse. It's the words written below it that strike me as peculiar.'

'St Luke, xi, 9,' she read. 'It's a text.'

'Yes. Doesn't that strike you as odd? Would an old lady of a religious persuasion write a text just under a charade?'

'It is rather odd,' agreed Tuppence thoughtfully.

'I presume that you, being a clergyman's daughter, have got your Bible with you?'

'As a matter of fact, I have. Aha! you didn't expect that. Wait a sec.'

Tuppence ran to her suitcase, extracted a small red volume and returned to the table. She turned the leaves rapidly. 'Here we are. Luke, chapter xi, verse 9. Oh! Tommy, look.'

Tommy bent over and looked where Tuppence's small finger pointed to a portion of the verse in question.

'Seek and ye shall find.'

'That's it,' cried Tuppence. 'We've got it! Solve the cryptogram and the treasure is ours—or rather Monica's.'

'Well, let's get to work on the cryptogram, as you call it. '*My first* you put on glowing coal.' What does that mean, I wonder? Then—'My *second* really is the first.' That's pure gibberish.'

'It's quite simple, really,' said Tuppence kindly. 'It's just a sort of knack. Let *me* have it.'

Tommy surrendered it willingly. Tuppence ensconced herself in an armchair, and began muttering to herself with bent brows.

'It's quite simple, really,' murmured Tommy when half an hour had elapsed.

'Don't crow! We're the wrong generation for this. I've a good mind to go back to town tomorrow and call on some old pussy who would probably read it as easy as winking. It's a knack, that's all.'

'Well, let's have one more try.'

'There aren't many things you can put on glowing coal,' said Tuppence thoughtfully. 'There's water, to put it out, or wood, or a kettle.'

'It must be one syllable, I suppose? What about *wood*, then?'

'You couldn't put anything *into* wood, though.'

'There's no one syllable word instead of *water*, but there must be one syllable things you can put on a fire in the kettle line.'

'Saucepans,' mused Tuppence. 'Frying pans. How about *pan?* or *pot?* What's a word beginning pan or pot that is something you cook?'

'Pottery,' suggested Tommy. 'You bake that in the fire. Wouldn't that be near enough?'

'The rest of it doesn't fit. Pancakes? No. Oh! bother.'

They were interrupted by the little serving-maid, who told them that dinner would be ready in a few minutes.

'Only Mrs Lumley, she wanted to know if you like your potatoes fried, or boiled in their jackets? She's got some of each.'

'Boiled in their jackets,' said Tuppence promptly. 'I love potatoes—' She stopped dead with her mouth open.

'What's the matter, Tuppence? Have you seen a ghost?'

'Tommy,' cried Tuppence. 'Don't you see? That's it! The word, I mean. *Potatoes*! 'My first you put on glowing coal"—that's pot. 'And into it you put my *whole*.' 'My *second* really is the first.' That's A, the first letter of the alphabet. 'My *third* mislikes the wintry blast"—cold *toes* of course!'

'You're right, Tuppence. Very clever of you. But I'm afraid we've wasted an awful lot of time over nothing. Potatoes don't fit in at all with missing treasure. Half a sec, though. What did you read out just now, when we were going through the box? Something about a recipe for New Potatoes. I wonder if there's anything in that.'

He rummaged hastily through the pile of recipes.

'Here it is. 'To KEEP NEW POTATOES. Put the new potatoes into tins and bury them in the garden. Even in the middle of winter, they will taste as though freshly dug.'

'We've got it,' screamed Tuppence. 'That's it. The treasure is in the garden, buried in a tin.'

'But I asked the gardener. He said he'd never buried anything.'

'Yes, I know, but that's because people never really answer what you say, they answer what they think you mean. He knew he'd never buried anything out of the common. We'll go tomorrow and ask him where he buried the potatoes.'

The following morning was Christmas Eve. By dint of inquiry they found the old gardener's cottage. Tuppence broached the subject after some minutes' conversation.

'I wish one could have new potatoes at Christmas time,' she remarked. 'Wouldn't they be good with turkey? Do people round here ever bury them in tins? I've heard that keeps them fresh.'

'Ay, that they do,' declared the old man. 'Old Miss Deane, up to the Red House, she allus had three tins buried every summer, and as often as not forgot to have 'em dug up again!'

'In the bed by the house, as a rule, didn't she?'

'No, over against the wall by the fir tree.'

Having got the information they wanted, they soon took their leave of the old man, presenting him with five shillings as a Christmas box.

'And now for Monica,' said Tommy.

'Tommy! You have no sense of the dramatic. Leave it

to me. I've got a beautiful plan. Do you think you could manage to beg, borrow or steal a spade?'

Somehow or other, a spade was duly produced, and that night, late, two figures might have been seen stealing into the grounds of the Red House. The place indicated by the gardener was easily found, and Tommy set to work. Presently his spade rang on metal, and a few seconds later he had unearthed a big biscuit tin. It was sealed round with adhesive plaster and firmly fastened down, but Tuppence, by the aid of Tommy's knife, soon managed to open it. Then she gave a groan. The tin was full of potatoes. She poured them out, so that the tin was completely empty, but there were no other contents.

'Go on digging, Tommy.'

It was some time before a second tin rewarded their search. As before, Tuppence unsealed it.

'Well?' demanded Tommy anxiously.

'Potatoes again!'

'Damn!' said Tommy, and set to once more.

'The third time is lucky,' said Tuppence consolingly.

'I believe the whole thing's a mare's nest,' said Tommy gloomily, but he continued to dig.

At last a third tin was brought to light.

'Potatoes aga—' began Tuppence, then stopped. 'Oh, Tommy, we've got it. It's only potatoes on top. Look!'

She held up a big old-fashioned velvet bag.

'Cut along home,' cried Tommy. 'It's icy cold. Take the bag with you. I must shovel back the earth. And may a thousand curses light upon your head, Tuppence, if you open that bag before I come!'

'I'll play fair. Ouch! I'm frozen.' She beat a speedy retreat.

On arrival at the inn she had not long to wait. Tommy

was hard upon her heels, perspiring freely after his digging and the final brisk run.

'Now then,' said Tommy, 'the private inquiry agents make good! Open the loot, Mrs Beresford.'

Inside the bag was a package done up in oil silk and a heavy chamois leather bag. They opened the latter first. It was full of gold sovereigns. Tommy counted them.

'Two hundred pounds. That was all they would let her have, I suppose. Cut open the package.'

Tuppence did so. It was full of closely folded banknotes. Tommy and Tuppence counted them carefully. They amounted to exactly twenty thousand pounds.

'Whew!' said Tommy. 'Isn't it lucky for Monica that we're both rich and honest? What's that done up in tissue paper?'

Tuppence unrolled the little parcel and drew out a magnificent string of pearls, exquisitely matched.

'I don't know much about these things,' said Tommy slowly. 'But I'm pretty sure that those pearls are worth another five thousand pounds at least. Look at the size of them. Now I see why the old lady kept that cutting about pearls being a good investment. She must have realised all her securities and turned them into notes and jewels.'

'Oh, Tommy, isn't it wonderful? Darling Monica. Now she can marry her nice young man and live happily ever afterwards, like me.'

'That's rather sweet of you, Tuppence. So you *are* happy with me?'

'As a matter of fact,' said Tuppence, 'I am. But I didn't mean to say so. It slipped out. What with being excited, and Christmas Eve, and one thing and another—'

'If you really love me,' said Tommy, 'will you answer me one question?'

'I hate these catches,' said Tuppence, 'but—well—all right.'

'Then how did you know that Monica was a clergyman's daughter?'

'Oh, that was just cheating,' said Tuppence happily. 'I opened her letter making an appointment, and a Mr Deane was father's curate once, and he had a little girl called Monica, about four or five years younger than me. So I put two and two together.'

'You are a shameless creature,' said Tommy. 'Hullo, there's twelve o'clock striking. Happy Christmas, Tuppence.'

'Happy Christmas, Tommy. It'll be a Happy Christmas for Monica too—and all owing to US. I am glad. Poor thing, she has been so miserable. Do you know, Tommy, I feel all queer and choky about the throat when I think of it.'

'Darling Tuppence,' said Tommy.

'Darling Tommy,' said Tuppence. 'How awfully sentimental we are getting.'

'Christmas comes but once a year,' said Tommy sententiously. 'That's what our great-grandmothers said, and I expect there's a lot of truth in it still.'

The Plymouth Express

Alec Simpson, RN, stepped from the platform at Newton Abbot into a first-class compartment of the Plymouth Express. A porter followed him with a heavy suitcase. He was about to swing it up to the rack, but the young sailor stopped him.

'No—leave it on the seat. I'll put it up later. Here you are.'

'Thank you, sir.' The porter, generously tipped, withdrew.

Doors banged; a stentorian voice shouted: 'Plymouth only. Change for Torquay. Plymouth next stop.' Then a whistle blew, and the train drew slowly out of the station.

Lieutenant Simpson had the carriage to himself. The December air was chilly, and he pulled up the window. Then he sniffed vaguely, and frowned. What a smell there was! Reminded him of that time in hospital, and the operation on his leg. Yes, chloroform; that was it!

He let the window down again, changing his seat to one with its back to the engine. He pulled a pipe out of his pocket and lit it. For a little time he sat inactive, looking out into the night and smoking.

At last he roused himself, and opening the suitcase, took out some papers and magazines, then closed the suitcase again and endeavoured to shove it under the opposite seat—without success. Some obstacle resisted it. He shoved harder with rising impatience, but it still stuck out half-way into the carriage.

'Why the devil won't it go in?' he muttered, and hauling it out completely, he stooped down and peered under the seat . . .

A moment later a cry rang out into the night, and the great train came to an unwilling halt in obedience to the imperative jerking of the communication cord.

'*Mon ami*,' said Poirot, 'you have, I know, been deeply interested in this mystery of the Plymouth Express. Read this.'

I picked up the note he flicked across the table to me. It was brief and to the point.

Dear Sir,

I shall be obliged if you will call upon me at your earliest convenience.

Yours faithfully,

EBENEZER HALLIDAY

The connection was not clear to my mind, and I looked inquiringly at Poirot.

For answer he took up the newspaper and read aloud: ''A sensational discovery was made last night. A young naval officer returning to Plymouth found under the seat of his compartment the body of a woman, stabbed through the heart. The officer at once pulled the communication cord, and the train was brought to a standstill. The woman, who was about thirty years of age, and richly dressed, has not yet been identified.'

'And later we have this: 'The woman found dead

in the Plymouth Express has been identified as the Honourable Mrs Rupert Carrington.' You see now, my friend? Or if you do not I will add this—Mrs Rupert Carrington was, before her marriage, Flossie Halliday, daughter of old man Halliday, the steel king of America.'

'And he has sent for you? Splendid!'

'I did him a little service in the past—an affair of bearer bonds. And once, when I was in Paris for a royal visit, I had Mademoiselle Flossie pointed out to me. *La jolie petite pensionnaire*! She had the *joli dot* too! It caused trouble. She nearly made a bad affair.'

'How was that?'

'A certain Count de la Rochefour. *Un bien mauvais sujet*! A bad hat, as you would say. An adventurer pure and simple, who knew how to appeal to a romantic young girl. Luckily her father got wind of it in time. He took her back to America in haste. I heard of her marriage some years later, but I know nothing of her husband.'

'H'm,' I said. 'The Honourable Rupert Carrington is no beauty, by all accounts. He'd pretty well run through his own money on the turf, and I should imagine old man Halliday's dollars came along in the nick of time. I should say that for a good-looking, well-mannered, utterly unscrupulous young scoundrel, it would be hard to find his mate!'

'Ah, the poor little lady! *Elle n'est pas bien tombée*!'

'I fancy he made it pretty obvious at once that it was her money, and not she, that had attracted him. I believe they drifted apart almost at once. I have heard rumours lately that there was to be a definite legal separation.'

'Old man Halliday is no fool. He would tie up her money pretty tight.'

'I dare say. Anyway, I know as a fact that the

Honourable Rupert is said to be extremely hard up.'

'Aha! I wonder—'

'You wonder what?'

'My good friend, do not jump down my throat like that. You are interested, I see. Suppose you accompany me to see Mr Halliday. There is a taxi-stand at the corner.'

A few minutes sufficed to whirl us to the superb house in Park Lane rented by the American magnate. We were shown into the library, and almost immediately we were joined by a large stout man, with piercing eyes and an aggressive chin.

'M. Poirot?' said Mr Halliday. 'I guess I don't need to tell you what I want you for. You've read the papers, and I'm never one to let the grass grow under my feet. I happened to hear you were in London, and I remembered the good work you did over those bombs. Never forget a name. I've the pick of Scotland Yard, but I'll have my own man as well. Money no object. All the dollars were made for my little girl—and now she's gone, I'll spend my last cent to catch the damned scoundrel that did it! See? So it's up to you to deliver the goods.'

Poirot bowed.

'I accept, monsieur, all the more willingly that I saw your daughter in Paris several times. And now I will ask you to tell me the circumstances of her journey to Plymouth and any other details that seem to you to bear upon the case.'

'Well, to begin with,' responded Halliday, 'she wasn't going to Plymouth. She was going to join a house-party at Avonmead Court, the Duchess of Swansea's place. She left London by the twelve-fourteen from Paddington, arriving at Bristol (where she had to change) at two-fifty. The principal Plymouth expresses, of course, run via Westbury, and do not go near Bristol at all. The twelve-fourteen does a non-stop run to Bristol, afterwards stopping at Weston, Taunton, Exeter and Newton Abbot. My daughter travelled alone in her carriage, which was reserved as far as Bristol, her maid being in a third class carriage in the next coach.'

Poirot nodded, and Mr Halliday went on: 'The party at Avonmead Court was to be a very gay one, with several balls, and in consequence my daughter had with her nearly all her jewels—amounting in value, perhaps, to about a hundred thousand dollars.'

'*Un moment*,' interrupted Poirot. 'Who had charge of the jewels? Your daughter, or the maid?'

'My daughter always took charge of them herself, carrying them in a small blue morocco case.'

'Continue, monsieur.'

'At Bristol the maid, Jane Mason, collected her mistress's dressing-bag and wraps, which were with her, and came to the door of Flossie's compartment. To her intense surprise, my daughter told her that she was not getting out at Bristol, but was going on farther. She directed Mason to get out the luggage and put it in the cloakroom. She could have tea in the refreshment-room, but she was to wait at the station for her mistress, who would return to Bristol by an up-train in the course of the afternoon. The maid, although very much astonished, did as she was told. She put the luggage in the cloakroom and had some tea. But up-train after up-train came in, and her mistress did not appear. After the arrival of the last train, she left the luggage where it was, and went to a hotel near the station for the night. This morning she read of the tragedy, and returned to town by the first available train.'

'Is there nothing to account for your daughter's sudden change of plan?'

'Well there is this: According to Jane Mason, at Bristol, Flossie was no longer alone in her carriage. There was a man in it who stood looking out of the farther window so that she could not see his face.'

'The train was a corridor one, of course?'

'Yes.'

'Which side was the corridor?'

'On the platform side. My daughter was standing in the corridor as she talked to Mason.'

'And there is no doubt in your mind—excuse me!' He got up, and carefully straightened the inkstand which was a little askew. '*Je vous demande pardon*,' he continued, re-seating himself. 'It affects my nerves to see anything crooked. Strange, is it not? I was saying, monsieur, that there is no doubt in your mind as to this probably unexpected meeting being the cause of your daughter's sudden change of plan?'

'It seems the only reasonable supposition.'

'You have no idea as to who the gentleman in question might be?'

The millionaire hesitated for a moment, and then replied: 'No—I do not know at all.'

'Now—as to the discovery of the body?'

'It was discovered by a young naval officer who at once gave the alarm. There was a doctor on the train. He examined the body. She had been first chloroformed, and then stabbed. He gave it as his opinion that she had been dead about four hours, so it must have been done not long after leaving Bristol—probably between there and Weston, possibly between Weston and Taunton.'

'And the jewel-case?'

'The jewel-case, M. Poirot, was missing.'

'One thing more, monsieur. Your daughter's fortune—to whom does it pass at her death?'

'Flossie made a will soon after her marriage, leaving everything to her husband.' He hesitated for a minute, and then went on: 'I may as well tell you, Monsieur Poirot, that I regard my son-in-law as an unprincipled scoundrel, and that, by my advice, my daughter was on the eve of freeing herself from him by legal means—no difficult matter. I settled her money upon her in such a way that he could not touch it during her lifetime, but although they have lived entirely apart for some years, she had frequently acceded to his demands for money, rather than face an open scandal. However, I was determined to put an end to this. At last Flossie agreed, and my lawyers were instructed to take proceedings.'

'And where is Monsieur Carrington?'

'In town. I believe he was away in the country yesterday, but he returned last night.'

Poirot considered a little while. Then he said: 'I think that is all, monsieur.'

'You would like to see the maid, Jane Mason?'

'If you please.'

Halliday rang the bell, and gave a short order to the footman.

A few minutes later Jane Mason entered the room, a respectable, hard-featured woman, as emotionless in the face of tragedy as only a good servant can be.

'You will permit me to put a few questions? Your mistress, she was quite as usual before starting yesterday morning? Not excited or flurried?'

'Oh no, sir!'

'But at Bristol she was quite different?'

'Yes, sir, regular upset—so nervous she didn't seem to know what she was saying.'

'What did she say exactly?'

'Well, sir, as near as I can remember, she said: 'Mason, I've got to alter my plans. Something has happened—I mean, I'm not getting out here after all. I must go on. Get out the luggage and put it in the cloakroom; then have some tea, and wait for me in the station.'

''Wait for you here, ma'am?' I asked.

''Yes, yes. Don't leave the station. I shall return by a later train. I don't know when. It mayn't be until quite late.'

''Very well, ma'am,' I says. It wasn't my place to ask questions, but I thought it very strange.'

'It was unlike your mistress, eh?'

'Very unlike her, sir.'

'What do you think?'

'Well, sir, I thought it was to do with the gentleman in the carriage. She didn't speak to him, but she turned round once or twice as though to ask him if she was doing right.'

'But you didn't see the gentleman's face?'

'No, sir; he stood with his back to me all the time.'

'Can you describe him at all?'

'He had on a light fawn overcoat, and a travelling-cap. He was tall and slender, like and the back of his head was dark.'

'You didn't know him?'

'Oh no, I don't think so, sir.'

'It was not your master, Mr Carrington, by any chance?'

Mason looked rather startled.

'Oh, I don't think so, sir!'

'But you are not *sure*?'

'It was about the master's build, sir—but I never thought of it being him. We so seldom saw him . . . I couldn't say it *wasn't* him!'

Poirot picked up a pin from the carpet, and frowned at it severely; then he continued: 'Would it be possible for the man to have entered the train at Bristol before you reached the carriage?'

Mason considered.

'Yes, sir, I think it would. My compartment was very crowded, and it was some minutes before I could get out—and then there was a very large crowd on the platform, and that delayed me too. But he'd only have had a minute or two to speak to the mistress, that way. I took it for granted that he'd come along the corridor.'

'That is more probable, certainly.'

He paused, still frowning.

'You know how the mistress was dressed, sir?'

'The papers give a few details, but I would like you to confirm them.'

'She was wearing a white fox fur toque, sir, with a white spotted veil, and a blue frieze coat and skirt—the shade of blue they call electric.'

'H'm, rather striking.'

'Yes,' remarked Mr Halliday. 'Inspector Japp is in hopes that that may help us to fix the spot where the crime took place. Anyone who saw her would remember her.'

'*Précisément*!—Thank you, mademoiselle.'

The maid left the room.

'Well!' Poirot got up briskly. 'That is all I can do here—except, monsieur, that I would ask you to tell me everything, but *everything*!'

'I have done so.'

'You are sure?'

'Absolutely.'

'Then there is nothing more to be said. I must decline the case.'

'Why?'

'Because you have not been frank with me.'

'I assure you—'

'No, you are keeping something back.'

There was a moment's pause, and then Halliday drew a paper from his pocket and handed it to my friend.

'I guess that's what you're after, Monsieur Poirot—though how you know about it fairly gets my goat!'

Poirot smiled, and unfolded the paper. It was a letter written in thin sloping handwriting. Poirot read it aloud.

> 'Chère Madame,
>
> It is with infinite pleasure that I look forward to the felicity of meeting you again. After your so amiable reply to my letter, I can hardly restrain my impatience. I have never forgotten those days in Paris. It is most cruel that you should be leaving London tomorrow. However, before very long, and perhaps sooner than you think, I shall have the joy of beholding once more the lady whose image has ever reigned supreme in my heart.
>
> Believe, chère madame, all the assurances of my most devoted and unaltered sentiments—
>
> ARMAND DE LA ROCHEFOUR.'

Poirot handed the letter back to Halliday with a bow.

'I fancy, monsieur, that you did not know that your daughter intended renewing her acquaintance with the Count de la Rochefour?'

'It came as a thunderbolt to me! I found this letter

in my daughter's handbag. As you probably know, Monsieur Poirot, this so-called count is an adventurer of the worst type.'

Poirot nodded.

'But I want to know how you knew of the existence of this letter?'

My friend smiled. 'Monsieur, I did not. But to track footmarks and recognize cigarette-ash is not sufficient for a detective. He must also be a good psychologist! I knew that you disliked and mistrusted your son-in-law. He benefits by your daughter's death; the maid's description of the mysterious man bears a sufficient resemblance to him. Yet you are not keen on his track! Why? Surely because your suspicions lie in another direction. Therefore you were keeping something back.'

'You're right, Monsieur Poirot. I was sure of Rupert's guilt until I found this letter. It unsettled me horribly.'

'Yes. The Count says 'Before very long, and perhaps sooner than you think.' Obviously he would not want to wait until you should get wind of his reappearance. Was it he who travelled down from London by the twelve-fourteen, and came along the corridor to your daughter's compartment? The Count de la Rochefour is also, if I remember rightly, tall and dark!'

The millionaire nodded.

'Well, monsieur, I will wish you good day. Scotland Yard has, I presume, a list of the jewels?'

'Yes, I believe Inspector Japp is here now if you would like to see him.'

Japp was an old friend of ours, and greeted Poirot with a sort of affectionate contempt.

'And how are you, monsieur? No bad feeling between us, though we *have* got our different ways of looking at things. How are the 'little grey cells'', eh? Going strong?'

Poirot beamed upon him. 'They function, my good Japp; assuredly they do!'

'Then that's all right. Think it was the Honourable Rupert, or a crook? We're keeping an eye on all the regular places, of course. We shall know if the shiners are disposed of, and of course whoever did it isn't going to keep them to admire their sparkle. Not likely! I'm trying to find out where Rupert Carrington was yesterday. Seems a bit of a mystery about it. I've got a man watching him.'

'A great precaution, but perhaps a day late,' suggested Poirot gently.

'You always will have your joke, Monsieur Poirot. Well, I'm off to Paddington. Bristol, Weston, Taunton, that's my beat. So long.'

'You will come round and see me this evening, and tell me the result?'

'Sure thing, if I'm back.'

'The good inspector believes in matter in motion,' murmured Poirot as our friend departed. 'He travels; he measures footprints; he collects mud and cigarette-ash! He is extremely busy! He is zealous beyond words! And if I mentioned psychology to him, do you know what he would do, my friend? He would smile! He would say to himself: 'Poor old Poirot! He ages! He grows senile!' Japp is the 'younger generation knocking on the door.' And *ma foi*! They are so busy knocking that they do not notice that the door is open!'

'And what are you going to do?'

'As we have *carte blanche*, I shall expend threepence in ringing up the Ritz—where you may have noticed our Count is staying. After that, as my feet are a little damp, and I have sneezed twice, I shall return to my rooms and make myself a *tisane* over the spirit lamp!'

I did not see Poirot again until the following morning. I found him placidly finishing his breakfast.

'Well?' I inquired eagerly. 'What has happened?'

'Nothing.'

'But Japp?'

'I have not seen him.'

'The Count?'

'He left the Ritz the day before yesterday.'

'The day of the murder?'

'Yes.'

'Then that settles it! Rupert Carrington is cleared.'

'Because the Count de la Rochefour has left the Ritz? You go too fast, my friend.'

'Anyway, he must be followed, arrested! But what could be his motive?'

'One hundred thousand dollars' worth of jewellery is a very good motive for anyone. No, the question to my mind is: why kill her? Why not simply steal the jewels? She would not prosecute.'

'Why not?'

'Because she is a woman, *mon ami*. She once loved this man. Therefore she would suffer her loss in silence. And the Count, who is an extremely good psychologist where women are concerned—hence his successes—would know that perfectly well! On the other hand, if Rupert Carrington killed her, why take the jewels which would incriminate him fatally?'

'As a blind.'

'Perhaps you are right, my friend. Ah, here is Japp! I recognize his knock.'

The inspector was beaming good-humouredly.

'Morning, Poirot. Only just got back. I've done some good work! And you?'

'Me, I have arranged my ideas,' replied Poirot placidly.

Japp laughed heartily.

'Old chap's getting on in years,' he observed beneath his breath to me. 'That won't do for us young folk,' he said aloud.

'*Quel dommage*?' Poirot inquired.

'Well, do you want to hear what I've done?'

'You permit me to make a guess? You have found the knife with which the crime was committed, by the side of the line between Weston and Taunton, and you have interviewed the paper-boy who spoke to Mrs Carrington at Weston!'

Japp's jaw fell. 'How on earth did you know? Don't tell me it was those almighty 'little grey cells" of yours!'

'I am glad you admit for once that they are *all mighty*! Tell me, did she give the paper-boy a shilling for himself?'

'No, it was half a crown!' Japp had recovered his temper, and grinned. 'Pretty extravagant, these rich Americans!'

'And in consequence the boy did not forget her?'

'Not he. Half-crowns don't come his way every day. She hailed him and bought two magazines. One had a picture of a girl in blue on the cover. 'That'll match me,' she said. Oh, he remembered her perfectly. Well, that was enough for me. By the doctor's evidence, the crime *must* have been committed before Taunton. I guessed they'd throw the knife away at once, and I walked down the line looking for it; and sure enough, there it was. I made inquiries at Taunton about our man, but of course it's a big station, and it wasn't likely they'd notice him. He probably got back to London by a later train.'

Poirot nodded. 'Very likely.'

'But I found another bit of news when I got back. They're passing the jewels, all right! That large emerald was pawned last night—by one of the regular lot. Who do you think it was?'

'I don't know—except that he was a short man.'

Japp stared. 'Well, you're right there. He's short enough. It was Red Narky.'

'Who is Red Narky?' I asked.

'A particularly sharp jewel-thief, sir. And not one to stick at murder. Usually works with a woman—Gracie Kidd; but she doesn't seem to be in it this time—unless she's got off to Holland with the rest of the swag.'

'You've arrested Narky?'

'Sure thing. But mind you, it's the other man we want—the man who went down with Mrs Carrington in the train. He was the one who planned the job, right enough. But Narky won't squeal on a pal.'

I noticed Poirot's eyes had become very green.

'I think,' he said gently, 'that I can find Narky's pal for you, all right.'

'One of your little ideas, eh?' Japp eyed Poirot sharply. 'Wonderful how you manage to deliver the goods sometimes, at your age and all. Devil's own luck, of course.'

'Perhaps, perhaps,' murmured my friend. 'Hastings, my hat. And the brush. So! My galoshes, if it still rains! We must not undo the good work of that *tisane*. *Au revoir*, Japp!'

'Good luck to you, Poirot.'

Poirot hailed the first taxi we met, and directed the driver to Park Lane.

When we drew up before Halliday's house, he skipped out nimbly, paid the driver and rang the bell. To the footman who opened the door he made a request in a low voice, and we were immediately taken upstairs. We went up to the top of the house, and were shown into a small neat bedroom. Poirot's eyes roved round the room and fastened themselves on a small black trunk. He knelt in front of it, scrutinized the labels on it, and took a small twist of wire from his pocket.

'Ask Mr Halliday if he will be so kind as to mount to me here,' he said over his shoulder to the footman.

The man departed, and Poirot gently coaxed the lock of the trunk with a practised hand. In a few minutes the lock gave, and he raised the lid of the trunk. Swiftly he began rummaging among the clothes it contained, flinging them out on the floor.

There was a heavy step on the stairs, and Halliday entered the room.

'What in hell are you doing here?' he demanded, staring.

'I was looking, monsieur, for *this*.' Poirot withdrew from the trunk a coat and skirt of bright blue frieze, and a small toque of white fox fur.

'What are you doing with my trunk?' I turned to see that the maid, Jane Mason, had entered the room.

'If you will just shut the door, Hastings. Thank you. Yes, and stand with your back against it. Now, Mr Halliday, let me introduce you to Gracie Kidd, otherwise Jane Mason, who will shortly rejoin her accomplice, Red Narky, under the kind escort of Inspector Japp.'

Poirot waved a deprecating hand. 'It was of the most simple!' He helped himself to more caviar.

'It was the maid's insistence on the clothes that her mistress was wearing that first struck me. Why was she so anxious that our attention should be directed to them? I reflected that we had only the maid's word for the mysterious man in the carriage at Bristol. As far as the doctor's evidence went, Mrs Carrington might easily have been murdered *before* reaching Bristol. But if so, then the maid must be an accomplice. And if she were an accomplice, she would not wish this point to rest on her evidence alone. The clothes Mrs Carrington was wearing were of a striking nature. A maid usually has a good deal of choice as to what her mistress shall wear. Now if, after Bristol, anyone saw a lady in a bright blue coat and skirt, and a fur toque, he will be quite ready to swear he had seen Mrs Carrington.

'I began to reconstruct. The maid would provide herself with duplicate clothes. She and her accomplice chloroform and stab Mrs Carrington between London and Bristol, probably taking advantage of a tunnel. Her body is rolled under the seat; and the maid takes her place. At Weston she must make herself noticed. How? In all probability, a newspaper-boy will be selected. She will insure his remembering her by giving him a large tip. She also drew his attention to the colour of her dress by a remark about one of the magazines. After leaving Weston, she throws the knife out of the window to mark the place where the crime presumably occurred, and changes her clothes, or buttons a long mackintosh over them. At Taunton she leaves the train and returns to Bristol as soon as possible, where her accomplice has duly left the luggage in the cloakroom. He hands over the ticket and himself returns to London. She waits on the platform, carrying out her role, goes to a hotel for the night and returns to town in the morning, exactly as she said.

'When Japp returned from his expedition, he confirmed all my deductions. He also told me that a well-known crook was passing the jewels. I knew that whoever it was would be the exact opposite of the man Jane Mason described. When I heard that it was Red Narky, who always worked with Gracie Kidd—well, I knew just where to find her.'

'And the Count?'

'The more I thought of it, the more I was convinced that he had nothing to do with it. That gentleman is much too careful of his own skin to risk murder. It would be out of keeping with his character.'

'Well, Monsieur Poirot,' said Halliday, 'I owe you a big debt. And the cheque I write after lunch won't go near to settling it.'

Poirot smiled modestly, and murmured to me: 'The good Japp, he shall get the official credit, all right, but though he has got his Gracie Kidd, I think that I, as the Americans say, have got his goat!'

Problem at Pollensa Bay

The steamer from Barcelona to Majorca landed Mr Parker Pyne at Palma in the early hours of the morning—and straightaway he met with disillusionment. The hotels were full! The best that could be done for him was an airless cupboard overlooking an inner court in a hotel in the centre of the town—and with that Mr Parker Pyne was not prepared to put up. The proprietor of the hotel was indifferent to his disappointment.

'What will you?' he observed with a shrug.

Palma was popular now! The exchange was favourable! Everyone—the English, the Americans—they all came to Majorca in the winter. The whole place was crowded. It was doubtful if the English gentleman would be able to get in anywhere—except perhaps at Formentor where the prices were so ruinous that even foreigners blenched at them.

Mr Parker Pyne partook of some coffee and a roll and went out to view the cathedral, but found himself in no mood for appreciating the beauties of architecture.

He next had a conference with a friendly taxi driver in inadequate French interlarded with native Spanish, and they discussed the merits and possibilities of Soller, Alcudia, Pollensa and Formentor—where there were fine hotels but very expensive.

Mr Parker Pyne was goaded to inquire how expensive.

They asked, said the taxi driver, an amount that it would be absurd and ridiculous to pay—was it not well known that the English came here because prices were cheap and reasonable?

Mr Parker Pyne said that that was quite so, but all the same what sums *did* they charge at Formentor?

A price incredible!

Perfectly—but WHAT PRICE EXACTLY?

The driver consented at last to reply in terms of figures.

Fresh from the exactions of hotels in Jerusalem and Egypt, the figure did not stagger Mr Parker Pyne unduly.

A bargain was struck, Mr Parker Pyne's suitcases were loaded on the taxi in a somewhat haphazard manner, and they started off to drive round the island, trying cheaper hostelries en route but with the final objective of Formentor.

But they never reached that final abode of plutocracy, for after they had passed through the narrow streets of Pollensa and were following the curved line of the seashore, they came to the Hotel Pino d'Oro—a small hotel standing on the edge of the sea looking out over a view that in the misty haze of a fine morning had the exquisite vagueness of a Japanese print. At once Mr Parker Pyne knew that this, and this only, was what he was looking for. He stopped the taxi, passed through the painted gate with the hope that he would find a resting place.

The elderly couple to whom the hotel belonged knew no English or French. Nevertheless the matter was concluded satisfactorily. Mr Parker Pyne was allotted a room overlooking the sea, the suitcases were unloaded, the driver congratulated his passenger upon avoiding the monstrous exigencies of 'these new hotels', received his fare and departed with a cheerful Spanish salutation.

Mr Parker Pyne glanced at his watch and perceiving that it was, even now, but a quarter to ten, he went out onto the small terrace now bathed in a dazzling morning light and ordered, for the second time that morning, coffee and rolls.

There were four tables there, his own, one from which breakfast was being cleared away and two occupied ones. At the one nearest him sat a family of father and mother and two elderly daughters—Germans. Beyond them, at the corner of the terrace, sat what were clearly an English mother and son.

The woman was about fifty-five. She had grey hair of a pretty tone—was sensibly but not fashionably dressed in a tweed coat and skirt—and had that comfortable self-possession which marks an Englishwoman used to much travelling abroad.

The young man who sat opposite her might have been twenty-five and he too was typical of his class and age. He was neither good-looking nor plain, tall nor short. He was clearly on the best of terms with his mother—they made little jokes together—and he was assiduous in passing her things.

As they talked, her eye met that of Mr Parker Pyne. It passed over him with well-bred nonchalance, but he knew that he had been assimilated and labelled.

He had been recognized as English and doubtless, in due course, some pleasant non-committal remark would be addressed to him.

Mr Parker Pyne had no particular objection. His own countrymen and women abroad were inclined to bore him slightly, but he was quite willing to pass the time of day in an amiable manner. In a small hotel it caused constraint if one did not do so. This particular woman, he felt sure, had excellent 'hotel manners', as he put it.

The English boy rose from his seat, made some laughing remark and passed into the hotel. The woman took her letters and bag and settled herself in a chair facing the sea. She unfolded a copy of the *Continental Daily Mail*. Her back was to Mr Parker Pyne.

As he drank the last drop of his coffee, Mr Parker Pyne glanced in her direction, and instantly he stiffened. He was alarmed—alarmed for the peaceful continuance of his holiday! That back was horribly expressive. In his time he had classified many such backs. Its rigidity—the tenseness of its poise—without seeing her face he knew well enough that the eyes were bright with unshed tears—that the woman was keeping herself in hand by a rigid effort.

Moving warily, like a much-hunted animal, Mr Parker Pyne retreated into the hotel. Not half an hour before he had been invited to sign his name in the book lying on the desk. There it was—a neat signature—C. Parker Pyne, London.

A few lines above Mr Parker Pyne noticed the entries: Mrs R. Chester, Mr Basil Chester—Holm Park, Devon.

Seizing a pen, Mr Parker Pyne wrote rapidly over his signature. It now read (with difficulty) Christopher Pyne.

If Mrs R. Chester was unhappy in Pollensa Bay, it was not going to be made easy for her to consult Mr Parker Pyne.

Already it had been a source of abiding wonder to that gentleman that so many people he had come across abroad should know his name and have noted his advertisements. In England many thousands of people read the *Times* every day and could have answered quite truthfully that they had never heard such a name in their lives. Abroad, he reflected, they read their newspapers more thoroughly. No item, not even the advertisement columns, escaped them.

Already his holidays had been interrupted on several occasions. He had dealt with a whole series of problems from murder to attempted blackmail. He was determined in Majorca to have peace. He felt instinctively that a distressed mother might trouble that peace considerably.

Mr Parker Pyne settled down at the Pino d'Oro very happily. There was a larger hotel not far off, the Mariposa, where a good many English people stayed. There was also quite an artist colony living all round. You could walk along by the sea to the fishing village where there was a cocktail bar where people met—there were a few shops. It was all very peaceful and pleasant. Girls strolled about in trousers with brightly coloured handkerchiefs tied round the upper halves of their bodies. Young men in berets with rather long hair held forth in 'Mac's Bar' on such subjects as plastic values and abstraction in art.

On the day after Mr Parker Pyne's arrival, Mrs Chester made a few conventional remarks to him on the subject of the view and the likelihood of the weather keeping fine. She then chatted a little with the German lady about knitting, and had a few pleasant words about the sadness of the political situation with two Danish gentlemen who spent their time rising at dawn and walking for eleven hours.

Mr Parker Pyne found Basil Chester a most likeable young man. He called Mr Parker Pyne 'sir' and listened most politely to anything the older man said. Sometimes the three English people had coffee together after dinner in the evening. After the third day, Basil left the party after ten minutes or so and Mr Parker Pyne was left tete-a-tete with Mrs Chester.

They talked about flowers and the growing of them, of the lamentable state of the English pound and of how expensive France had become, and of the difficulty of getting good afternoon tea.

Every evening when her son departed, Mr Parker Pyne saw the quickly concealed tremor of her lips, but immediately she recovered and discoursed pleasantly on the above-mentioned subjects.

Little by little she began to talk of Basil—of how well he had done at school—'he was in the First XI, you know'—of how everyone liked him, of how proud his father would have been of the boy had he lived, of how thankful she had been that Basil had never been 'wild'. 'Of course I always urge him to be with young people, but he really seems to prefer being with me.'

She said it with a kind of nice modest pleasure in the fact.

But for once Mr Parker Pyne did not make the usual tactful response he could usually achieve so easily. He said instead:

'Oh! well, there seem to be plenty of young people here—not in the hotel, but round about.'

At that, he noticed, Mrs Chester stiffened. She said: Of course there were a lot of *artists*. Perhaps she was very old-fashioned—*real* art, of course, was different, but a lot of young people just made that sort of thing an excuse for lounging about and doing nothing—and the girls drank a lot too much.

On the following day Basil said to Mr Parker Pyne:

'I'm awfully glad you turned up here, sir—especially for my mother's sake. She likes having you to talk to in the evenings.'

'What did you do when you were first here?'

'As a matter of fact we used to play piquet.'

'I see.'

'Of course one gets rather tired of piquet. As a matter of fact I've got some friends here—frightfully cheery crowd. I don't really think my mother approves of them—' He laughed as though he felt this ought to be amusing. 'The mater's very old-fashioned . . . Even girls in trousers shock her!'

'Quite so,' said Mr Parker Pyne.

'What I tell her is—one's got to move with the times . . . The girls at home round us are frightfully dull . . .'

'I see,' said Mr Parker Pyne.

All this interested him well enough. He was a spectator of a miniature drama, but he was not called upon to take part in it.

And then the worst—from Mr Parker Pyne's point of view—happened. A gushing lady of his acquaintance came to stay at the Mariposa. They met in the tea shop in the presence of Mrs Chester.

The newcomer screamed:

'Why—if it isn't Mr Parker Pyne—the one and only Mr Parker Pyne! And Adela Chester! Do you know each other? Oh, you do? You're staying at the same hotel? He's the one and only original wizard, Adela—the marvel of the century—all your troubles smoothed out while you wait! Didn't you *know*? You must have *heard* about him? Haven't you read his advertisements? '*Are you in trouble? Consult Mr Parker Pyne.*' There's just nothing he can't do. Husbands and wives flying at each other's throats and he brings 'em together—if you've lost interest in life he gives you the most thrilling adventures. As I say the man's just a *wizard*!'

It went on a good deal longer—Mr Parker Pyne at intervals making modest disclaimers. He disliked the look that Mrs Chester turned upon him. He disliked even more seeing her return along the beach in close confabulation with the garrulous singer of his praises.

The climax came quicker than he expected. That evening, after coffee, Mrs Chester said abruptly,

'Will you come into the little salon, Mr Pyne? There is something I want to say to you.'

He could but bow and submit.

Mrs Chester's self-control had been wearing thin—as the door of the little salon closed behind them, it snapped. She sat down and burst into tears.

'My boy, Mr Parker Pyne. You must save him. *We* must save him. It's breaking my heart!'

'My dear lady, as a mere outsider—'

'Nina Wycherley says you can do *anything*. She said I was to have the utmost confidence in you. She advised me to tell you everything—and that you'd put the whole thing right.'

Inwardly Mr Parker Pyne cursed the obtrusive Mrs Wycherley. Resigning himself he said:

'Well, let us thrash the matter out. A girl, I suppose?'

'Did he tell you about her?'

'Only indirectly.'

Words poured in a vehement stream from Mrs Chester. 'The girl was dreadful. She drank, she swore—she wore no clothes to speak of. Her sister lived out here—was married to an artist—a Dutchman. The whole set was most undesirable. Half of them were living together without being married. Basil was completely changed. He had always been so quiet, so interested in serious subjects. He had thought at one time of taking up archaeology—'

'Well, well,' said Mr Parker Pyne. 'Nature will have her revenge.'

'What do you mean?'

'It isn't healthy for a young man to be interested in serious subjects. He ought to be making an idiot of himself over one girl after another.'

'Please be serious, Mr Pyne.'

'I'm perfectly serious. Is the young lady, by any chance, the one who had tea with you yesterday?'

He had noticed her—her grey flannel trousers—the scarlet handkerchief tied loosely around her breast—the vermilion mouth and the fact that she had chosen a cocktail in preference to tea.

'You saw her? Terrible! Not the kind of girl Basil has ever admired.'

'You haven't given him much chance to admire a girl, have you?'

'I?'

'He's been too fond of *your* company! Bad! However, I daresay he'll get over this—if you don't precipitate matters.'

'You don't understand. He wants to marry this girl—Betty Gregg—they're *engaged*.'

'It's gone as far as that?'

'Yes. Mr Parker Pyne, you *must* do something. You must get my boy out of this disastrous marriage! His whole life will be ruined.'

'Nobody's life can be ruined except by themselves.'

'Basil's will be,' said Mrs Chester positively.

'I'm not worrying about Basil.'

'You're not worrying about the *girl*?'

'No, I'm worrying about *you*. You've been squandering your birthright.'

Mrs Chester looked at him, slightly taken aback.

'What are the years from twenty to forty? Fettered and bound by personal and emotional relationships. That's bound to be. That's living. But later there's a new stage. You can think, observe life, discover something about other people and the truth about yourself. Life becomes real—significant. You see it as a whole. Not just one scene—the scene you, as an actor, are playing. No man or woman is actually himself (or herself) till after forty-five. That's when individuality has a chance.'

Mrs Chester said:

'I've been wrapped up in Basil. He's been *everything* to me.'

'Well, he shouldn't have been. That's what you're paying for now. Love him as much as you like—but you're Adela Chester, remember, a person—not just Basil's mother.'

'It will break my heart if Basil's life is ruined,' said Basil's mother.

He looked at the delicate lines of her face, the wistful droop of her mouth. She was, somehow, a lovable woman. He did not want her to be hurt. He said:

'I'll see what I can do.'

He found Basil Chester only too ready to talk, eager to urge his point of view.

'This business is being just hellish. Mother's hopeless—prejudiced, narrow-minded. If only she'd let herself, she'd *see* how fine Betty is.'

'And Betty?'

He sighed.

'Betty's being damned difficult! If she'd just conform a bit—I mean leave off the lipstick for a day—it might make all the difference. She seems to go out of her way to be—well—modern—when Mother's about.'

Mr Parker Pyne smiled.

'Betty and Mother are two of the dearest people in the world, I should have thought they would have taken to each other like hot cakes.'

'You have a lot to learn, young man,' said Mr Parker Pyne.

'I wish you'd come along and see Betty and have a good talk about it all.'

Mr Parker Pyne accepted the invitation readily.

Betty and her sister and her husband lived in a small dilapidated villa a little way back from the sea. Their life was of a refreshing simplicity. Their furniture comprised three chairs, a table and beds. There was a cupboard in the wall that held the bare requirements of cups and plates. Hans was an excitable young man with wild blond hair that stood up all over his head. He spoke very odd English with incredible rapidity, walking up and down as he did so. Stella, his wife, was small and fair. Betty Gregg had red hair and freckles and a mischievous eye. She was, he noticed, not nearly so made-up as she had been the previous day at the Pino d'Oro.

She gave him a cocktail and said with a twinkle:

'You're in on the big bust-up?'

Mr Parker Pyne nodded.

'And whose side are you on, big boy? The young lovers—or the disapproving dame?'

'May I ask you a question?'

'Certainly.'

'Have you been very tactful over all this?'

'Not at all,' said Miss Gregg frankly. 'But the old cat put my back up.' (She glanced round to make sure that Basil was out of earshot) 'That woman just makes me feel mad. She's kept Basil tied to her apron strings all these years—that sort of thing makes a man look a fool. Basil isn't a fool really. Then she's so terribly *pukka sahib*.'

'That's not really such a bad thing. It's merely 'unfashionable" just at present.'

Betty Gregg gave a sudden twinkle.

'You mean it's like putting Chippendale chairs in the attic in Victorian days? Later you get them down again and say, 'Aren't they marvellous?' '

'Something of the kind.'

Betty Gregg considered.

'Perhaps you're right. I'll be honest. It was Basil who put my back up—being so anxious about what impression I'd make on his mother. It drove me to extremes. Even now I believe he might give me up—if his mother worked on him good and hard.'

'He might,' said Mr Parker Pyne. 'If she went about it the right way.'

'Are you going to tell her the right way? She won't think of it herself, you know. She'll just go on disapproving and that won't do the trick. But if you prompted her—'

She bit her lip—raised frank blue eyes to his.

'I've heard about you, Mr Parker Pyne. You're supposed to know something about human nature.

Do you think Basil and I could make a go of it—or not?'

'I should like an answer to three questions.'

'Suitability test? All right, go ahead.'

'Do you sleep with your window open or shut?'

'Open. I like lots of air.'

'Do you and Basil enjoy the same kind of food?'

'Yes.'

'Do you like going to bed early or late?'

'Really, under the rose, early. At half past ten I yawn—and I secretly feel rather hearty in the mornings—but of course I daren't admit it.'

'You ought to suit each other very well,' said Mr Parker Pyne.

'Rather a superficial test.'

'Not at all. I have known seven marriages at least, entirely wrecked, because the husband liked sitting up till midnight and the wife fell asleep at half past nine and vice versa.'

'It's a pity,' said Betty, 'that everybody can't be happy. Basil and I, and his mother giving us her blessing.'

Mr Parker Pyne coughed.

'I think,' he said, 'that that could possibly be managed.'

She looked at him doubtfully.

'Now I wonder,' she said, 'if you're double-crossing me?'

Mr Parker Pyne's face told nothing.

To Mrs Chester he was soothing, but vague. An engagement was not marriage. He himself was going to Soller for a week. He suggested that her line of action should be non-committal. Let her appear to acquiesce.

He spent a very enjoyable week at Soller.

On his return he found that a totally unexpected development had arisen.

As he entered the Pino d'Oro the first thing he saw was Mrs Chester and Betty Gregg having tea together. Basil was not there. Mrs Chester looked haggard. Betty, too, was looking off colour. She was hardly made-up at all, and her eyelids looked as though she had been crying.

They greeted him in a friendly fashion, but neither of them mentioned Basil.

Suddenly he heard the girl beside him draw in her breath sharply as though something had hurt her. Mr Parker Pyne turned his head.

Basil Chester was coming up the steps from the sea front. With him was a girl so exotically beautiful that it quite took your breath away. She was dark and her figure was marvellous. No one could fail to notice the fact since she wore nothing but a single garment of pale blue crêpe. She was heavily made-up with ochre powder and an orange scarlet mouth—but the unguents only displayed her remarkable beauty in a more pronounced fashion. As for young Basil, he seemed unable to take his eyes from her face.

'You're very late, Basil,' said his mother. 'You were to have taken Betty to Mac's.'

'My fault,' drawled the beautiful unknown. 'We just drifted.' She turned to Basil. 'Angel—get me something with a kick in it!'

She tossed off her shoe and stretched out her manicured toenails which were done emerald green to match her fingernails.

She paid no attention to the two women, but she leaned a little towards Mr Parker Pyne.

'Terrible island this,' she said. 'I was just dying with boredom before I met Basil. He is rather a pet!'

'Mr Parker Pyne—Miss Ramona,' said Mrs Chester.

The girl acknowledged the introduction with a lazy smile.

'I guess I'll call you Parker almost at once,' she murmured. 'My name's Dolores.'

Basil returned with the drinks. Miss Ramona divided her conversation (what there was of it—it was mostly glances) between Basil and Mr Parker Pyne. Of the two women she took no notice whatever. Betty attempted once or twice to join in the conversation but the other girl merely stared at her and yawned.

Suddenly Dolores rose.

'Guess I'll be going along now. I'm at the other hotel. Anyone coming to see me home?'

Basil sprang up.

'I'll come with you.'

Mrs Chester said: 'Basil, my dear—'

'I'll be back presently, Mother.'

'Isn't he the mother's boy?' Miss Ramona asked of the world at large. 'Just toots round after her, don't you?'

Basil flushed and looked awkward. Miss Ramona gave a nod in Mrs Chester's direction, a dazzling smile to Mr Parker Pyne and she and Basil moved off together.

After they had gone there was rather an awkward silence. Mr Parker Pyne did not like to speak first. Betty Gregg was twisting her fingers and looking out to sea. Mrs Chester looked flushed and angry.

Betty said: 'Well, what do you think of our new acquisition in Pollensa Bay?' Her voice was not quite steady.

Mr Parker Pyne said cautiously:

'A little—er—exotic.'

'Exotic?' Betty gave a short bitter laugh.

Mrs Chester said: 'She's terrible—terrible. Basil must be quite mad.'

Betty said sharply: 'Basil's all right.'

'Her toenails,' said Mrs Chester with a shiver of nausea.

Betty rose suddenly.

'I think, Mrs Chester, I'll go home and not stay to dinner after all.'

'Oh, my dear—Basil will be so disappointed.'

'Will he?' asked Betty with a short laugh. 'Anyway, I think I will. I've got rather a headache.'

She smiled at them both and went off. Mrs Chester turned to Mr Parker Pyne.

'I wish we had never come to this place—never!'

Mr Parker Pyne shook his head sadly.

'You shouldn't have gone away,' said Mrs Chester. 'If you'd been here this wouldn't have happened.'

Mr Parker Pyne was stung to respond.

'My dear lady, I can assure you that when it comes to a question of a beautiful young woman, I should have no influence over your son whatever. He—er—seems to be of a very susceptible nature.'

'He never used to be,' said Mrs Chester tearfully.

'Well,' said Mr Parker Pyne with an attempt at cheerfulness, 'this new attraction seems to have broken the back of his infatuation for Miss Gregg. That must be some satisfaction to you.'

'I don't know what you mean,' said Mrs Chester. 'Betty is a dear child and devoted to Basil. She is behaving extremely well over this. I think my boy must be mad.'

Mr Parker Pyne received this startling change of face without wincing. He had met inconsistency in women before. He said mildly:

'Not exactly mad—just bewitched.'

'She's impossible.'

'But extremely good-looking.'

Mrs Chester snorted.

Basil ran up the steps from the sea front.

'Hullo, Mater, here I am. Where's Betty?'

'Betty's gone home with a headache. I don't wonder.'

'Sulking, you mean.'

'I consider, Basil, that you are being extremely unkind to Betty.'

'For God's sake, Mother, don't jaw. If Betty is going to make this fuss every time I speak to another girl a nice sort of life we'll lead together.'

'You *are* engaged.'

'Oh, we're engaged all right. That doesn't mean that we're not going to have any friends of our own.

Nowadays people have to lead their own lives and try to cut out jealousy.'

He paused.

'Look here, if Betty isn't going to dine with us—I think I'll go back to the Mariposa. They did ask me to dine . . .'

'Oh, Basil—'

The boy gave her an exasperated look, then ran off down the steps.

Mrs Chester looked eloquently at Mr Parker Pyne.

'You see,' she said.

He saw.

Matters came to a head a couple of days later. Betty and Basil were to have gone for a long walk, taking a picnic lunch with them. Betty arrived at the Pino d'Oro to find that Basil had forgotten the plan and gone over to Formentor for the day with Dolores Ramona's party.

Beyond a tightening of the lips the girl made no sign. Presently, however, she got up and stood in front of Mrs Chester (the two women were alone on the terrace).

'It's quite all right,' she said. 'It doesn't matter. But I think—all the same—that we'd better call the whole thing off.'

She slipped from her finger the signet ring that Basil had given her—he would buy the real engagement ring later.

'Will you give him back this Mrs Chester? And tell him it's all right—not to worry . . .'

'Betty dear, don't! He *does* love you—really.'

'It looks like it, doesn't it?' said the girl with a short laugh. 'No—I've got some pride. Tell him everything's all right and that I—I wish him luck.'

When Basil returned at sunset he was greeted by a storm.

He flushed a little at the sight of his ring.

'So that's how she feels, is it? Well, I daresay it's the best thing.'

'Basil!'

'Well, frankly, Mother, we don't seem to have been hitting it off lately.'

'Whose fault was that?'

'I don't see that it was mine particularly. Jealousy's beastly and I really don't see why *you* should get all worked up about it. You begged me yourself not to marry Betty.'

'That was before I knew her. Basil—my dear—you're not thinking of marrying this other creature.'

Basil Chester said soberly:

'I'd marry her like a shot if she'd have me—but I'm afraid she won't.'

Cold chills went down Mrs Chester's spine. She sought and found Mr Parker Pyne, placidly reading a book in a sheltered corner.

'You must *do* something! You *must* do something! My boy's life will be ruined.'

Mr Parker Pyne was getting a little tired of Basil Chester's life being ruined.

'What can I do?'

'Go and see this terrible creature. If necessary buy her off.'

'That may come very expensive.'

'I don't care.'

'It seems a pity. Still there are, possibly, other ways.'

She looked a question. He shook his head.

'I'll make no promises—but I'll see what I can do. I have handled that kind before. By the way, not a word to Basil—that would be fatal.'

'Of course not.'

Mr Parker Pyne returned from the Mariposa at midnight. Mrs Chester was sitting up for him.

'Well?' she demanded breathlessly.

His eyes twinkled.

'The Señorita Dolores Ramona will leave Pollensa tomorrow morning and the island tomorrow night.'

'Oh, Mr Parker Pyne! How did you manage it?'

'It won't cost a cent,' said Mr Parker Pyne. Again his eyes twinkled. 'I rather fancied I might have a hold over her—and I was right.'

'You are wonderful. Nina Wycherley was quite right. You must let me know—er—your fees—'

Mr Parker Pyne held up a well-manicured hand.

'Not a penny. It has been a pleasure. I hope all will go well. Of course the boy will be very upset at first when he finds she's disappeared and left no address. Just go easy with him for a week or two.'

'If only Betty will forgive him—'

'She'll forgive him all right. They're a nice couple. By the way, I'm leaving tomorrow, too.'

'Oh, Mr Parker Pyne, we shall miss you.'

'Perhaps it's just as well I should go before that boy of yours gets infatuated with yet a third girl.'

Mr Parker Pyne leaned over the rail of the steamer and looked at the lights of Palma. Beside him stood Dolores Ramona. He was saying appreciatively:

'A very nice piece of work, Madeleine. I'm glad I wired you to come out. It's odd when you're such a quiet, stay-at-home girl really.'

Madeleine de Sara, alias Dolores Ramona, alias Maggie Sayers, said primly: 'I'm glad you're pleased, Mr Parker Pyne. It's been a nice little change. I think I'll go below now and get to bed before the boat starts. I'm such a bad sailor.'

A few minutes later a hand fell on Mr Parker Pyne's shoulder. He turned to see Basil Chester.

'Had to come and see you off, Mr Parker Pyne, and give you Betty's love and her and my best thanks. It was a grand stunt of yours. Betty and Mother are as thick as thieves. Seemed a shame to deceive the old darling—but she *was* being difficult. Anyway it's all right now. I must just be careful to keep up the annoyance stuff a couple of days longer. We're no end grateful to you, Betty and I.'

'I wish you every happiness,' said Mr Parker Pyne.

'Thanks.'

There was a pause, then Basil said with somewhat overdone carelessness:

'Is Miss—Miss de Sara—anywhere about? I'd like to thank her, too.'

Mr Parker Pyne shot a keen glance at him.

He said:

'I'm afraid Miss de Sara's gone to bed.'

'Oh, too bad—well, perhaps I'll see her in London sometime.'

'As a matter of fact she is going to America on business for me almost at once.'

'Oh!' Basil's tone was blank. 'Well,' he said. 'I'll be getting along . . .'

Mr Parker Pyne smiled. On his way to his cabin he tapped on the door of Madeleine's.

'How are you, my dear? All right? Our young friend has been along. The usual slight attack of Madeleinitis. He'll get over it in a day or two, but you are rather distracting.'

Sanctuary

The vicar's wife came round the corner of the vicarage with her arms full of chrysanthemums. A good deal of rich garden soil was attached to her strong brogue shoes and a few fragments of earth were adhering to her nose, but of that fact she was perfectly unconscious.

She had a slight struggle in opening the vicarage gate which hung, rustily, half off its hinges. A puff of wind caught at her battered felt hat, causing it to sit even more rakishly than it had done before. 'Bother!' said Bunch.

Christened by her optimistic parents Diana, Mrs Harmon had become Bunch at an early age for somewhat obvious reasons and the name had stuck to her ever since. Clutching the chrysanthemums, she made her way through the gate to the churchyard, and so to the church door.

The November air was mild and damp. Clouds scudded across the sky with patches of blue here and there. Inside, the church was dark and cold; it was unheated except at service times.

'Brrrrrh!' said Bunch expressively. 'I'd better get on with this quickly. I don't want to die of cold.'

With the quickness born of practice she collected the necessary paraphernalia: vases, water, flower-holders. 'I wish we had lilies,' thought Bunch to herself. 'I get so tired of these scraggy chrysanthemums.' Her nimble fingers arranged the blooms in their holders.

There was nothing particularly original or artistic about the decorations, for Bunch Harmon herself was neither original nor artistic, but it was a homely and pleasant arrangement. Carrying the vases carefully, Bunch stepped up the aisle and made her way towards the altar. As she did so the sun came out.

It shone through the east window of somewhat crude coloured glass, mostly blue and red—the gift of a wealthy Victorian churchgoer. The effect was almost startling in its sudden opulence. 'Like jewels,' thought Bunch. Suddenly she stopped, staring ahead of her. On the chancel steps was a huddled dark form.

Putting down the flowers carefully, Bunch went up to it and bent over it. It was a man lying there, huddled over on himself. Bunch knelt down by him and slowly, carefully, she turned him over. Her fingers went to his pulse—a pulse so feeble and fluttering that it told its own story, as did the almost greenish pallor of his face. There was no doubt, Bunch thought, that the man was dying.

He was a man of about forty-five, dressed in a dark, shabby suit. She laid down the limp hand she had picked up and looked at his other hand. This seemed clenched like a fist on his breast. Looking more closely she saw that the fingers were closed over what seemed to be a large wad or handkerchief which he was holding tightly to his chest. All round the clenched hand there were splashes of a dry brown fluid which, Bunch guessed, was dry blood. Bunch sat back on her heels, frowning.

Up till now the man's eyes had been closed but at this point they suddenly opened and fixed themselves on Bunch's face. They were neither dazed nor wandering.

They seemed fully alive and intelligent. His lips moved, and Bunch bent forward to catch the words, or rather the word. It was only one word that he said:

'Sanctuary.'

There was, she thought, just a very faint smile as he breathed out this word. There was no mistaking it, for after a moment he said it again, 'Sanctuary . . .'

Then, with a faint, long-drawn-out sigh, his eyes closed again. Once more Bunch's fingers went to his pulse. It was still there, but fainter now and more intermittent. She got up with decision.

'Don't move,' she said, 'or try to move. I'm going for help.'

The man's eyes opened again but he seemed now to be fixing his attention on the coloured light that came through the east window. He murmured something that Bunch could not quite catch. She thought, startled, that it might have been her husband's name.

'Julian?' she said. 'Did you come here to find Julian?' But there was no answer. The man lay with eyes closed, his breathing coming in slow, shallow fashion.

Bunch turned and left the church rapidly. She glanced at her watch and nodded with some satisfaction. Dr Griffiths would still be in his surgery. It was only a couple of minutes' walk from the church. She went in, without waiting to knock or ring, passing through the waiting room and into the doctor's surgery.

'You must come at once,' said Bunch. 'There's a man dying in the church.'

Some minutes later Dr Griffiths rose from his knees after a brief examination.

'Can we move him from here into the vicarage? I can attend to him better there—not that it's any use.'

'Of course,' said Bunch. 'I'll go along and get things

ready. I'll get Harper and Jones, shall I? To help you carry him.'

'Thanks. I can telephone from the vicarage for an ambulance, but I'm afraid—by the time it comes . . .' He left the remark unfinished.

Bunch said, 'Internal bleeding?'

Dr Griffiths nodded. He said, 'How on earth did he come here?'

'I think he must have been here all night,' said Bunch, considering. 'Harper unlocks the church in the morning as he goes to work, but he doesn't usually come in.'

It was about five minutes later when Dr Griffiths put down the telephone receiver and came back into the morning-room where the injured man was lying on quickly arranged blankets on the sofa. Bunch was moving a basin of water and clearing up after the doctor's examination.

'Well, that's that,' said Griffiths. 'I've sent for an ambulance and I've notified the police.' He stood, frowning, looking down on the patient who lay with closed eyes. His left hand was plucking in a nervous, spasmodic way at his side.

'He was shot,' said Griffiths. 'Shot at fairly close quarters. He rolled his handkerchief up into a ball and plugged the wound with it so as to stop the bleeding.'

'Could he have gone far after that happened?' Bunch asked.

'Oh, yes, it's quite possible. A mortally wounded man has been known to pick himself up and walk along a street as though nothing had happened, and then suddenly collapse five or ten minutes later. So he needn't have been shot in the church. Oh no. He may have been shot some distance away. Of course, he may have shot himself and then dropped the revolver and staggered blindly towards the church. I don't quite know why he made for the church and not for the vicarage.'

'Oh, I know *that*,' said Bunch. 'He said it: 'Sanctuary.''

The doctor stared at her. 'Sanctuary?'

'Here's Julian,' said Bunch, turning her head as she heard her husband's steps in the hall. 'Julian! Come here.'

The Reverend Julian Harmon entered the room. His vague, scholarly manner always made him appear much older than he really was. 'Dear me!' said Julian Harmon, staring in a mild, puzzled manner at the surgical appliances and the prone figure on the sofa.

Bunch explained with her usual economy of words. 'He was in the church, dying. He'd been shot. Do you know him, Julian? I thought he said your name.'

The vicar came up to the sofa and looked down at the dying man. 'Poor fellow,' he said, and shook his head. 'No, I don't know him. I'm almost sure I've never seen him before.'

At that moment the dying man's eyes opened once more. They went from the doctor to Julian Harmon and from him to his wife. The eyes stayed there, staring into Bunch's face. Griffiths stepped forward.

'If you could tell us,' he said urgently.

But with eyes fixed on Bunch, the man said in a weak voice, 'Please—*please*—' And then, with a slight tremor, he died . . .

Sergeant Hayes licked his pencil and turned the page of his notebook.

'So that's all you can tell me, Mrs Harmon?'

'That's all,' said Bunch. 'These are the things out of his coat pockets.'

On a table at Sergeant Hayes's elbow was a wallet, a

rather battered old watch with the initials W.S. and the return half of a ticket to London. Nothing more.

'You've found out who he is?' asked Bunch.

'A Mr and Mrs Eccles phoned up the station. He's her brother, it seems. Name of Sandbourne. Been in a low state of health and nerves for some time. He's been getting worse lately. The day before yesterday he walked out and didn't come back. He took a revolver with him.'

'And he came out here and shot himself with it?' said Bunch. 'Why?'

'Well, you see, he'd been depressed . . .'

Bunch interrupted him. 'I don't mean *that*. I mean, why here?'

Since Sergeant Hayes obviously did not know the answer to that one, he replied in an oblique fashion, 'Come out here, he did, on the five-ten bus.'

'Yes,' said Bunch again. 'But *why*?'

'I don't know, Mrs Harmon,' said Sergeant Hayes. 'There's no accounting. If the balance of the mind is disturbed—'

Bunch finished for him. 'They may do it anywhere. But it still seems to me unnecessary to take a bus out to a small country place like this. He didn't know anyone here, did he?'

'Not so far as can be ascertained,' said Sergeant Hayes. He coughed in an apologetic manner and said, as he rose to his feet, 'It may be as Mr and Mrs Eccles will come out and see you, ma'am—if you don't mind, that is.'

'Of course I don't mind,' said Bunch. 'It's very natural. I only wish I had something to tell them.'

'I'll be getting along,' said Sergeant Hayes.

'I'm only so thankful,' said Bunch, going with him to the front door, 'that it wasn't murder.'

A car had driven up at the vicarage gate. Sergeant Hayes, glancing at it, remarked: 'Looks as though that's Mr and Mrs Eccles come here now, ma'am, to talk with you.'

Bunch braced herself to endure what, she felt, might be rather a difficult ordeal. 'However,' she thought, 'I can always call Julian to help me. A clergyman's a great help when people are bereaved.'

Exactly what she had expected Mr and Mrs Eccles to be like, Bunch could not have said, but she was conscious, as she greeted them, of a feeling of surprise. Mr Eccles was a stout florid man whose natural manner would have been cheerful and facetious. Mrs Eccles had a vaguely flashy look about her. She had a small, mean, pursed-up mouth. Her voice was thin and reedy.

'It's been a terrible shock, Mrs Harmon, as you can imagine,' she said.

'Oh, I know,' said Bunch. 'It must have been. Do sit down. Can I offer you—well, perhaps it's a little early for tea—'

Mr Eccles waved a pudgy hand. 'No, no, nothing for us,' he said. 'It's very kind of you, I'm sure. Just wanted to . . . well . . . what poor William said and all that, you know?'

'He's been abroad a long time,' said Mrs Eccles, 'and I think he must have had some very nasty experiences. Very quiet and depressed he's been, ever since he came home. Said the world wasn't fit to live in and there was nothing to look forward to. Poor Bill, he was always moody.'

Bunch stared at them both for a moment or two without speaking.

'Pinched my husband's revolver, he did,' went on Mrs Eccles. 'Without our knowing. Then it seems he come here by bus. I suppose that was nice feeling on his part. He wouldn't have liked to do it in our house.'

'Poor fellow, poor fellow,' said Mr Eccles, with a sigh. 'It doesn't do to judge.'

There was another short pause, and Mr Eccles said, 'Did he leave a message? Any last words, nothing like that?'

His bright, rather pig-like eyes watched Bunch closely. Mrs Eccles, too, leaned forward as though anxious for the reply.

'No,' said Bunch quietly. 'He came into the church when he was dying, for sanctuary.'

Mrs Eccles said in a puzzled voice. 'Sanctuary? I don't think I quite . . .'

Mr Eccles interrupted. 'Holy place, my dear,' he said impatiently. 'That's what the vicar's wife means. It's a sin—suicide, you know. I expect he wanted to make amends.'

'He tried to say something just before he died,' said Bunch. 'He began, 'Please,' but that's as far as he got.'

Mrs Eccles put her handkerchief to her eyes and sniffed. 'Oh, dear,' she said. 'It's terribly upsetting, isn't it?'

'There, there, Pam,' said her husband. 'Don't take on. These things can't be helped. Poor Willie. Still, he's at peace now. Well, thank you very much, Mrs Harmon. I hope we haven't interrupted you. A vicar's wife is a busy lady, we know that.'

They shook hands with her. Then Eccles turned back suddenly to say, 'Oh yes, there's just one other thing. I think you've got his coat here, haven't you?'

'His coat?' Bunch frowned.

Mrs Eccles said, 'We'd like all his things, you know. Sentimental-like.'

'He had a watch and a wallet and a railway ticket in the pockets,' said Bunch. 'I gave them to Sergeant Hayes.'

'That's all right, then,' said Mr Eccles. 'He'll hand them over to us, I expect. His private papers would be in the wallet.'

'There was a pound note in the wallet,' said Bunch. 'Nothing else.'

'No letters? Nothing like that?'

Bunch shook her head.

'Well, thank you again, Mrs Harmon. The coat he was wearing—perhaps the sergeant's got that too, has he?'

Bunch frowned in an effort of remembrance.

'No,' she said. 'I don't think . . . let me see. The doctor and I took his coat off to examine his wound.' She looked round the room vaguely. 'I must have taken it upstairs with the towels and basin.'

'I wonder now, Mrs Harmon, if you don't mind . . . We'd like his coat, you know, the last thing he wore. Well, the wife feels rather sentimental about it.'

'Of course,' said Bunch. 'Would you like me to have it cleaned first? I'm afraid it's rather—well—stained.'

'Oh, no, no, no, that doesn't matter.'

Bunch frowned. 'Now I wonder where . . . excuse me a moment.' She went upstairs and it was some few minutes before she returned.

'I'm so sorry,' she said breathlessly, 'my daily woman must have put it aside with other clothes that were going to the cleaners. It's taken me quite a long time to find it. Here it is. I'll do it up for you in brown paper.'

Disclaiming their protests she did so; then once more effusively bidding her farewell the Eccleses departed.

Bunch went slowly back across the hall and entered the study. The Reverend Julian Harmon looked up and his brow cleared. He was composing a sermon and was fearing that he'd been led astray by the interest of the political relations between Judaea and Persia, in the reign of Cyrus.

'Yes, dear?' he said hopefully.

'Julian,' said Bunch. 'What's *Sanctuary* exactly?'

Julian Harmon gratefully put aside his sermon paper.

'Well,' he said. 'Sanctuary in Roman and Greek temples applied to the *cella* in which stood the statue of a god. The Latin word for altar '*ara*'' also means protection.' He continued learnedly: 'In three hundred and ninety-nine A.D. the right of sanctuary in Christian churches was finally and definitely recognized. The earliest mention of the right of sanctuary in England is in the Code of Laws issued by Ethelbert in A.D. six hundred . . .'

He continued for some time with his exposition but was, as often, disconcerted by his wife's reception of his erudite pronouncement.

'Darling,' she said. 'You *are* sweet.'

Bending over, she kissed him on the tip of his nose. Julian felt rather like a dog who has been congratulated on performing a clever trick.

'The Ecdeses have been here,' said Bunch.

The vicar frowned. 'The Eccleses? I don't seem to remember . . .'

'You don't know them. They're the sister and her husband of the man in the church.'

'My dear, you ought to have called me.'

'There wasn't any need,' said Bunch. 'They were not in need of consolation. I wonder now . . .' She frowned. 'If I put a casserole in the oven tomorrow, can you manage, Julian? I think I shall go up to London for the sales.'

'The sails?' Her husband looked at her blankly. 'Do you mean a yacht or a boat or something?'

Bunch laughed. 'No, darling. There's a special white sale at Burrows and Portman's. You know, sheets, table cloths and towels and glass-cloths. I don't know what we do with our glass-cloths, the way they wear through. Besides,' she added thoughtfully, 'I think I ought to go and see Aunt Jane.'

That sweet old lady, Miss Jane Marple, was enjoying the delights of the metropolis for a fortnight, comfortably installed in her nephew's studio flat.

'So kind of dear Raymond,' she murmured. 'He and Joan have gone to America for a fortnight and they insisted I should come up here and enjoy myself. And now, dear Bunch, do tell me what it is that's worrying you.'

Bunch was Miss Marple's favourite godchild, and the old lady looked at her with great affection as Bunch, thrusting her best felt hat farther on the back of her head, started her story.

Bunch's recital was concise and clear. Miss Marple nodded her head as Bunch finished. 'I see,' she said. 'Yes, I see.'

'That's why I felt I had to see you,' said Bunch. 'You see, not being clever—'

'But you *are* clever, my dear.'

'No, I'm not. Not clever like Julian.'

'Julian, of course, has a very solid intellect,' said Miss Marple.

'That's it,' said Bunch. 'Julian's got the intellect, but on the other hand, I've got the *sense*.'

'You have a lot of common sense, Bunch, and you're very intelligent.'

'You see, I don't really know what I ought to do.

I can't ask Julian because—well, I mean, Julian's so full of rectitude . . .'

This statement appeared to be perfectly understood by Miss Marple, who said, 'I know what you mean, dear. We women—well, it's different.' She went on. 'You told me what happened, Bunch, but I'd like to know first exactly what you think.'

'It's all wrong,' said Bunch. 'The man who was there in the church, dying, knew all about Sanctuary. He said it just the way Julian would have said it. I mean, he was a well-read, educated man. And if he'd shot himself, he wouldn't drag himself to a church afterwards and say 'sanctuary". Sanctuary means that you're pursued, and when you get into a church you're safe. Your pursuers can't touch you. At one time even the law couldn't get at you.'

She looked questioningly at Miss Marple. The latter nodded. Bunch went on, 'Those people, the Eccleses, were quite different. Ignorant and coarse. And there's another thing. That watch—the dead man's watch. It had the initials W.S. on the back of it. But inside—I opened it—in very small lettering there was 'To Walter from his father" and a date. *Walter.* But the Eccleses kept talking of him as William or Bill.'

Miss Marple seemed about to speak but Bunch rushed on. 'Oh, I know you're not always called the name you're baptized by. I mean, I can understand that you might be christened William and called 'Porgy" or 'Carrots" or something. But your sister wouldn't call you William or Bill if your name was Walter.'

'You mean that she wasn't his sister?'

'I'm quite sure she wasn't his sister. They were horrid—both of them. They came to the vicarage to get his things and to find out if he'd said anything before he died. When I said he hadn't I saw it in their faces—relief. I think myself,' finished Bunch, 'it was Eccles who shot him.'

'Murder?' said Miss Marple.

'Yes,' said Bunch. 'Murder. That's why I came to you, darling.'

Bunch's remark might have seemed incongruous to an ignorant listener, but in certain spheres Miss Marple had a reputation for dealing with murder.

'He said 'please'' to me before he died,' said Bunch. 'He wanted me to do something for him. The awful thing is I've no idea what.'

Miss Marple considered for a moment or two, and then pounced on the point that had already occurred to Bunch. 'But why was he there at all?' she asked.

'You mean,' said Bunch, 'if you wanted sanctuary you might pop into a church anywhere. There's no need to take a bus that only goes four times a day and come out to a lonely spot like ours for it.'

'He must have come there for a purpose,' Miss Marple thought. 'He must have come to see someone. Chipping Cleghorn's not a big place, Bunch. Surely you must have some idea of who it was he came to see?'

Bunch reviewed the inhabitants of her village in her mind before rather doubtfully shaking her head. 'In a way,' she said, 'it could be anybody.'

'He never mentioned a name?'

'He said Julian, or I thought he said Julian. It might have been Julia, I suppose. As far as I know, there isn't any Julia living in Chipping Cleghorn.'

She screwed up her eyes as she thought back to the scene. The man lying there on the chancel steps, the light coming through the window with its jewels of red and blue light.

'Jewels,' said Miss Marple thoughtfully.

'I'm coming now,' said Bunch, 'to the most important thing of all. The reason why I've really come here today. You see, the Eccleses made a great fuss about having his coat. We took it off when the doctor was seeing him. It was an old, shabby sort of coat—there was no reason they should have wanted it. They pretended it was sentimental, but that was nonsense.

'Anyway, I went up to find it, and as I was just going up the stairs I remembered how he'd made a kind of picking gesture with his hand, as though he was fumbling with the coat. So when I got hold of the coat I looked at it very carefully and I saw that in one place the lining had been sewn up again with a different thread. So I unpicked it and I found a little piece of paper inside. I took it out and I sewed it up again properly with thread that matched. I was careful and I don't really think that the Eccleses would know I've done it. I don't *think* so, but I can't be sure. And I took the coat down to them and made some excuse for the delay.'

'The piece of paper?' asked Miss Marple.

Bunch opened her handbag. 'I didn't show it to Julian,' she said, 'because he would have said that I ought to have given it to the Eccleses. But I thought I'd rather bring it to you instead.'

'A cloakroom ticket,' said Miss Marple, looking at it. 'Paddington Station.'

'He had a return ticket to Paddington in his pocket,' said Bunch.

The eyes of the two women met.

'This calls for action,' said Miss Marple briskly. 'But it would be advisable, I think, to be careful. Would you have noticed at all, Bunch dear, whether you were followed when you came to London today?'

'Followed!' exclaimed Bunch. 'You don't think—'

'Well, I think it's *possible*,' said Miss Marple. 'When anything is possible, I think we ought to take precautions.' She rose with a brisk movement. 'You came up here ostensibly, my dear, to go to the sales. I think the right thing to do, therefore, would be for us to *go* to the sales. But before we set out, we might put one or two little arrangements in hand. I don't suppose,' Miss Marple added obscurely, 'that I shall need the old speckled tweed with the beaver collar just at present.'

It was about an hour and a half later that the two ladies, rather the worse for wear and battered in appearance, and both clasping parcels of hardly-won household linen, sat down at a small and sequestered hostelry called the Apple Bough to restore their forces with steak and kidney pudding followed by apple tart and custard.

'Really a prewar quality face towel,' gasped Miss Marple, slightly out of breath. 'With a J on it, too. So fortunate that Raymond's wife's name is Joan. I shall put them aside until I really need them and then they will do for her if I pass on sooner than I expect.'

'I really did need the glass-cloths,' said Bunch. 'And they were very cheap, though not as cheap as the ones that woman with the ginger hair managed to snatch from me.'

A smart young woman with a lavish application of rouge and lipstick entered the Apple Bough at that moment. After looking around vaguely for a moment or two, she hurried to their table. She laid down an envelope by Miss Marple's elbow.

'There you are, miss,' she said briskly.

'Oh, thank you, Gladys,' said Miss Marple. 'Thank you very much. So kind of you.'

'Always pleased to oblige, I'm sure,' said Gladys.

'Ernie always says to me, 'Everything what's good you learned from that Miss Marple of yours that you were in service with,' and I'm sure I'm always glad to oblige you, miss.'

'Such a dear girl,' said Miss Marple as Gladys departed again. 'Always so willing and so kind.'

She looked inside the envelope and then passed it on to Bunch. 'Now be very careful, dear,' she said. 'By the way, is there still that nice young inspector at Melchester that I remember?'

'I don't know,' said Bunch. 'I expect so.'

'Well, if not,' said Miss Marple thoughtfully. 'I can always ring up the Chief Constable. I *think* he would remember me.'

'Of course he'd remember you,' said Bunch. 'Everybody would remember *you*. You're quite unique.' She rose.

Arrived at Paddington, Bunch went to the luggage office and produced the cloakroom ticket. A moment or two later a rather shabby old suitcase was passed across to her, and carrying this she made her way to the platform.

The journey home was uneventful. Bunch rose as the train approached Chipping Cleghorn and picked up the old suitcase. She had just left her carriage when a man, sprinting along the platform, suddenly seized the suitcase from her hand and rushed off with it.

'Stop!' Bunch yelled. 'Stop him, stop him. He's taken my suitcase.'

The ticket collector who, at this rural station, was a man of somewhat slow processes, had just begun to say, 'Now, look here, you can't do that—' when a smart blow on the chest pushed him aside, and the man with the suitcase rushed out from the station. He made his way towards a waiting car. Tossing the suitcase in, he was about to climb after it, but before he could move a hand fell on his shoulder, and the voice of Police Constable Abel said, 'Now then, what's all this?'

Bunch arrived, panting, from the station. 'He snatched my suitcase. I just got out of the train with it.'

'Nonsense,' said the man. 'I don't know what this lady means. It's my suitcase. I just got out of the train with it.'

He looked at Bunch with a bovine and impartial stare. Nobody would have guessed that Police Constable Abel and Mrs Harmon spent long half-hours in Police Constable Abel's off-time discussing the respective merits of manure and bone meal for rose bushes.

'You say, madam, that this is your suitcase?' said Police Constable Abel.

'Yes,' said Bunch. 'Definitely.'

'And you, sir?'

'I say this suitcase is mine.'

The man was tall, dark and well dressed, with a drawling voice and a superior manner. A feminine voice from inside the car said, 'Of course it's your suitcase, Edwin. I don't know what this woman means.'

'We'll have to get this clear,' said Police Constable Abel. 'If it's your suitcase, madam, what do you say is inside it?'

'Clothes,' said Bunch. 'A long speckled coat with a beaver collar, two wool jumpers and a pair of shoes.'

'Well, that's clear enough,' said Police Constable Abel. He turned to the other.

'I am a theatrical costumer,' said the dark man importantly. 'This suitcase contains theatrical properties which I brought down here for an amateur performance.'

'Right, sir,' said Police Constable Abel. 'Well, we'll

just look inside, shall we, and see? We can go along to the police station, or if you're in a hurry we'll take the suitcase back to the station and open it there.'

'It'll suit me,' said the dark man. 'My name is Moss, by the way, Edwin Moss.'

The police constable, holding the suitcase, went back into the station. 'Just taking this into the parcels office, George,' he said to the ticket collector.

Police Constable Abel laid the suitcase on the counter of the parcels office and pushed back the clasp. The case was not locked. Bunch and Mr Edwin Moss stood on either side of him, their eyes regarding each other vengefully.

'Ah!' said Police Constable Abel, as he pushed up the lid.

Inside, neatly folded, was a long rather shabby tweed coat with a beaver fur collar. There were also two wool jumpers and a pair of country shoes.

'Exactly as you say, madam,' said Police Constable Abel, turning to Bunch.

Nobody could have said that Mr Edwin Moss underdid things. His dismay and compunction were magnificent.

'I do apologize,' he said. 'I really *do* apologize. Please believe me, dear lady, when I tell you how very, very sorry I am. Unpardonable—quite unpardonable—my behaviour has been.' He looked at his watch. 'I must rush now. Probably my suitcase has gone on the train.' Raising his hat once more, he said meltingly to Bunch, 'Do, *do* forgive me,' and rushed hurriedly out of the parcels office.

'Are you going to let him get away?' asked Bunch in a conspiratorial whisper to Police Constable Abel.

The latter slowly closed a bovine eye in a wink.

'He won't get too far, ma'am,' he said. 'That's to say he won't get far unobserved, if you take my meaning.'

'Oh,' said Bunch, relieved.

'That old lady's been on the phone,' said Police Constable Abel, 'the one as was down here a few years ago. Bright she is, isn't she? But there's been a lot cooking up all today. Shouldn't wonder if the inspector or sergeant was out to see you about it tomorrow morning.'

It was the inspector who came, the Inspector Craddock whom Miss Marple remembered. He greeted Bunch with a smile as an old friend.

'Crime in Chipping Cleghorn again,' he said cheerfully. 'You don't lack for sensation here, do you, Mrs Harmon?'

'I could do with rather less,' said Bunch. 'Have you come to ask me questions or are you going to tell me things for a change?'

'I'll tell you some things first,' said the inspector. 'To begin with, Mr and Mrs Eccles have been having an eye kept on them for some time. There's reason to believe they've been connected with several robberies in this part of the world. For another thing, although Mrs Eccles *has* a brother called Sandbourne who has recently come back from abroad, the man you found dying in the church yesterday was definitely not Sandbourne.'

'I knew that he wasn't,' said Bunch. 'His name was Walter, to begin with, not William.'

The inspector nodded. 'His name was Walter St John, and he escaped forty-eight hours ago from Charrington Prison.'

'Of course,' said Bunch softly to herself, 'he was being hunted down by the law, and he took sanctuary.' Then she asked, 'What had he done?'

'I'll have to go back rather a long way. It's a complicated story. Several years ago there was a certain dancer doing turns at the music halls. I don't expect you'll have ever heard of her, but she specialized in an Arabian Night turn, 'Aladdin in the Cave of Jewels" it was called. She wore bits of rhinestone and not much else.

'She wasn't much of a dancer, I believe, but she was—well—attractive. Anyway, a certain Asian royalty fell for her in a big way. Amongst other things he gave her a very magnificent emerald necklace.'

'The historic jewels of a Rajah?' murmured Bunch ecstatically.

Inspector Craddock coughed. 'Well, a rather more modern version, Mrs Harmon. The affair didn't last very long, broke up when our potentate's attention was captured by a certain film star whose demands were not quite so modest.

'Zobeida, to give the dancer her stage name, hung on to the necklace, and in due course it was stolen. It disappeared from her dressing-room at the theatre, and there was a lingering suspicion in the minds of the authorities that she herself might have engineered its disappearance. Such things have been known as a publicity stunt, or indeed from more dishonest motives.

'The necklace was never recovered, but during the course of the investigation the attention of the police was drawn to this man, Walter St John. He was a man of education and breeding who had come down in the world, and who was employed as a working jeweller with a rather obscure firm which was suspected of acting as a fence for jewel robberies.

'There was evidence that this necklace had passed through his hands. It was, however, in connection with the theft of some other jewellery that he was finally brought to trial and convicted and sent to prison. He had not very much longer to serve, so his escape was rather a surprise.'

'But why did he come here?' asked Bunch.

'We'd like to know that very much, Mrs Harmon. Following up his trial, it seems that he went first to London. He didn't visit any of his old associates but he visited an elderly woman, a Mrs Jacobs who had formerly been a theatrical dresser. She won't say a word of what he came for, but according to other lodgers in the house he left carrying a suitcase.'

'I see,' said Bunch. 'He left it in the cloakroom at Paddington and then he came down here.'

'By that time,' said Inspector Craddock, 'Eccles and the man who calls himself Edwin Moss were on his trail. They wanted that suitcase. They saw him get on the bus. They must have driven out in a car ahead of him and been waiting for him when he left the bus.'

'And he was murdered?' said Bunch.

'Yes,' said Craddock. 'He was shot. It was Eccles's revolver, but I rather fancy it was Moss who did the shooting. Now, Mrs Harmon, what we want to know is, where is the suitcase that Walter St John actually deposited at Paddington Station?'

Bunch grinned. 'I expect Aunt Jane's got it by now,' she said. 'Miss Marple, I mean. That was her plan. She sent a former maid of hers with a suitcase packed with her things to the cloakroom at Paddington and we exchanged tickets. I collected her suitcase and brought it down by train. She seemed to expect that an attempt would be made to get it from me.'

It was Inspector Craddock's turn to grin. 'So she said when she rang up. I'm driving up to London to see her. Do you want to come, too, Mrs Harmon?'

'Wel-l,' said Bunch, considering. 'Wel-l, as a matter of fact, it's very fortunate. I had a toothache last night so I really ought to go to London to see the dentist, oughtn't I?'

'Definitely,' said Inspector Craddock . . .

Miss Marple looked from Inspector Craddock's face to the eager face of Bunch Harmon. The suitcase lay on the table. 'Of course, I haven't opened it,' the old lady said. 'I wouldn't dream of doing such a thing till somebody official arrived. Besides,' she added, with a demurely mischievous Victorian smile, 'it's locked.'

'Like to make a guess at what's inside, Miss Marple?' asked the inspector.

'I should imagine, you know,' said Miss Marple, 'that it would be Zobeida's theatrical costumes. Would you like a chisel, Inspector?'

The chisel soon did its work. Both women gave a slight gasp as the lid flew up. The sunlight coming through the window lit up what seemed like an inexhaustible treasure of sparkling jewels, red, blue, green, orange.

'Aladdin's Cave,' said Miss Marple. 'The flashing jewels the girl wore to dance.'

'Ah,' said Inspector Craddock. 'Now, what's so precious about it, do you think, that a man was murdered to get hold of it?'

'She was a shrewd girl, I expect,' said Miss Marple thoughtfully. 'She's dead, isn't she, Inspector?'

'Yes, died three years ago.'

'She had this valuable emerald necklace,' said Miss Marple, musingly. 'Had the stones taken out of their setting and fastened here and there on her theatrical costume, where everyone would take them for merely coloured rhinestones. Then she had a replica made of the real necklace, and that, of course, was what was stolen. No wonder it never came on the market. The thief soon discovered the stones were false.'

'Here is an envelope,' said Bunch, pulling aside some of the glittering stones.

Inspector Craddock took it from her and extracted two official-looking papers from it. He read aloud, ''Marriage Certificate between Walter Edmund St John and Mary Moss.' That was Zobeida's real name.'

'So they were married,' said Miss Marple. 'I see.'

'What's the other?' asked Bunch.

'A birth certificate of a daughter, Jewel.'

'Jewel?' cried Bunch. 'Why, of course. Jewel! *Jill!* That's it. I see now why he came to Chipping Cleghorn. *That's* what he was trying to say to me. Jewel. The Mundys, you know. Laburnum Cottage. They look after a little girl for someone. They're devoted to her. She's been like their own granddaughter. Yes, I remember now, her name *was* Jewel, only, of course, they call her Jill.

'Mrs Mundy had a stroke about a week ago, and the old man's been very ill with pneumonia. They were both going to go to the infirmary. I've been trying hard to find a good home for Jill somewhere. I didn't want her taken away to an institution.

'I suppose her father heard about it in prison and he managed to break away and get hold of this suitcase from the old dresser he or his wife left it with. I suppose if the jewels really belonged to her mother, they can be used for the child now.'

'I should imagine so, Mrs Harmon. *If* they're here.'

'Oh, they'll be here all right,' said Miss Marple cheerfully . . .

⋆ ⋆ ⋆

'Thank goodness you're back, dear,' said the Reverend Julian Harmon, greeting his wife with affection and a sigh of content. 'Mrs Burt always tries to do her best when you're away, but she really gave me some *very* peculiar fish-cakes for lunch. I didn't want to hurt her feelings so I gave them to Tiglath Pileser, but even *he* wouldn't eat them so I had to throw them out of the window.'

'Tiglath Pileser,' said Bunch, stroking the vicarage cat, who was purring against her knee, 'is *very* particular about what fish he eats. I often tell him he's got a proud stomach!'

'And your tooth, dear? Did you have it seen to?'

'Yes,' said Bunch. 'It didn't hurt much, and I went to see Aunt Jane again, too . . .'

'Dear old thing,' said Julian. 'I hope she's not failing at all.'

'Not in the least,' said Bunch, with a grin.

The following morning Bunch took a fresh supply of chrysanthemums to the church. The sun was once more pouring through the east window, and Bunch stood in the jewelled light on the chancel steps. She said very softly under her breath, 'Your little girl will be all right. *I'll* see that she is. I promise.'

Then she tidied up the church, slipped into a pew and knelt for a few moments to say her prayers before returning to the vicarage to attack the piled-up chores of two neglected days.

The Mystery of Hunter's Lodge

'After all,' murmured Poirot, 'it is possible that I shall not die this time.'

Coming from a convalescent influenza patient, I hailed the remark as showing a beneficial optimism. I myself had been the first sufferer from the disease. Poirot in his turn had gone down. He was now sitting up in bed, propped up with pillows, his head muffled in a woollen shawl, and was slowly sipping a particularly noxious *tisane* which I had prepared according to his directions. His eye rested with pleasure upon a neatly graduated row of medicine bottles which adorned the mantelpiece.

'Yes, yes,' my little friend continued. 'Once more shall I be myself again, the great Hercule Poirot, the terror of evildoers! Figure to yourself, *mon ami*, that I have a little paragraph to myself in *Society Gossip*. But yes! Here it is: 'Go it—criminals—all out! Hercule Poirot—and believe me, girls, he's some Hercules!—our own pet society detective can't get a grip on you. 'Cause why? 'Cause he's got *la grippe* himself"!'

I laughed.

'Good for you, Poirot. You are becoming quite a public character. And fortunately you haven't missed anything of particular interest during this time.'

'That is true. The few cases I have had to decline did not fill me with any regret.'

Our landlady stuck her head in at the door.

'There's a gentleman downstairs. Says he must see Monsieur Poirot or you, Captain. Seeing as he was in a great to-do—and with all that quite the gentleman—I brought up 'is card.'

She handed me a bit of pasteboard. 'Mr Roger Havering,' I read.

Poirot motioned with his head towards the bookcase, and I obediently pulled forth *Who's Who*. Poirot took it from me and scanned the pages rapidly.

'Second son of fifth Baron Windsor. Married 1913 Zoe, fourth daughter of William Crabb.'

'H'm!' I said. 'I rather fancy that's the girl who used to act at the Frivolity—only she called herself Zoe Carrisbrook. I remember she married some young man about town just before the War.'

'Would it interest you, Hastings, to go down and hear what our visitor's particular little trouble is? Make him all my excuses.'

Roger Havering was a man of about forty, well set up and of smart appearance. His face, however, was haggard, and he was evidently labouring under great agitation.

'Captain Hastings? You are Monsieur Poirot's partner, I understand. It is imperative that he should come with me to Derbyshire today.'

'I'm afraid that's impossible,' I replied. 'Poirot is ill in bed—influenza.'

His face fell.

'Dear me, that is a great blow to me.'

'The matter on which you want to consult him is serious?'

'My God, yes! My uncle, the best friend I have in the world, was foully murdered last night.'

'Here in London?'

'No, in Derbyshire. I was in town and received a telegram from my wife this morning. Immediately upon its receipt I determined to come round and beg Monsieur Poirot to undertake the case.'

'If you will excuse me a minute,' I said, struck by a sudden idea.

I rushed upstairs, and in a few brief words acquainted Poirot with the situation. He took any further words out of my mouth.

'I see. I see. You want to go yourself, is it not so? Well, why not? You should know my methods by now. All I ask is that you should report to me fully every day, and follow implicitly any instructions I may wire you.'

To this I willingly agreed.

An hour later I was sitting opposite Mr Havering in a first-class carriage on the Midland Railway, speeding rapidly away from London.

'To begin with, Captain Hastings, you must understand that Hunter's Lodge, where we are going, and where the tragedy took place, is only a small shooting-box in the heart of the Derbyshire moors. Our real home is near Newmarket, and we usually rent a flat in town for the season. Hunter's Lodge is looked after by a housekeeper who is quite capable of doing all we need when we run down for an occasional weekend. Of course, during the shooting season, we take down some of our own servants from Newmarket. My uncle, Mr Harrington Pace (as you may know, my mother was a Miss Pace of New York), has, for the last three years, made his home with us. He never got on well with my father, or my elder brother, and I suspect that my being somewhat of a prodigal son myself rather increased than diminished his affection towards me. Of course I am a poor man, and my uncle was a rich one—in other words, he paid the piper! But, though exacting in many ways, he was not really hard to get on with, and we all three lived very harmoniously together. Two days ago, my uncle, rather wearied with some recent gaieties of ours in town, suggested that we should run down to Derbyshire for a day or two. My wife telegraphed to Mrs Middleton, the housekeeper, and we went down that same afternoon. Yesterday evening I was forced to return to town, but my wife and my uncle remained on. This morning I received this telegram.' He handed it over to me:

> 'Come at once uncle Harrington murdered last night bring good detective if you can but do come—Zoe.'

'Then, as yet you know no details?'

'No, I suppose it will be in the evening papers. Without doubt the police are in charge.'

It was about three o'clock when we arrived at the little station of Elmer's Dale. From there a five-mile drive brought us to a small grey stone building in the midst of the rugged moors.

'A lonely place,' I observed with a shiver.

Havering nodded.

'I shall try and get rid of it. I could never live here again.'

We unlatched the gate and were walking up the narrow path to the oak door when a familiar figure emerged and came to meet us.

'Japp!' I ejaculated.

The Scotland Yard inspector grinned at me in a friendly fashion before addressing my companion.

'Mr Havering, I think? I've been sent down from London to take charge of this case, and I'd like a word with you, if I may, sir.'

'My wife—'

'I've seen your good lady, sir—and the housekeeper. I won't keep you a moment, but I am anxious to get back to the village now that I've seen all there is to see here.'

'I know nothing as yet as to what—'

'Ex-actly,' said Japp soothingly. 'But there are just one or two little points I'd like your opinion about all the same. Captain Hastings here, he knows me, and he'll go on up to the house and tell them you're coming. What have you done with the little man, by the way, Captain Hastings?'

'He's ill in bed with influenza.'

'Is he now? I'm sorry to hear that. Rather the case of the cart without the horse, you being here without him, isn't it?'

And on his rather ill-timed jest I went on to the house. I rang the bell, as Japp had closed the door behind him. After some moments it was opened to me by a middle-aged woman in black.

'Mr Havering will be here in a moment,' I explained. 'He has been detained by the inspector. I have come down with him from London to look into the case. Perhaps you can tell me briefly what occurred last night.'

'Come inside, sir.' She closed the door behind me, and we stood in the dimly-lighted hall. 'It was after dinner last night, sir, that the man came. He asked to see Mr Pace, sir, and, seeing that he spoke the same way, I thought it was an American gentleman friend of Mr Pace's and I showed him into the gun-room, and then went to tell Mr Pace. He wouldn't give any name, which, of course, was a bit odd, now I come to think of it. I told Mr Pace, and he seemed puzzled like, but he said to the mistress: 'Excuse me, Zoe, while I see what this fellow wants.' He went off to the gun-room, and I went back to the kitchen, but after a while I heard loud voices, as if they were quarrelling, and I came out into the hall. At the same time, the mistress she comes out too, and just then there was a shot and then a dreadful silence. We both ran to the gun-room door, but it was locked and we had to go round to the window. It was open, and there inside was Mr Pace, all shot and bleeding.'

'What became of the man?'

'He must have got away through the window, sir, before we got to it.'

'And then?'

'Mrs Havering sent me to fetch the police. Five miles to walk it was. They came back with me, and the constable he stayed all night, and this morning the police gentleman from London arrived.'

'What was this man like who called to see Mr Pace?'

The housekeeper reflected.

'He had a black beard, sir, and was about middle-aged, and had on a light overcoat. Beyond the fact that he spoke like an American I didn't notice much about him.'

'I see. Now I wonder if I can see Mrs Havering?'

'She's upstairs, sir. Shall I tell her?'

'If you please. Tell her that Mr Havering is outside with Inspector Japp, and that the gentleman he has brought back with him from London is anxious to speak to her as soon as possible.'

'Very good, sir.'

I was in a fever of impatience to get all the facts. Japp had two or three hours' start on me, and his anxiety to be gone made me keen to be close at his heels.

Mrs Havering did not keep me waiting long. In a few minutes I heard a light step descending the stairs, and looked up to see a very handsome young woman coming towards me. She wore a flame-coloured jumper, that set off the slender boyishness of her figure. On her dark head was a little hat of flame-coloured leather. Even the present tragedy could not dim the vitality of her personality.

I introduced myself, and she nodded in quick comprehension.

'Of course I have often heard of you and your colleague, Monsieur Poirot. You have done some wonderful things together, haven't you? It was very clever of my husband to get you so promptly. Now will you ask me questions? That is the easiest way, isn't it, of getting to know all you want to about this dreadful affair?'

'Thank you, Mrs Havering. Now what time was it that this man arrived?'

'It must have been just before nine o'clock. We had finished dinner, and were sitting over our coffee and cigarettes.'

'Your husband had already left for London?'

'Yes, he went up by the 6.15.'

'Did he go by car to the station, or did he walk?'

'Our own car isn't down here. One came out from the garage in Elmer's Dale to fetch him in time for the train.'

'Was Mr Pace quite his usual self?'

'Absolutely. Most normal in every way.'

'Now, can you describe this visitor at all?'

'I'm afraid not. I didn't see him. Mrs Middleton showed him straight into the gun-room and then came to tell my uncle.'

'What did your uncle say?'

'He seemed rather annoyed, but went off at once. It was about five minutes later that I heard the sound of raised voices. I ran out into the hall and almost collided with Mrs Middleton. Then we heard the shot. The gun-room door was locked on the inside, and we had to go right round the house to the window. Of course that took some time, and the murderer had been able to get well away. My poor uncle'—her voice faltered—'had been shot through the head. I saw at once that he was dead. I sent Mrs Middleton for the police, I was careful to touch nothing in the room but to leave it exactly as I found it.'

I nodded approval.

'Now, as to the weapon?'

'Well, I can make a guess at it, Captain Hastings. A pair of revolvers of my husband's were mounted upon the wall. One of them is missing. I pointed this out to the police, and they took the other one away with them. When they have extracted the bullet, I suppose they will know for certain.'

'May I go to the gun-room?'

'Certainly. The police have finished with it. But the body has been removed.'

She accompanied me to the scene of the crime. At that moment Havering entered the hall, and with a quick apology his wife ran to him. I was left to undertake my investigations alone.

I may as well confess at once that they were rather disappointing. In detective novels clues abound, but here I could find nothing that struck me as out of the ordinary except a large blood-stain on the carpet where I judged the dead man had fallen. I examined everything with painstaking care and took a couple of pictures of the room with my little camera which I had brought with me. I also examined the ground outside the window, but it appeared to have been so heavily trampled underfoot that I judged it was useless to waste time over it. No, I had seen all that Hunter's Lodge had to show me. I must go back to Elmer's Dale and get into touch with Japp. Accordingly I took leave of the Haverings, and was driven off in the car that had brought us from the station.

I found Japp at the Matlock Arms and he took me forthwith to see the body. Harrington Pace was a small, spare, clean-shaven man, typically American in appearance. He had been shot through the back of the head, and the revolver had been discharged at close quarters.

'Turned away for a moment,' remarked Japp, 'and the other fellow snatched up a revolver and shot him. The one Mrs Havering handed over to us was fully loaded and I suppose the other one was also. Curious what darn fool things people do. Fancy keeping two loaded revolvers hanging up on your wall.'

'What do you think of the case?' I asked, as we left the gruesome chamber behind us.

'Well, I'd got my eye on Havering to begin with. Oh, yes!'—noting my exclamation of astonishment. 'Havering has one or two shady incidents in his past. When he was a boy at Oxford there was some funny business about the signature on one of his father's cheques. All hushed up of course. Then, he's pretty heavily in debt now, and they're the kind of debts he wouldn't like to go to his uncle about, whereas you may be sure the uncle's will would be in his favour. Yes, I'd got my eye on him, and that's why I wanted to speak to him before he saw his wife, but their statements dovetail all right, and I've been to the station and there's no doubt whatever that he left by the 6.15. That gets up to London about 10.30. He went straight to his club, he says, and if that's confirmed all right—why, he couldn't have been shooting his uncle here at nine o'clock in a black beard!'

'Ah, yes, I was going to ask you what you thought about that beard?'

Japp winked.

'I think it grew pretty fast—grew in the five miles from Elmer's Dale to Hunter's Lodge. Americans that I've met are mostly clean-shaven. Yes, it's amongst Mr Pace's American associates that we'll have to look for the murderer. I questioned the housekeeper first, and then her mistress, and their stories agree all right, but I'm sorry Mrs Havering didn't get a look at the fellow. She's a smart woman, and she might have noticed something that would set us on the track.'

I sat down and wrote a minute and lengthy account to Poirot. I was able to add various further items of information before I posted the letter.

The bullet had been extracted and was proved to have been fired from a revolver identical with the one held by the police. Furthermore, Mr Havering's movements on the night in question had been checked and verified, and it was proved beyond doubt that he had actually arrived in London by the train in question. And, thirdly, a sensational development had occurred. A city gentleman, living at Ealing, on crossing Haven Green to get to the District Railway Station that morning, had observed a brown-paper parcel stuck between the railings. Opening it, he found that it contained a revolver. He handed the parcel over to the local police station, and before night it was proved to be the one we were in search of, the fellow to that given us by Mrs Havering. One bullet had been fired from it.

All this I added to my report. A wire from Poirot arrived whilst I was at breakfast the following morning:

'Of course black-bearded man was not Havering only you or Japp would have such an idea wire me description of housekeeper and what clothes she wore this morning same of Mrs Havering do not waste time taking photographs of interiors they are underexposed and not in the least artistic.'

It seemed to me that Poirot's style was unnecessarily facetious. I also fancied he was a shade jealous of my position on the spot with full facilities for handling the case. His request for a description of the clothes worn by the two women appeared to me to be simply ridiculous, but I complied as well as I, a mere man, was able to.

At eleven a reply wire came from Poirot:

'Advise Japp arrest housekeeper before it is too late.'

Dumbfounded, I took the wire to Japp. He swore softly under his breath.

'He's the goods, Monsieur Poirot: if he says so, there's something in it. And I hardly noticed the woman. I don't know that I can go so far as arresting her, but I'll have her watched. We'll go up right away, and take another look at her.'

But it was too late, Mrs Middleton, that quiet middle-aged woman, who had appeared so normal and respectable, had vanished into thin air. Her box had been left behind. It contained only ordinary wearing apparel. There was no clue to her identity, or as to her whereabouts.

From Mrs Havering we elicited all the facts we could:

'I engaged her about three weeks ago when Mrs Emery, our former housekeeper, left. She came to me from Mrs Selbourne's Agency in Mount Street—a very well-known place. I get all my servants from there. They sent several women to see me, but this Mrs Middleton seemed much the nicest, and had splendid references. I engaged her on the spot, and notified the Agency of the fact. I can't believe that there was anything wrong with her. She was such a nice quiet woman.'

The thing was certainly a mystery. Whilst it was clear that the woman herself could not have committed the crime, since at the moment the shot was fired Mrs Havering was with her in the hall, nevertheless she must have some connection with the murder, or why should she suddenly take to her heels and bolt?

I wired the latest development to Poirot and suggested returning to London and making inquiries at Selbourne's Agency.

Poirot's reply was prompt:

> 'Useless to inquire at agency they will never have heard of her find out what vehicle took her up to hunters lodge when she first arrived there.'

Though mystified, I was obedient. The means of transport in Elmer's Dale were limited. The local garage had two battered Ford cars, and there were two station flies. None of these had been requisitioned on the date in question. Questioned, Mrs Havering explained that she had given the woman the money for her fare down to Derbyshire and sufficient to hire a car or fly to take her up to Hunter's Lodge. There was usually one of the Fords at the station on the chance of its being required. Taking into consideration the further fact that nobody at the station had noticed the arrival of a stranger, black-bearded or otherwise, on the fatal evening, everything seemed to point to the conclusion that the murderer had come to the spot in a car, which had been waiting near at hand to aid his escape, and that the same car had brought the mysterious housekeeper to her new post. I may mention that inquiries at the Agency in London bore out Poirot's prognostication. No such woman as 'Mrs Middleton' had ever been on their books. They had received the Hon. Mrs Havering's application for a housekeeper, and had sent her various applicants for the post. When she sent them the engagement fee, she omitted to mention which woman she had selected.

Somewhat crestfallen, I returned to London. I found Poirot established in an armchair by the fire in a garish, silk dressing-gown. He greeted me with much affection.

'*Mon ami* Hastings! But how glad I am to see you. Veritably I have for you a great affection! And you have enjoyed yourself? You have run to and fro with the good Japp? You have interrogated and investigated to your heart's content?'

'Poirot,' I cried, 'the thing's a dark mystery! It will never be solved.'

'It is true that we are not likely to cover ourselves with glory over it.'

'No, indeed. It's a hard nut to crack.'

'Oh, as far as that goes, I am very good at cracking the nuts! A veritable squirrel! It is not that which embarrasses me. I know well enough who killed Mr Harrington Pace.'

'You know? How did you find out?'

'Your illuminating answers to my wires supplied me with the truth. See here, Hastings, let us examine the facts methodically and in order. Mr Harrington Pace is a man with a considerable fortune which at his death will doubtless pass to his nephew. Point No 1. His nephew is known to be desperately hard up. Point No 2. His nephew is also known to be—shall we say a man of rather loose moral fibre? Point No 3.'

'But Roger Havering is proved to have journeyed straight up to London.'

'*Précisément*—and therefore, as Mr Havering left Elmer's Dale at 6.15, and since Mr Pace cannot have been killed before he left, or the doctor would have spotted the time of the crime as being given wrongly when he examined the body, we conclude quite rightly, that Mr Havering did *not* shoot his uncle. But there is a Mrs Havering, Hastings.'

'Impossible! The housekeeper was with her when the shot was fired.'

'Ah, yes, the housekeeper. But she has disappeared.'

'She will be found.'

'I think not. There is something peculiarly elusive about that housekeeper, don't you think so, Hastings? It struck me at once.'

'She played her part, I suppose, and then got out in the nick of time.'

'And what was her part?'

'Well, presumably to admit her confederate, the black-bearded man.'

'Oh, no, that was not her part! Her part was what you have just mentioned, to provide an alibi for Mrs Havering at the moment the shot was fired. And no one will ever find her, *mon ami*, because she does not exist! 'There's no such person,' as your so great Shakespeare says.'

'It was Dickens,' I murmured, unable to suppress a smile. 'But what do you mean, Poirot?'

'I mean that Zoe Havering was an actress before her

marriage, that you and Japp only saw the housekeeper in a dark hall, a dim middle-aged figure in black with a faint subdued voice, and finally that neither you nor Japp, nor the local police whom the housekeeper fetched, ever saw Mrs Middleton and her mistress at one and the same time. It was child's play for that clever and daring woman. On the pretext of summoning her mistress, she runs upstairs, slips on a bright jumper and a hat with black curls attached which she jams down over the grey transformation. A few deft touches, and the make-up is removed, a slight dusting of rouge, and the brilliant Zoe Havering comes down with her clear ringing voice. Nobody looks particularly at the housekeeper. Why should they? There is nothing to connect her with the crime. She, too, has an alibi.'

'But the revolver that was found at Ealing? Mrs Havering could not have placed it there?'

'No, that was Roger Havering's job—but it was a mistake on their part. It put me on the right track. A man who has committed murder with a revolver which he found on the spot would fling it away at once, he would not carry it up to London with him. No, the motive was clear, the criminals wished to focus the interest of the police on a spot far removed from Derbyshire, they were anxious to get the police away as soon as possible from the vicinity of Hunter's Lodge. Of course the revolver found at Ealing was not the one with which Mr Pace was shot. Roger Havering discharged one shot from it, brought it up to London, went straight to his club to establish his alibi, then went quickly out to Ealing by the District, a matter of about twenty minutes only, placed the parcel where it was found and so back to town. That charming creature, his wife, quietly shoots Mr Pace after dinner—you remember he was shot from behind? Another significant point, that!—reloads the revolver and puts it back in its place, and then starts off with her desperate little comedy.'

'It's incredible,' I muttered, fascinated, 'and yet—'

'And yet it is true. *Bien sur*, my friend, it is true. But to bring that precious pair to justice, that is another matter. Well, Japp must do what he can—I have written him fully—but I very much fear, Hastings, that we shall be obliged to leave them to Fate, or *le bon Dieu*, whichever you prefer.'

'The wicked flourish like a green bay tree,' I reminded him.

'But at a price, Hastings, always at a price, *croyez-moi*!'

Poirot's forebodings were confirmed, Japp, though convinced of the truth of his theory, was unable to get together the necessary evidence to ensure a conviction.

Mr Pace's huge fortune passed into the hands of his murderers. Nevertheless, Nemesis did overtake them, and when I read in the paper that the Hon. Roger and Mrs Havering were amongst those killed in the crashing of the Air Mail to Paris I knew that Justice was satisfied.

The World's End

Mr Satterthwaite had come to Corsica because of the Duchess. It was out of his beat. On the Riviera he was sure of his comforts, and to be comfortable meant a lot to Mr Satterthwaite. But though he liked his comfort, he also liked a Duchess. In his way, a harmless, gentlemanly, old-fashioned way, Mr Satterthwaite was a snob. He liked the best people. And the Duchess of Leith was a very authentic Duchess. There were no Chicago pork butchers in her ancestry. She was the daughter of a Duke as well as the wife of one.

For the rest, she was rather a shabby-looking old lady, a good deal given to black bead trimmings on her clothes. She had quantities of diamonds in old-fashioned settings, and she wore them as her mother before her had worn them: pinned all over her indiscriminately. Someone had suggested once that the Duchess stood in the middle of the room whilst her maid flung brooches at her haphazard. She subscribed generously to charities, and looked well after her tenants and dependents, but was extremely mean over small sums. She cadged lifts from her friends, and did her shopping in bargain basements.

The Duchess was seized with a whim for Corsica. Cannes bored her and she had a bitter argument with the hotel proprietor over the price of her rooms.

'And you shall go with me, Satterthwaite,' she said firmly. 'We needn't be afraid of scandal at our time of life.'

Mr Satterthwaite was delicately flattered. No one had ever mentioned scandal in connection with him before. He was far too insignificant. Scandal—and a Duchess—delicious!

'Picturesque you know,' said the Duchess. 'Brigands—all that sort of thing. And extremely cheap, so I've heard. Manuel was positively impudent this morning. These hotel proprietors need putting in their place. They can't expect to get the best people if they go on like this. I told him so plainly.'

'I believe,' said Mr Satterthwaite, 'that one can fly over quite comfortably. From Antibes.'

'They probably charge you a pretty penny for it,' said the Duchess sharply. 'Find out, will you?'

'Certainly, Duchess.'

Mr Satterthwaite was still in a flutter of gratification despite the fact that his role was clearly to be that of a glorified courier.

When she learned the price of a passage by Avion, the Duchess turned it down promptly.

'They needn't think I'm going to pay a ridiculous sum like that to go in one of their nasty dangerous things.'

So they went by boat, and Mr Satterthwaite endured ten hours of acute discomfort. To begin with, as the boat sailed at seven, he took it for granted that there would be dinner on board. But there was no dinner. The boat was small and the sea was rough. Mr Satterthwaite was decanted at Ajaccio in the early hours of the morning more dead than alive.

The Duchess, on the contrary, was perfectly fresh. She never minded discomfort if she could feel she was saving money. She waxed enthusiastic over the scene on the quay, with the palm trees and the rising sun. The whole population seemed to have turned out to watch the arrival of the boat, and the launching of the gangway was attended with excited cries and directions.

'*On dirait,*' said a stout Frenchman who stood beside them, '*que jamais avant on n'a fait cette manoeuvre là!*'

'That maid of mine has been sick all night,' said the Duchess. 'The girl's a perfect fool.'

Mr Satterthwaite smiled in a pallid fashion.

'A waste of good food, I call it,' continued the Duchess robustly.

'Did she get any food?' asked Mr Satterthwaite enviously.

'I happened to bring some biscuits and a stick of chocolate on board with me,' said the Duchess. 'When I found there was no dinner to be got, I gave the lot to her. The lower classes always make such a fuss about going without their meals.'

With a cry of triumph the launching of the gangway was accomplished. A Musical Comedy chorus of brigands rushed aboard and wrested hand-luggage from the passengers by main force.

'Come on, Satterthwaite,' said the Duchess. 'I want a hot bath and some coffee.'

So did Mr Satterthwaite. He was not wholly successful, however. They were received at the hotel by a bowing manager and were shown to their rooms. The Duchess's had a bathroom attached. Mr Satterthwaite, however, was directed to a bath that appeared to be situated in somebody else's bedroom. To expect the water to be hot at that hour in the morning was, perhaps, unreasonable. Later he drank intensely black coffee, served in a pot without a lid. The shutters and the window of his room had been flung open, and the crisp morning air came in fragrantly. A day of dazzling blue and green.

The waiter waved his hand with a flourish to call attention to the view.

'*Ajaccio*,' he said solemnly. '*Le plus beau port du monde!*'

And he departed abruptly.

Looking out over the deep blue of the bay, with the snowy mountains beyond, Mr Satterthwaite was almost inclined to agree with him. He finished his coffee, and lying down on the bed, fell fast asleep.

At *déjeuner* the Duchess was in great spirits.

'This is just what will be good for you, Satterthwaite,' she said. 'Get you out of all those dusty little old-maidish ways of yours.' She swept a *lorgnette* round the room. 'Upon my word, there's Naomi Carlton Smith.'

She indicated a girl sitting by herself at a table in the window. A round-shouldered girl, who slouched as she sat. Her dress appeared to be made of some kind of brown sacking. She had black hair, untidily bobbed.

'An artist?' asked Mr Satterthwaite.

He was always good at placing people.

'Quite right,' said the Duchess. 'Calls herself one anyway. I knew she was mooching around in some queer quarter of the globe. Poor as a church mouse, proud as Lucifer, and a bee in her bonnet like all the Carlton Smiths. Her mother was my first cousin.'

'She's one of the Knowlton lot then?'

The Duchess nodded.

'Been her own worst enemy,' she volunteered. 'Clever girl too. Mixed herself up with a most undesirable young man. One of that Chelsea crowd. Wrote plays or poems or something unhealthy. Nobody took 'em, of course. Then he stole somebody's jewels and got caught out. I forget what they gave him. Five years, I think. But you must remember? It was last winter.'

'Last winter I was in Egypt,' explained Mr Satterthwaite. 'I had 'flu very badly the end of January, and the doctors insisted on Egypt afterwards. I missed a lot.'

His voice rang with a note of real regret.

'That girl seems to me to be moping,' said the Duchess, raising her *lorgnette* once more. 'I can't allow that.'

On her way out, she stopped by Miss Carlton Smith's table and tapped the girl on the shoulder.

'Well, Naomi, you don't seem to remember me?'

Naomi rose rather unwillingly to her feet.

'Yes, I do, Duchess. I saw you come in. I thought it was quite likely you mightn't recognize me.'

She drawled the words lazily, with a complete indifference of manner.

'When you've finished your lunch, come and talk to me on the terrace,' ordered the Duchess.

'Very well.'

Naomi yawned.

'Shocking manners,' said the Duchess, to Mr Satterthwaite, as she resumed her progress. 'All the Carlton Smiths have.'

They had their coffee outside in the sunshine. They had been there about six minutes when Naomi Carlton Smith lounged out from the hotel and joined them. She let herself fall slackly on to a chair with her legs stretched out ungracefully in front of her.

An odd face, with its jutting chin and deep-set grey eyes. A clever, unhappy face—a face that only just missed being beautiful.

'Well, Naomi,' said the Duchess briskly. 'And what are you doing with yourself?'

'Oh, I dunno. Just marking time.'

'Been painting?'

'A bit.'

'Show me your things.'

Naomi grinned. She was not cowed by the autocrat. She was amused. She went into the hotel and came out again with a portfolio.

'You won't like 'em, Duchess,' she said warningly. 'Say what you like. You won't hurt my feelings.'

Mr Satterthwaite moved his chair a little nearer. He was interested. In another minute he was more interested still. The Duchess was frankly unsympathetic.

'I can't even see which way the things ought to be,' she complained. 'Good gracious, child, there was never a sky that colour—or a sea either.'

'That's the way I see 'em,' said Naomi placidly.

'Ugh!' said the Duchess, inspecting another. 'This gives me the creeps.'

'It's meant to,' said Naomi. 'You're paying me a compliment without knowing it.'

It was a queer vorticist study of a prickly pear—just recognizable as such. Grey-green with slodges of violent colour where the fruit glittered like jewels. A swirling mass of evil, fleshy—festering. Mr Satterthwaite shuddered and turned his head aside.

He found Naomi looking at him and nodding her head in comprehension.

'I know,' she said. 'But it *is* beastly.'

The Duchess cleared her throat.

'It seems quite easy to be an artist nowadays,' she observed witheringly. 'There's no attempt to copy things. You just shovel on some paint—I don't know what with, not a brush, I'm sure—'

'Palette knife,' interposed Naomi, smiling broadly once more.

'A good deal at a time,' continued the Duchess. 'In lumps. And there you are! Everyone says: 'How clever.' Well, I've no patience with that sort of thing. Give me—'

'A nice picture of a dog or a horse, by Edwin Landseer.'

'And why not?' demanded the Duchess. 'What's wrong with Landseer?'

'Nothing,' said Naomi. 'He's all right. And you're all right. The tops of things are always nice and shiny and smooth. I respect you, Duchess, you've got force. You've met life fair and square and you've come out on top. But the people who are underneath see the under side of things. And that's interesting in a way.'

The Duchess stared at her.

'I haven't the faintest idea what you're talking about,' she declared.

Mr Satterthwaite was still examining the sketches. He realized, as the Duchess could not, the perfection of technique behind them. He was startled and delighted. He looked up at the girl.

'Will you sell me one of these, Miss Carlton Smith?' he asked.

'You can have any one you like for five guineas,' said the girl indifferently.

Mr Satterthwaite hesitated a minute or two and then he selected a study of prickly pear and aloe. In the foreground was a vivid blur of yellow mimosa, the scarlet of the aloe flower danced in and out of the picture, and inexorable, mathematically underlying the whole, was the oblong pattern of the prickly pear and the sword motif of the aloe.

He made a little bow to the girl.

'I am very happy to have secured this, and I think I have made a bargain. Some day, Miss Carlton Smith, I shall be able to sell this sketch at a very good profit—if I want to!'

The girl leant forward to see which one he had taken. He saw a new look come into her eyes. For the first time she was really aware of his existence, and there was respect in the quick glance she gave him.

'You have chosen the best,' she said. 'I—I am glad.'

'Well, I suppose you know what you're doing,' said the Duchess. 'And I daresay you're right. I've heard that you are quite a connoisseur. But you can't tell me that all this new stuff is art, because it isn't. Still, we needn't go into that. Now I'm only going to be here a few days and I want to see something of the island. You've got a car, I suppose, Naomi?'

The girl nodded.

'Excellent,' said the Duchess. 'We'll make a trip somewhere tomorrow.'

'It's only a two-seater.'

'Nonsense, there's a dickey, I suppose, that will do for Mr Satterthwaite?'

A shuddering sigh went through Mr Satterthwaite. He had observed the Corsican roads that morning. Naomi was regarding him thoughtfully.

'I'm afraid my car would be no good to you,' she said. 'It's a terribly battered old bus. I bought it second-hand for a mere song. It will just get me up the hills—with coaxing. But I can't take passengers. There's quite a good garage, though, in the town. You can hire a car there.'

'Hire a car?' said the Duchess, scandalized. 'What an idea. Who's that nice-looking man who drove up in a four-seater just before lunch?'

'I expect you mean Mr Tomlinson. He's a retired Indian judge.'

He seems quite a decent sort of man. I shall talk to him.'

That evening, on coming down to dinner, Mr Satterthwaite found the Duchess resplendent in black velvet and diamonds, talking earnestly to the owner of the four-seater car. She beckoned authoritatively.

'Come here, Mr Satterthwaite, Mr Tomlinson is telling me the most interesting things, and what do you think?—he is actually going to take us on an expedition tomorrow in his car.'

Mr Satterthwaite regarded her with admiration.

'We must go in to dinner,' said the Duchess. 'Do come and sit at our table, Mr Tomlinson, and then you can go on with what you were telling me.'

'Quite a decent sort of man,' the Duchess pronounced later.

'With quite a decent sort of car,' retorted Mr Satterthwaite.

'Naughty,' said the Duchess, and gave him a resounding blow on the knuckles with the dingy black fan she always carried. Mr Satterthwaite winced with pain.

'Naomi is coming too,' said the Duchess. 'In her car. That girl wants taking out of herself. She's very selfish. Not exactly self-centred, but totally indifferent to everyone and everything. Don't you agree?'

'I don't think that's possible,' said Mr Satterthwaite, slowly. 'I mean, everyone's interest must go *somewhere*. There are, of course, the people who revolve round themselves—but I agree with you, she's not one of that kind. She's totally uninterested in herself. And yet she's got a strong character—there must be *something*. I thought at first it was her art—but it isn't. I've never met anyone so detached from life. That's dangerous.'

'Dangerous? What do you mean?'

'Well, you see—it must mean an obsession of some kind, and obsessions are always dangerous.'

'Satterthwaite,' said the Duchess, 'don't be a fool. And listen to me. About tomorrow—'

Mr Satterthwaite listened. It was very much his role in life.

They started early the following morning, taking their lunch with them. Naomi, who had been six months in the island, was to be the pioneer. Mr Satterthwaite went over to her as she sat waiting to start.

'You are sure that—I can't come with you?' he said wistfully.

She shook her head.

'You'll be much more comfortable in the back of the other car. Nicely padded seats and all that. This is a regular old rattle trap. You'd leap in the air going over the bumps.'

'And then, of course, the hills.'

Naomi laughed.

'Oh, I only said that to rescue you from the dickey. The Duchess could perfectly well afford to have hired a car. She's the meanest woman in England. All the same, the old thing is rather a sport, and I can't help liking her.'

'Then I could come with you after all?' said Mr Satterthwaite eagerly.

She looked at him curiously.

'Why are you so anxious to come with me?'

'Can you ask?' Mr Satterthwaite made his funny old-fashioned bow.

She smiled, but shook her head.

'That isn't the reason,' she said thoughtfully. 'It's odd . . . But you can't come with me—not today.'

'Another day, perhaps,' suggested Mr Satterthwaite politely.

'Oh, another day!' she laughed suddenly, a very queer laugh, Mr Satterthwaite thought. 'Another day! Well, we'll see.'

They started. They drove through the town, and then round the long curve of the bay, winding inland to cross a river and then back to the coast with its hundreds of little sandy coves. And then they began to climb. In and out, round nerve-shattering curves, upwards, ever upwards on the tortuous winding road. The blue bay was far below them, and on the other side of it Ajaccio sparkled in the sun, white, like a fairy city.

In and out, in and out, with a precipice first one side of them, then the other. Mr Satterthwaite felt slightly giddy, he also felt slightly sick. The road was not very wide. And still they climbed.

It was cold now. The wind came to them straight off the snow peaks. Mr Satterthwaite turned up his coat collar and buttoned it tightly under his chin.

It was very cold. Across the water, Ajaccio was still bathed in sunlight, but up here thick grey clouds came drifting across the face of the sun. Mr Satterthwaite ceased to admire the view. He yearned for a steam-heated hotel and a comfortable armchair.

Ahead of them Naomi's little two-seater drove steadily forward. Up, still up. They were on top of the world now. On either side of them were lower hills, hills sloping down to valleys. They looked straight across to the snow peaks. And the wind came tearing over them, sharp, like a knife. Suddenly Naomi's car stopped, and she looked back.

'We've arrived,' she said. 'At the World's End. And I don't think it's an awfully good day for it.'

They all got out. They had arrived in a tiny village, with half a dozen stone cottages. An imposing name was printed in letters a foot high.

'Coti Chiaveeri.'

Naomi shrugged her shoulders.

'That's its official name, but I prefer to call it the World's End.'

She walked on a few steps, and Mr Satterthwaite joined her. They were beyond the houses now. The road stopped. As Naomi had said, this was the end, the back of beyond, the beginning of nowhere. Behind them the white ribbon of the road, in front of them—nothing. Only far, far below, the sea . . .

Mr Satterthwaite drew a deep breath.

'It's an extraordinary place. One feels that anything might happen here, that one might meet—anyone—'

He stopped, for just in front of them a man was sitting on a boulder, his face turned to the sea. They had not seen him till this moment, and his appearance had the suddenness of a conjuring trick. He might have sprung from the surrounding landscape.

'I wonder—' began Mr Satterthwaite.

But at that minute the stranger turned, and Mr Satterthwaite saw his face.

'Why, Mr Quin! How extraordinary. Miss Carlton Smith, I want to introduce my friend Mr Quin to you. He's the most unusual fellow. You are, you know. You always turn up in the nick of time—'

He stopped, with the feeling that he had said something awkwardly significant, and yet for the life of him he could not think what it was.

Naomi had shaken hands with Mr Quin in her usual abrupt style.

'We're here for a picnic,' she said. 'And it seems to me we shall be pretty well frozen to the bone.'

Mr Satterthwaite shivered.

'Perhaps,' he said uncertainly, 'we shall find a sheltered spot?'

'Which this isn't,' agreed Naomi. 'Still, it's worth seeing, isn't it?'

'Yes, indeed.' Mr Satterthwaite turned to Mr Quin. 'Miss Carlton Smith calls this place the World's End. Rather a good name, eh?'

Mr Quin nodded his head slowly several times.

'Yes—a very suggestive name. I suppose one only comes once in one's life to a place like that—a place where one can't go on any longer.'

'What do you mean?' asked Naomi sharply.

He turned to her.

'Well, usually, there's a choice, isn't there? To the right or to the left. Forward or back. Here—there's the road behind you and in front of you—nothing.'

Naomi stared at him. Suddenly she shivered and began to retrace her steps towards the others. The two men fell in beside her. Mr Quin continued to talk, but his tone was now easily conversational.

'Is the small car yours, Miss Carlton Smith?'

'Yes.'

'You drive yourself? One needs, I think, a good deal of nerve to do that round here. The turns are rather appalling. A moment of inattention, a brake that failed to hold, and—over the edge—down—down—down. It would be—very easily done.'

They had now joined the others. Mr Satterthwaite introduced his friend. He felt a tug at his arm. It was Naomi. She drew him apart from the others.

'Who is he?' she demanded fiercely.

Mr Satterthwaite gazed at her in astonishment.

'Well, I hardly know. I mean, I have known him for some years now—we have run across each other from time to time, but in the sense of knowing actually—'

He stopped. These were futilities that he was uttering, and the girl by his side was not listening. She was standing with her head bent down, her hands clenched by her sides.

'He knows things,' she said. 'He knows things . . . How does he know?'

Mr Satterthwaite had no answer. He could only look at her dumbly, unable to comprehend the storm that shook her.

'I'm afraid,' she muttered.

'Afraid of Mr Quin?'

'I'm afraid of his eyes. He sees things . . .'

Something cold and wet fell on Mr Satterthwaite's cheek. He looked up.

'Why, it's snowing,' he exclaimed, in great surprise.

'A nice day to have chosen for a picnic,' said Naomi.

She had regained control of herself with an effort.

What was to be done? A babel of suggestions broke out. The snow came down thick and fast. Mr Quin made a suggestion and everyone welcomed it. There was a little stone Cassecroute at the end of the row of houses. There was a stampede towards it.

'You have your provisions,' said Mr Quin, 'and they will probably be able to make you some coffee.'

It was a tiny place, rather dark, for the one little window did little towards lighting it, but from one end came a grateful glow of warmth. An old Corsican woman was just throwing a handful of branches on the fire. It blazed up, and by its light the newcomers realized that others were before them.

Three people were sitting at the end of a bare wooden table. There was something unreal about the scene to Mr Satterthwaite's eye, there was something even more unreal about the people.

The woman who sat at the end of the table looked like a duchess—that is, she looked more like a popular conception of a duchess. She was the ideal stage *grande dame.* Her aristocratic head was held high, her exquisitely dressed hair was of a snowy white. She was dressed in grey—soft draperies that fell about her in artistic folds. One long white hand supported her chin, the other was holding a roll spread with *pâté de foie gras*. On her right was a man with a very white face, very black hair, and horn-rimmed spectacles. He was marvellously and beautifully dressed. At the moment his head was thrown back, and his left arm was thrown out as though he were about to declaim something.

On the left of the white-haired lady was a jolly-looking little man with a bald head. After the first glance, nobody looked at him.

There was just a moment of uncertainty, and then the Duchess (the authentic Duchess) took charge.

'Isn't this storm too dreadful?' she said pleasantly, coming forward, and smiling a purposeful and efficient smile that she had found very useful when serving on Welfare and other committees. 'I suppose you've been caught in it just like we have? But Corsica is a marvellous place. I only arrived this morning.'

The man with the black hair got up, and the Duchess with a gracious smile slipped into his seat.

The white-haired lady spoke.

'We have been here a week,' she said.

Mr Satterthwaite started. Could anyone who had once heard that voice ever forget it? It echoed round the stone room, charged with emotion—with exquisite melancholy. It seemed to him that she had said something wonderful, memorable, full of meaning. She had spoken from her heart.

He spoke in a hurried aside to Mr Tomlinson.

'The man in spectacles is Mr Vyse—the producer, you know.'

The retired Indian judge was looking at Mr Vyse with a good deal of dislike.

'What does he produce?' he asked. 'Children?'

'Oh, dear me, no,' said Mr Satterthwaite, shocked by the mere mention of anything so crude in connection with Mr Vyse. 'Plays.'

'I think,' said Naomi, 'I'll go out again. It's too hot in here.'

Her voice, strong and harsh, made Mr Satterthwaite jump. She made almost blindly, as it seemed, for the door, brushing Mr Tomlinson aside. But in the doorway itself she came face to face with Mr Quin, and he barred her way.

'Go back and sit down,' he said.

His voice was authoritative. To Mr Satterthwaite's surprise the girl hesitated a minute and then obeyed. She sat down at the foot of the table as far from the others as possible.

Mr Satterthwaite bustled forward and button-holed the producer.

'You may not remember me,' he began, 'my name is Satterthwaite.'

'Of course!' A long bony hand shot out and enveloped

the other's in a painful grip. 'My dear man. Fancy meeting you here. You know Miss Nunn, of course?'

Mr Satterthwaite jumped. No wonder that voice had been familiar. Thousands, all over England, had thrilled to those wonderful emotion-laden tones. Rosina Nunn! England's greatest emotional actress. Mr Satterthwaite too had lain under her spell. No one like her for interpreting a part—for bringing out the finer shades of meaning. He had thought of her always as an intellectual actress, one who comprehended and got inside the soul of her part.

He might be excused for not recognizing her. Rosina Nunn was volatile in her tastes. For twenty-five years of her life she had been a blonde. After a tour in the States she had returned with the locks of the raven, and she had taken up tragedy in earnest. This 'French Marquise' effect was her latest whim.

'Oh, by the way, Mr Judd—Miss Nunn's husband,' said Vyse, carelessly introducing the man with the bald head.

Rosina Nunn had had several husbands, Mr Satterthwaite knew. Mr Judd was evidently the latest.

Mr Judd was busily unwrapping packages from a hamper at his side. He addressed his wife.

'Some more *pâté*, dearest? That last wasn't as thick as you like it.'

Rosina Nunn surrendered her roll to him, as she murmured simply:

'Henry thinks of the most enchanting meals. I always leave the commissariat to him.'

'Feed the brute,' said Mr Judd, and laughed. He patted his wife on the shoulder.

'Treats her just as though she were a dog,' murmured the melancholy voice of Mr Vyse in Mr Satterthwaite's ear. 'Cuts up her food for her. Odd creatures, women.'

Mr Satterthwaite and Mr Quin between them unpacked lunch. Hard-boiled eggs, cold ham and Gruyère cheese were distributed round the table. The Duchess and Miss Nunn appeared to be deep in murmured confidences. Fragments came along in the actress's deep contralto.

'The bread must be lightly toasted, you understand? Then just a *very* thin layer of marmalade. Rolled up and put in the oven for one minute—not more. Simply delicious.'

'That woman lives for food,' murmured Mr Vyse. 'Simply lives for it. She can't think of anything else. I remember in Riders to the Sea—you know 'and it's the fine quiet time I'll be having.' I could *not* get the effect I wanted. At last I told her to think of peppermint creams—she's very fond of peppermint creams. I got the effect at once—a sort of far-away look that went to your very soul.'

Mr Satterthwaite was silent. He was remembering.

Mr Tomlinson opposite cleared his throat preparatory to entering into conversation.

'You produce plays, I hear, eh? I'm fond of a good play myself. Jim the Penman, now, that was a play.'

'My God,' said Mr Vyse, and shivered down all the long length of him.

'A tiny clove of garlic,' said Miss Nunn to the Duchess. 'You tell your cook. It's wonderful.'

She sighed happily and turned to her husband.

'Henry,' she said plaintively, 'I've never even *seen* the caviare.'

'You're as near as nothing to sitting on it,' returned Mr Judd cheerfully. 'You put it behind you on the chair.'

Rosina Nunn retrieved it hurriedly, and beamed round the table.

'Henry is too wonderful. I'm so terribly absent-minded. I never know where I've put anything.'

'Like the day you packed your pearls in your sponge bag,' said Henry jocosely. 'And then left it behind at the hotel. My word, I did a bit of wiring and phoning that day.'

'They were insured,' said Miss Nunn dreamily. 'Not like my opal.'

A spasm of exquisite heartrending grief flitted across her face.

Several times, when in the company of Mr Quin, Mr Satterthwaite had had the feeling of taking part in a play. The illusion was with him very strongly now. This was a dream. Everyone had his part. The words 'my opal' were his own cue. He leant forward.

'Your opal, Miss Nunn?'

'Have you got the butter, Henry? Thank you. Yes, my opal. It was stolen, you know. And I never got it back.'

'Do tell us,' said Mr Satterthwaite.

'Well—I was born in October—so it was lucky for me to wear opals, and because of that I wanted a real beauty. I waited a long time for it. They said it was one of the most perfect ones known. Not very large—about the size of a two-shilling piece—but oh! the colour and the fire.'

She sighed. Mr Satterthwaite observed that the Duchess was fidgeting and seemed uncomfortable, but nothing could stop Miss Nunn now. She went on, and the exquisite inflections of her voice made the story sound like some mournful Saga of old.

'It was stolen by a young man called Alec Gerard. He wrote plays.'

'Very good plays,' put in Mr Vyse professionally. 'Why, I once kept one of his plays for six months.'

'Did you produce it?' asked Mr Tomlinson.

'Oh, *no*,' said Mr Vyse, shocked at the idea. 'But do you know, at one time I actually thought of doing so?'

'It had a wonderful part in it for me,' said Miss Nunn. 'Rachel's Children, it was called—though there wasn't anyone called Rachel in the play. He came to talk to me about it—at the theatre. I liked him. He was a nice-looking—and very shy, poor boy. I remember'—a beautiful far-away look stole over her face—'he bought me some peppermint creams. The opal was lying on the dressing-table. He'd been out in Australia, and he knew something about opals. He took it over to the light to look at it. I suppose he must have slipped it into his pocket then. I missed it as soon as he'd gone. There *was* a to-do. You remember?'

She turned to Mr Vyse.

'Oh, I remember,' said Mr Vyse with a groan.

'They found the empty case in his rooms,' continued the actress. 'He'd been terribly hard up, but the very next day he was able to pay large sums into his bank. He pretended to account for it by saying that a friend of his had put some money on a horse for him, but he couldn't produce the friend. He said he must have put the case in his pocket by mistake. I think that was a terribly weak thing to say, don't you? He might have thought of something better than that . . . I had to go and give evidence. There were pictures of me in all the papers. My press agent said it was very good publicity—but I'd much rather have had my opal back.'

She shook her head sadly.

'Have some preserved pineapple?' said Mr Judd.

Miss Nunn brightened up.

'Where is it?'

'I gave it to you just now.'

Miss Nunn looked behind her and in front of her, eyed her grey silk pochette, and then slowly drew up a large purple silk bag that was reposing on the ground beside her. She began to turn the contents out slowly on the table, much to Mr Satterthwaite's interest.

There was a powder puff, a lip-stick, a small jewel case, a skein of wool, another powder puff, two handkerchiefs, a box of chocolate creams, an enamelled paper knife, a mirror, a little dark brown wooden box, five letters, a walnut, a small square of mauve crêpe de chine, a piece of ribbon and the end of a *croissant*. Last of all came the preserved pineapple.

'*Eureka*,' murmured Mr Satterthwaite softly.

'I beg your pardon?'

'Nothing,' said Mr Satterthwaite hastily. 'What a charming paper knife.'

'Yes, isn't it? Somebody gave it to me. I can't remember who.'

'That's an Indian box,' remarked Mr Tomlinson. 'Ingenious little things, aren't they?'

'Somebody gave me that too,' said Miss Nunn. 'I've had it a long time. It used always to stand on my dressing-table at the theatre. I don't think it's very pretty, though, do you?'

The box was of plain dark brown wood. It pushed open from the side. On the top of it were two plain flaps of wood that could be turned round and round.

'Not pretty, perhaps,' said Mr Tomlinson with a chuckle. 'But I'll bet you've never seen one like it.'

Mr Satterthwaite leaned forward. He had an excited feeling.

'Why did you say it was ingenious?' he demanded.

'Well, isn't it?'

The judge appealed to Miss Nunn. She looked at him blankly.

'I suppose I mustn't show them the trick of it—eh?' Miss Nunn still looked blank.

'What trick?' asked Mr Judd.

'God bless my soul, don't you know?'

He looked round the inquiring faces.

'Fancy that now. May I take the box a minute? Thank you.'

He pushed it open.

'Now then, can anyone give me something to put in it—not too big. Here's a small piece of Gruyère cheese. That will do capitally. I place it inside, shut the box.'

He fumbled for a minute or two with his hands.

'Now see—'

He opened the box again. It was empty.

'Well, I never,' said Mr Judd. 'How do you do it?'

'It's quite simple. Turn the box upside down, and move the left hand flap half-way round, then shut the right hand flap. Now to bring our piece of cheese back again we must reverse that. The right hand flap halfway round, and the left one closed, still keeping the box upside down. And now—Hey Presto!'

The box slid open. A gasp went round the table. The cheese was there but so was something else. A round thing that blinked forth every colour of the rainbow.

'My opal!'

It was a clarion note. Rosina Nunn stood upright, her hands clasped to her breast.

'My opal! How did it get there?'

Henry Judd cleared his throat.

'I—er—I rather think, Rosy, my girl, you must have put it there yourself.'

Someone got up from the table and blundered out into the air. It was Naomi Carlton Smith. Mr Quin followed her.

'But when? Do you mean—?'

Mr Satterthwaite watched her while the truth dawned on her. It took over two minutes before she got it.

'You mean last year—at the theatre.'

'You know,' said Henry apologetically. 'You *do* fiddle with things, Rosy. Look at you with the caviare today.'

Miss Nunn was painfully following out her mental processes.

'I just slipped it in without thinking, and then I suppose I turned the box about and did the thing by accident, but then—but then—' At last it came. 'But then Alec Gerard didn't steal it after all. Oh!'—a full-throated cry, poignant, moving—'How dreadful!'

'Well,' said Mr Vyse, 'that can be put right now.'

'Yes, but he's been in prison a year.' And then she startled them. She turned sharp on the Duchess. 'Who is that girl—that girl who has just gone out?'

'Miss Carlton Smith,' said the Duchess, 'was engaged to Mr Gerard. She—took the thing very hard.'

Mr Satterthwaite stole softly away. The snow had stopped, Naomi was sitting on the stone wall. She had a sketch book in her hand, some coloured crayons were scattered around. Mr Quin was standing beside her.

She held out the sketch book to Mr Satterthwaite. It was a very rough affair—but it had genius. A kaleidoscopic whirl of snowflakes with a figure in the centre.

'Very good,' said Mr Satterthwaite.

Mr Quin looked up at the sky.

'The storm is over,' he said. 'The roads will be slippery, but I do not think there will be any accident—now.'

'There will be no accident,' said Naomi. Her voice was charged with some meaning that Mr Satterthwaite did not understand. She turned and smiled at him—a sudden dazzling smile. 'Mr Satterthwaite can drive back with me if he likes.'

He knew then to what length desperation had driven her.

'Well,' said Mr Quin, 'I must bid you goodbye.'

He moved away.

'Where is he going?' said Mr Satterthwaite, staring after him.

'Back where he came from, I suppose,' said Naomi in an odd voice.

'But—but there isn't anything there,' said Mr Satterthwaite, for Mr Quin was making for that spot on the edge of the cliff where they had first seen him. 'You know you said yourself it was the World's End.'

He handed back the sketch book.

'It's very good,' he said. 'A very good likeness. But why—er—why did you put him in Fancy Dress?'

Her eyes met his for a brief second.

'I see him like that,' said Naomi Carlton Smith.

The Manhood of Edward Robinson

'With a swing of his mighty arms, Bill lifted her right off her feet, crushing her to his breast. With a deep sigh she yielded her lips in such a kiss as he had never dreamed of—'

With a sigh, Mr Edward Robinson put down *When Love is King* and stared out of the window of the underground train. They were running through Stamford Brook. Edward Robinson was thinking about Bill. Bill was the real hundred per cent he-man beloved of lady novelists. Edward envied him his muscles, his rugged good looks and his terrific passions. He picked up the book again and read the description of the proud Marchesa Bianca (she who had yielded her lips). So ravishing was her beauty, the intoxication of her was so great, that strong men went down before her like ninepins, faint and helpless with love.

'Of course,' said Edward to himself, 'it's all bosh, this sort of stuff. All bosh, it is. And yet, I wonder—'

His eyes looked wistful. Was there such a thing as a world of romance and adventure somewhere? Were there women whose beauty intoxicated? Was there such a thing as love that devoured one like a flame?

'This is real life, this is,' said Edward. 'I've got to go on the same just like all the other chaps.'

On the whole, he supposed, he ought to consider

himself a lucky young man. He had an excellent berth—a clerkship in a flourishing concern. He had good health, no one dependent upon him, and he was engaged to Maud.

But the mere thought of Maud brought a shadow over his face. Though he would never have admitted it, he was afraid of Maud. He loved her—yes—he still remembered the thrill with which he had admired the back of her white neck rising out of the cheap four and elevenpenny blouse on the first occasion they had met. He had sat behind her at the cinema, and the friend he was with had known her and had introduced them. No doubt about it, Maud was very superior. She was good looking and clever and very lady-like, and she was always right about everything. The kind of girl, everyone said, who would make such an excellent wife.

Edward wondered whether the Marchesa Bianca would have made an excellent wife. Somehow, he doubted it. He couldn't picture the voluptuous Bianca, with her red lips and her swaying form, tamely sewing on buttons, say, for the virile Bill. No, Bianca was Romance, and this was real life. He and Maud would be very happy together. She had so much common sense . . .

But all the same, he wished that she wasn't quite so—well, sharp in manner. So prone to 'jump upon him".

It was, of course, her prudence and her common sense which made her do so. Maud was very sensible. And, as a rule, Edward was very sensible too, but sometimes—He had wanted to get married this Christmas, for instance. Maud had pointed out how much more prudent it would be to wait a while—a year or two, perhaps. His salary was not large. He had wanted to give her an expensive ring—she had been horror stricken, and had forced him to take it back and exchange it for a cheaper one. Her qualities were all excellent qualities, but sometimes Edward wished that she had more faults and less virtues. It was her virtues that drove him to desperate deeds.

For instance—

A blush of guilt overspread his face. He had got to tell her—and tell her soon. His secret guilt was already making him behave strangely. Tomorrow was the first of three days holiday, Christmas Eve, Christmas Day and Boxing Day. She had suggested that he should come round and spend the day with her people, and in a clumsy foolish manner, a manner that could not fail to arouse her suspicions, he had managed to get out of it—had told a long, lying story about a pal of his in the country with whom he had promised to spend the day.

And there was no pal in the country. There was only his guilty secret.

Three months ago, Edward Robinson, in company with a few hundred thousand other young men, had gone in for a competition in one of the weekly papers. Twelve girls' names had to be arranged in order of popularity. Edward had had a brilliant idea. His own preference was sure to be wrong—he had noticed that in several similar competitions. He wrote down the twelve names arranged in his own order of merit, then he wrote them down again this time placing one from the top and one from the bottom of the list alternately.

When the result was announced, Edward had got eight right out of the twelve, and was awarded the first prize of £500. This result, which might easily be ascribed to luck, Edward persisted in regarding as the direct outcome of his 'system.' He was inordinately proud of himself.

The next thing was, what do do with the £500? He knew very well what Maud would say. Invest it. A nice little nest egg for the future. And, of course, Maud would be quite right, he knew that. But to win money as the result of a competition is an entirely different feeling from anything else in the world.

Had the money been left to him as a legacy, Edward would have invested it religiously in Conversion Loan or Savings Certificates as a matter of course. But money that one has achieved by a mere stroke of the pen, by a lucky and unbelievable chance, comes under the same heading as a child's sixpence—'for your very own—to spend as you like'.

And in a certain rich shop which he passed daily on his way to the office, was the unbelievable dream, a small two-seater car, with a long shining nose, and the price clearly displayed on it—£465.

'If I were rich,' Edward had said to it, day after day. 'If I were rich, I'd have you.'

And now he was—if not rich—at least possessed of a lump sum of money sufficient to realize his dream. That car, that shining alluring piece of loveliness, was his if he cared to pay the price.

He had meant to tell Maud about the money. Once he had told her, he would have secured himself against temptation. In face of Maud's horror and disapproval, he would never have the courage to persist in his madness. But, as it chanced, it was Maud herself who clinched the matter. He had taken her to the cinema—and to the best seats in the house. She had pointed out to him, kindly but firmly, the criminal folly of his behaviour—wasting good money—three and sixpence against two and fourpence, when one saw just as well from the latter places.

Edward took her reproaches in sullen silence. Maud felt contentedly that she was making an impression. Edward could not be allowed to continue in these extravagant ways. She loved Edward, but she realized that he was weak—hers the task of being ever at hand to influence him in the way he should go. She observed his worm-like demeanour with satisfaction.

Edward was indeed worm-like. Like worms, he turned. He remained crushed by her words, but it was at that precise minute that he made up his mind to buy the car.

'Damn it,' said Edward to himself. 'For once in my life, I'll do what I like. Maud can go hang!'

And the very next morning he had walked into that palace of plate glass, with its lordly inmates in their glory of gleaming enamel and shimmering metal, and with an insouciance that surprised himself, he bought the car. It was the easiest thing in the world, buying a car!

It had been his for four days now. He had gone about, outwardly calm, but inwardly bathed in ecstasy. And to Maud he had as yet breathed no word. For four days, in his luncheon hour, he had received instruction in the handling of the lovely creature. He was an apt pupil.

Tomorrow, Christmas Eve, he was to take her out into the country. He had lied to Maud, and he would lie again if need be. He was enslaved body and soul by his new possession. It stood to him for Romance, for Adventure, for all the things that he had longed for and had never had. Tomorrow, he and his mistress would take the road together. They would rush through the keen cold air, leaving the throb and fret of London far behind—out into the wide clear spaces . . .

At this moment, Edward, though he did not know it, was very near to being a poet.

Tomorrow—

He looked down at the book in his hand—*When Love is King.* He laughed and stuffed it into his pocket. The car, and the red lips of the Marchesa Bianca, and the amazing prowess of Bill seemed all mixed up together. Tomorrow—

The weather, usually a sorry jade to those who count upon her, was kindly disposed towards Edward. She gave him the day of his dreams, a day of glittering frost, and pale-blue sky, and a primrose-yellow sun.

So, in a mood of high adventure, of dare-devil wickedness, Edward drove out of London. There was trouble at Hyde Park Corner, and a sad *contretemps* at Putney Bridge, there was much protesting of gears, and a frequent jarring of brakes, and much abuse was freely showered upon Edward by the drivers of other vehicles. But for a novice he did not acquit himself so badly, and presently he came out on to one of those fair wide roads that are the joy of the motorist. There was little congestion on this particular road today. Edward drove on and on, drunk with his mastery over this creature of the gleaming sides, speeding through the cold white world with the elation of a god.

It was a delirious day. He stopped for lunch at an old-fashioned inn, and again later for tea. Then reluctantly he turned homewards—back again to London, to Maud, to the inevitable explanation, recriminations . . .

He shook off the thought with a sigh. Let tomorrow look after itself. He still had today. And what could be more fascinating than this? Rushing through the darkness with the headlights searching out the way in front. Why, this was the best of all!

He judged that he had no time to stop anywhere for dinner. This driving through the darkness was a ticklish business. It was going to take longer to get back to London than he had thought. It was just eight o'clock when he passed through Hindhead and came out upon the rim of the Devil's Punch Bowl. There was moonlight, and the snow that had fallen two days ago was still unmelted.

He stopped the car and stood staring. What did it matter if he didn't get back to London until midnight? What did it matter if he never got back? He wasn't going to tear himself away from this at once.

He got out of the car, and approached the edge. There was a path winding down temptingly near him. Edward yielded to the spell. For the next half-hour he wandered deliriously in a snowbound world. Never had he imagined anything quite like this. And it was his, his very own, given to him by his shining mistress who waited for him faithfully on the road above.

He climbed up again, got into the car and drove off, still a little dizzy from that discovery of sheer beauty which comes to the most prosaic men once in a while.

Then, with a sigh, he came to himself, and thrust his hand into the pocket of the car where he had stuffed an additional muffler earlier in the day.

But the muffler was no longer there. The pocket was empty. No, not completely empty—there was something scratchy and hard—like pebbles.

Edward thrust his hand deep down. In another minute he was staring like a man bereft of his senses. The object that he held in his hand, dangling from his fingers, with the moonlight striking a hundred fires from it, was a diamond necklace.

Edward stared and stared. But there was no doubting possible. A diamond necklace worth probably thousands of pounds (for the stones were large ones) had been casually reposing in the side-pocket of the car.

But who had put it there? It had certainly not been there when he started from town. Someone must have come along when he was walking about in the snow, and deliberately thrust it in. But why? Why choose *his* car? Had the owner of the necklace made a mistake? Or was it—could it possibly be *a stolen* necklace?

And then, as all these thoughts went whirling through his brain, Edward suddenly stiffened and went cold all over. *This was not his car.*

It was very like it, yes. It was the same brilliant shade of scarlet—red as the Marchesa Bianca's lips—it had the same long and gleaming nose, but by a thousand small signs, Edward realized that it was not his car. Its shining newness was scarred here and there, it bore signs, faint but unmistakeable, of wear and tear. In that case ...

Edward, without more ado, made haste to turn the car. Turning was not his strong point. With the car in reverse, he invariably lost his head and twisted the wheel the wrong way. Also, he frequently became entangled between the accelerator and the foot brake with disastrous results. In the end, however, he succeeded, and straight away the car began purring up the hill again.

Edward remembered that there had been another car standing some little distance away. He had not noticed it particularly at the time. He had returned from his walk by a different path from that by which he had gone down into the hollow. This second path had brought him out on the road immediately behind, as he had thought, his own car. It must really have been the other one.

In about ten minutes he was once more at the spot where he had halted. But there was now no car at all by the roadside. Whoever had owned this car must now have gone off in Edward's—he also, perhaps, misled by the resemblance.

Edward took out the diamond necklace from his pocket and let it run through his fingers perplexedly.

What to do next? Run on to the nearest police station? Explain the circumstances, hand over the necklace, and give the number of his own car.

By the by, what was the number of his car? Edward thought and thought, but for the life of him he couldn't remember. He felt a cold sinking sensation. He was going to look the most utter fool at the police station. There was an eight in it, that was all that he could remember. Of course, it didn't really matter—at least . . . He looked uncomfortably at the diamonds. Supposing they should think—oh, but they wouldn't—and yet again they might—that he had stolen the car and the diamonds? Because, after all, when one came to think of it, would anyone in their senses thrust a valuable diamond necklace carelessly into the open pocket of a car?

Edward got out and went round to the back of the motor. Its number was XR10061. Beyond the fact that that was certainly not the number of his car, it conveyed nothing to him. Then he set to work systematically to search all the pockets. In the one where he had found the diamonds he made a discovery—a small scrap of paper with some words pencilled on it. By the light of the headlights, Edward read them easily enough.

'*Meet me, Greane, corner of Salter's Lane, ten o'clock.*'

He remembered the name Greane. He had seen it on a sign-post earlier in the day. In a minute, his mind was made up. He would go to this village, Greane, find Salter's Lane, meet the person who had written the note, and explain the circumstances. That would be much better than looking a fool in the local police station.

He started off almost happily. After all, this was an adventure. This was the sort of thing that didn't happen every day. The diamond necklace made it exciting and mysterious.

He had some little difficulty in finding Greane, and still more difficulty in finding Salter's Lane, but after knocking up two cottages, he succeeded.

Still, it was a few minutes after the appointed hour when he drove cautiously along a narrow road, keeping a sharp look-out on the left-hand side where he had been told Salter's Lane branched off.

He came upon it quite suddenly round a bend, and even as he drew up, a figure came forward out of the darkness.

'At last!' a girl's voice cried. 'What an age you've been, Gerald!'

As she spoke, the girl stepped right into the glare of the headlights, and Edward caught his breath. She was the most glorious creature he had ever seen.

She was quite young, with hair black as night, and wonderful scarlet lips. The heavy cloak that she wore swung open, and Edward saw that she was in full evening dress—a kind of flame-coloured sheath, outlining her perfect body. Round her neck was a row of exquisite pearls.

Suddenly the girl started.

'Why,' she cried; 'it isn't Gerald.'

'No,' said Edward hastily. 'I must explain.' He took the diamond necklace from his pocket and held it out to her. 'My name is Edward—'

He got no further, for the girl clapped her hands and broke in:

'Edward, of course! I am so glad. But that idiot Jimmy told me over the phone that he was sending Gerald along with the car. It's awfully sporting of you to come. I've been dying to meet you. Remember I haven't seen you since I was six years old. I see you've got the necklace all right. Shove it in your pocket again. The village policeman might come along and see it. Brrr, it's cold as ice waiting here! Let me get in.'

As though in a dream Edward opened the door, and she sprang lightly in beside him. Her furs swept his cheek, and an elusive scent, like that of violets after rain, assailed his nostrils.

He had no plan, no definite thought even. In a minute, without conscious volition, he had yielded himself to the adventure. She had called him Edward—what matter if he were the wrong Edward? She would find him out soon enough. In the meantime, let the game go on. He let in the clutch and they glided off.

Presently the girl laughed. Her laugh was just as wonderful as the rest of her.

'It's easy to see you don't know much about cars. I suppose they don't have them out there?'

'I wonder where 'out there" is?' thought Edward. Aloud he said, 'Not much.'

'Better let me drive,' said the girl. 'It's tricky work finding your way round these lanes until we get on the main road again.'

He relinquished his place to her gladly. Presently they were humming through the night at a pace and with a recklessness that secretly appalled Edward. She turned her head towards him.

'I like pace. Do you? You know—you're not a bit like Gerald. No one would ever take you to be brothers. You're not a bit like what I imagined, either.'

'I suppose,' said Edward, 'that I'm so completely ordinary. Is that it?'

'Not ordinary—different. I can't make you out. How's poor old Jimmy? Very fed up, I suppose?'

'Oh, Jimmy's all right,' said Edward.

'It's easy enough to say that—but it's rough luck on him having a sprained ankle. Did he tell you the whole story?'

'Not a word. I'm completely in the dark. I wish you'd enlighten me.'

'Oh, the thing worked like a dream. Jimmy went in at the front door, togged up in his girl's clothes. I gave him a minute or two, and then shinned up to the window. Agnes Larella's maid was there laying out Agnes's dress and jewels, and all the rest. Then there was a great yell downstairs, and the squib went off, and everyone shouted fire. The maid dashed out, and I hopped in, helped myself to the necklace, and was out and down in a flash, and out of the place by the back way across the Punch Bowl. I shoved the necklace and the notice where to pick me up in the pocket of the car in passing. Then I joined Louise at the hotel, having shed my snow boots of course. Perfect alibi for me. She'd no idea I'd been out at all.'

'And what about Jimmy?'

'Well, you know more about that than I do.'

'He didn't tell me anything,' said Edward easily.

'Well, in the general rag, he caught his foot in his skirt and managed to sprain it. They had to carry him to the car, and the Larellas' chauffeur drove him home. Just fancy if the chauffeur had happened to put his hand in the pocket!'

Edward laughed with her, but his mind was busy. He understood the position more or less now. The name of Larella was vaguely familiar to him—it was a name that spelt wealth. This girl, and an unknown man called Jimmy, had conspired together to steal the necklace, and had succeeded. Owing to his sprained ankle and the presence of the Larellas' chauffeur Jimmy had not been able to look in the pocket of the car before telephoning to the girl—probably had had no wish to do so. But it was almost certain that the other unknown 'Gerald' would do so at any early opportunity. And in it, he would find Edward's muffler!

'Good going,' said the girl.

A tram flashed past them, they were on the outskirts of London. They flashed in and out of the traffic. Edward's heart stood in his mouth. She was a wonderful driver, this girl, but she took risks!

Quarter of an hour later they drew up before an imposing house in a frigid square.

'We can shed some of our clothing here,' said the girl, 'before we go on to Ritson's.'

'Ritson's?' queried Edward. He mentioned the famous night-club almost reverently.

'Yes, didn't Gerald tell you?'

'He did not,' said Edward grimly. 'What about my clothes?'

She frowned.

'Didn't they tell you *anything*? We'll rig you up somehow. We've got to carry this through.'

A stately butler opened the door and stood aside to let them enter.

'Mr Gerald Champneys rang up, your ladyship. He was very anxious to speak to you, but he wouldn't leave a message.'

'I bet he was anxious to speak to her,' said Edward to himself. 'At any rate, I know my full name now. Edward Champneys. But who is she? Your ladyship, they called her. What does she want to steal a necklace for? Bridge debts?'

In the *feuilletons* which he occasionally read, the beautiful and titled heroine was always driven desperate by bridge debts.

Edward was led away by the stately butler, and delivered over to a smooth-mannered valet. A quarter of an hour later he rejoined his hostess in the hall, exquisitely attired in evening clothes made in Savile Row which fitted him to a nicety.

Heavens! What a night!

They drove in the car to the famous Ritson's. In common with everyone else Edward had read scandalous paragraphs concerning Ritson's. Anyone who was anyone turned up at Ritson's sooner or later. Edward's only fear was that someone who knew the real Edward Champneys might turn up. He consoled himself by the reflection that the real man had evidently been out of England for some years.

Sitting at a little table against the wall, they sipped cocktails. Cocktails! To the simple Edward they represented the quintessence of the fast life. The girl, wrapped in a wonderful embroidered shawl, sipped nonchalantly. Suddenly she dropped the shawl from her shoulders and rose.

'Let's dance.'

Now the one thing that Edward could do to perfection was to dance. When he and Maud took the floor together at the Palais de Danse, lesser lights stood still and watched in admiration.

'I nearly forgot,' said the girl suddenly. 'The necklace?'

She held out her hand. Edward, completely bewildered, drew it from his pocket and gave it to her. To his utter amazement, she coolly clasped it round her neck. Then she smiled up at him intoxicatingly.

'Now,' she said softly, 'we'll dance.'

They danced. And in all Ritson's nothing more perfect could be seen.

Then, as at length they returned to their table, an old gentleman with a would-be rakish air accosted Edward's companion.

'Ah! Lady Noreen, always dancing! Yes, yes. Is Captain Folliot here tonight?'

'Jimmy's taken a toss—racked his ankle.'

'You don't say so? How did that happen?'

'No details as yet.'

She laughed and passed on.

Edward followed, his brain in a whirl. He knew now. Lady Noreen Eliot, the famous Lady Noreen herself, perhaps the most talked of girl in England. Celebrated for her beauty, for her daring—the leader of that set known as the Bright Young People. Her engagement to Captain James Folliot, V.C., of the Household Calvalry, had been recently announced.

But the necklace? He still couldn't understand the necklace. He must risk giving himself away, but know he must.

As they sat down again, he pointed to it.

'Why that, Noreen?' he said. 'Tell me why?'

She smiled dreamily, her eyes far away, the spell of the dance still holding her.

'It's difficult for you to understand, I suppose. One gets so tired of the same thing—always the same thing. Treasure hunts were all very well for a while, but one gets used to everything. 'Burglaries" were my idea. Fifty pounds entrance fee, and lots to be drawn. This is the third. Jimmy and I drew Agnes Larella. You know the rules? Burglary to be carried out within three days and the loot to be worn for at least an hour in a public place, or you forfeit your stake and a hundred-pound fine. It's rough luck on Jimmy spraining his ankle, but we'll scoop the pool all right.'

'I see,' said Edward, drawing a deep breath. 'I see.'

Noreen rose suddenly, pulling her shawl round her.

'Drive me somewhere in the car. Down to the docks. Somewhere horrible and exciting. Wait a minute—' She reached up and unclasped the diamonds from her neck. 'You'd better take these again. I don't want to be murdered for them.'

They went out of Ritson's together. The car stood in a small by-street, narrow and dark. As they turned the corner towards it, another car drew up to the curb, and a young man sprang out.

'Thank the Lord, Noreen, I've got hold of you at last,' he cried. 'There's the devil to pay. That ass Jimmy got off with the wrong car. God knows where those diamonds are at this minute. We're in the devil of a mess.'

Lady Noreen stared at him.

'What do you mean? We've got the diamonds—at least Edward has.'

'Edward?'

'Yes.' She made a slight gesture to indicate the figure by her side.

'It's I who am in the devil of a mess,' thought Edward. 'Ten to one this is brother Gerald.'

The young man stared at him.

'What do you mean?' he said slowly. 'Edward's in Scotland.'

'Oh!' cried the girl. She stared at Edward. 'Oh!'

Her colour came and went.

'So you,' she said, in a low voice, 'are the real thing?'

It took Edward just one minute to grasp the situation.

There was awe in the girl's eyes—was it, could it be—admiration? Should he explain? Nothing so tame! He would play up to the end.

He bowed ceremoniously.

'I have to thank you, Lady Noreen,' he said, in the best highwayman manner, 'for a most delightful evening.'

One quick look he cast at the car from which the other had just alighted. A scarlet car with a shining bonnet. His car!

'And I will wish you good-evening.'

One quick spring and he was inside, his foot on the clutch. The car started forward. Gerald stood paralysed, but the girl was quicker. As the car slid past she leapt for it, alighting on the running board.

The car swerved, shot blindly round the corner and pulled up. Noreen, still panting from her spring, laid her hand on Edward's arm.

'You must give it me—oh, you must give it me. I've got to return it to Agnes Larella. Be a sport—we've had a good evening together—we've danced—we've been—pals. Won't you give it to me? To *me*?'

A woman who intoxicated you with her beauty. There were such women then . . .

Also, Edward was only too anxious to get rid of the necklace. It was a heaven-sent opportunity for a *beau geste*.

He took it from his pocket and dropped it into her outstretched hand.

'We've been—pals,' he said.

'Ah!' Her eyes smouldered—lit up.

Then surprisingly she bent her head to him. For a moment he held her, her lips against his . . .

Then she jumped off. The scarlet car sped forward with a great leap.

Romance!

Adventure!

At twelve o'clock on Christmas Day, Edward Robinson strode into the tiny drawing-room of a house in Clapham with the customary greeting of 'Merry Christmas'.

Maud, who was rearranging a piece of holly, greeted him coldly.

'Have a good day in the country with that friend of yours?' she inquired.

'Look here,' said Edward. 'That was a lie I told you. I won a competition—£500, and I bought a car with it. I didn't tell you because I knew you'd kick up a row about it. That's the first thing. I've bought the car and there's nothing more to be said about it. The second thing is this—I'm not going to hang about for years. My prospects are quite good enough and I mean to marry you next month. See?'

'Oh!' said Maud faintly.

Was this—could this be—*Edward* speaking in this masterful fashion?

'Will you?' said Edward. 'Yes or no?'

She gazed at him, fascinated. There was awe and admiration in her eyes, and the sight of that look was intoxicating to Edward. Gone was that patient motherliness which had roused him to exasperation.

So had the Lady Noreen looked at him last night. But the Lady Noreen had receded far away, right into the region of Romance, side by side with the Marchesa Bianca. This was the Real Thing. This was his woman.

'Yes or no?' he repeated, and drew a step nearer.

'Ye—ye-es,' faltered Maud. 'But, oh, Edward, what has happened to you? You're quite different today.'

'Yes,' said Edward. 'For twenty-four hours I've been a man instead of a worm—and, by God, it pays!'

He caught her in his arms almost as Bill the superman might have done.

'Do you love me, Maud? Tell me, do you love me?'

'Oh, Edward!' breathed Maud. 'I adore you . . .'

Christmas Adventure

The big logs crackled merrily in the wide, open fire-place, and above their crackling rose the babel of six tongues all wagging industriously together. The house-party of young people were enjoying their Christmas.

Old Miss Endicott, known to most of those present as Aunt Emily, smiled indulgently on the clatter.

'Bet you you can't eat six mince-pies, Jean.'

'Yes, I can.'

'No, you can't.'

'You'll get the pig out of the trifle if you do.'

'Yes, *and* three helps of trifle, *and* two helps of plum-pudding.'

'I hope the pudding will be good,' said Miss Endicott apprehensively. 'But they were only made three days ago. Christmas puddings ought to be made a long time before Christmas. Why, I remember when I was a child, I thought the last Collect before Advent—'Stir up, O Lord, we beseech Thee . . .'—referred in some way to stirring up the Christmas puddings!'

There was a polite pause while Miss Endicott was speaking. Not because any of the young people were in the least interested in her reminiscences of bygone days, but because they felt that some show of attention was due by good manners to their hostess. As soon as she stopped, the babel burst out again. Miss Endicott sighed, and glanced towards the only member of the party whose years approached her own, as though in search of sympathy—a little man with a curious egg-shaped head and fierce upstanding moustaches. Young people were not what they were, reflected Miss Endicott. In olden days there would have been a mute, respectful circle, listening to the pearls of wisdom dropped by their elders. Instead of which there was all this nonsensical chatter, most of it utterly incomprehensible. All the same, they were dear children! Her eyes softened as she passed them in review—tall, freckled Jean; little Nancy Cardell, with her dark, gipsy beauty; the two younger boys home from school, Johnnie and Eric, and their friend, Charlie Pease; and fair, beautiful Evelyn Haworth . . . At thought of the last, her brow contracted a little, and her eyes wandered to where her eldest nephew, Roger, sat morosely silent, taking no part in the fun, with his eyes fixed on the exquisite Northern fairness of the young girl.

'Isn't the snow ripping?' cried Johnnie, approaching the window. 'Real Christmas weather. I say, let's have a snowball fight. There's lots of time before dinner, isn't there, Aunt Emily?'

'Yes, my dear. We have it at two o'clock. That reminds me, I had better see to the table.'

She hurried out of the room.

'I tell you what. We'll make a snowman!' screamed Jean.

'Yes, what fun! I know; we'll do a snow statue of M. Poirot. Do you hear, M. Poirot? The great detective, Hercule Poirot, modelled in snow, by six celebrated artists!'

The little man in the chair bowed his acknowledgements with a twinkling eye.

'Make him very handsome, my children,' he urged. 'I insist on that.'

'Ra-ther!'

The troop disappeared like a whirlwind, colliding in the doorway with a stately butler who was entering with a note on a salver. The butler, his calm re-established, advanced towards Poirot.

Poirot took the note and tore it open. The butler departed. Twice the little man read the note through, then he folded it up and put it in his pocket. Not a muscle of his face had moved, and yet the contents of the note were sufficiently surprising. Scrawled in an illiterate hand were the words: '*Don't eat any plum-pudding.*'

'Very interesting,' murmured M. Poirot to himself. 'And quite unexpected.'

He looked across to the fireplace. Evelyn Haworth had not gone out with the rest. She was sitting staring at the fire, absorbed in thought, nervously twisting a ring on the third finger of her left hand round and round.

'You are lost in a dream, Mademoiselle,' said the little man at last. 'And the dream is not a happy one, eh?'

She started, and looked across at him uncertainly. He nodded reassuringly.

'It is my business to know things. No, you are not happy. Me, too, I am not very happy. Shall we confide in each other? See you, I have the big sorrow because a friend of mine, a friend of many years, has gone away across the sea to the South America. Sometimes, when we were together, this friend made me impatient, his stupidity enraged me; but now that he is gone, I can remember only his good qualities. That is the way of life, is it not? And now, Mademoiselle, what is your trouble? You are not like me, old and alone—you are young and beautiful; and the man you love loves you—oh yes, it is so: I have been watching him for the last half-hour.'

The girl's colour rose.

'You mean Roger Endicott? Oh, but you have made a mistake; it is not Roger I am engaged to.'

'No, you are engaged to Mr Oscar Levering. I know that perfectly. But why are you engaged to him, since you love another man?'

The girl did not seem to resent his words; indeed, there was something in his manner which made that impossible. He spoke with a mixture of kindliness and authority that was irresistible.

'Tell me all about it,' said Poirot gently; and he added the phrase he had used before, the sound of which was oddly comforting to the girl. 'It is my business to know things.'

'I am so miserable, M. Poirot—so very miserable. You see, once we were very well off. I was supposed to be an heiress, and Roger was only a younger son; and—and although I'm sure he cared for me, he never said anything, but went off to Australia.'

'It is droll, the way they arrange the marriages over here,' interpolated M. Poirot. 'No order. No method. Everything left to chance.' Evelyn continued.

'Then suddenly we lost all our money. My mother and I were left almost penniless. We moved into a tiny house, and we could just manage. But my mother became very ill. The only chance for her was to have a serious operation and go abroad to a warm climate. And we hadn't the money, M. Poirot—we hadn't the money! It meant that she must die. Mr Levering had proposed to me once or twice already. He again asked me to marry him, and promised to do everything that could be done for my mother. I said yes—what else could I do? He kept his word. The operation was performed by the greatest specialist of the day, and we went to Egypt for the winter. That was a year ago. My mother is well and strong again; and I—I am to marry Mr Levering after Christmas.'

'I see,' said M. Poirot; 'and in the meantime, M. Roger's elder brother has died, and he has come home—to find his dream shattered. All the same, you are not yet married, Mademoiselle.'

'A Haworth does not break her word, M. Poirot,' said the girl proudly.

Almost as she spoke, the door opened, and a big man with a rubicund face, narrow, crafty eyes, and a bald head stood on the threshold.

'What are you moping in here for, Evelyn? Come out for a stroll.'

'Very well, Oscar.'

She rose listlessly. Poirot rose also and demanded politely:

'Mademoiselle Levering, she is still indisposed?'

'Yes, I'm sorry to say my sister is still in bed. Too bad, to be laid up on Christmas Day.'

'It is indeed,' agreed the detective politely.

A few minutes sufficed for Evelyn to put on her snow-boots and some wraps, and she and her fiancé went out into the snow-covered grounds. It was an ideal Christmas Day, crisp and sunny. The rest of the house-party were busy with the erection of the snowman. Levering and Evelyn paused to watch them.

'Love's young dream, yah!' cried Johnnie, and threw a snowball at them.

'What do you think of it, Evelyn?' cried Jean. 'M. Hercule Poirot, the great detective.'

'Wait till the moustache goes on,' said Eric. 'Nancy's going to clip off a bit of her hair for it. *Vivent les braves Belges!* Pom, pom!'

'Fancy having a real-live detective in the house!'—this from Charlie—'I wish there could be a murder, too.'

'Oh, oh, oh!' cried Jean, dancing about. 'I've got an idea. Let's get up a murder—a spoof one, I mean. And take him in. Oh, do let's—it would be no end of a rag.'

Five voices began to talk at once.

'How should we do it?'

'Awful groans!'

'No, you stupid, out here.'

'Footprints in the snow, of course.'

'Jean in her nightie.'

'You do it with red paint.'

'In your hand—and clap it to your head.'

'I say, I wish we had a revolver.'

'I tell you, Father and Aunt Em won't hear. Their rooms are the other side of the house.'

'No, he won't mind a bit; he's no end of a sport.'

'Yes, but what kind of red paint? Enamel?'

'We could get some in the village.'

'Fat-head, not on Christmas Day.'

'No, watercolour. Crimson lake.'

'Jean can be it.'

'Never mind if you *are* cold. It won't be for long.'

'No, Nancy can be it, Nancy's got those posh pyjamas.'

'Let's see if Graves knows where there's any paint.'

A stampede to the house.

'In a brown study, Endicott?' said Levering, laughing disagreeably.

Roger roused himself abruptly. He had heard little of what had passed.

'I was just wondering,' he said quietly.

'Wondering?'

'Wondering what M. Poirot was doing down here at all.'

Levering seemed taken aback; but at that moment the big gong pealed out, and everybody went in to Christmas dinner. The curtains were drawn in the dining-room, and the lights on, illuminating the long table piled high with crackers and other decorations. It was a real old-fashioned Christmas dinner. At one end of the table was the Squire, red-faced and jovial; his sister faced him at the other. M. Poirot, in honour of the occasion, had donned a red waistcoat, and his plumpness, and the way he carried his head on one side, reminded one irresistibly of a robin redbreast.

The Squire carved rapidly, and everyone fell to on turkey. The carcasses of two turkeys were removed, and there fell a breathless hush. Then Graves, the butler, appeared in state, bearing the plum-pudding aloft—a gigantic pudding wreathed in flames. A hullabaloo broke out.

'Quick. Oh! my piece is going out. Buck up, Graves; unless it's still burning, I shan't get my wish.'

Nobody had leisure to notice a curious expression on the face of M. Poirot as he surveyed the portion of pudding on his plate. Nobody observed the lightning glance he sent round the table. With a faint, puzzled frown he began to eat his pudding. Everybody began to eat pudding. The conversation was more subdued. Suddenly the Squire uttered an exclamation. His face became purple and his hand went to his mouth.

'Confound it, Emily!' he roared. 'Why do you let the cook put glass in the puddings?'

'Glass?' cried Miss Endicott, astonished.

The Squire withdrew the offending substance from his mouth.

'Might have broken a tooth,' he grumbled. 'Or swallowed it and had appendicitis.'

In front of each person was a small finger-bowl of water, designed to receive the sixpences and other matters found in the trifle. Mr Endicott dropped the piece of glass into this, rinsed it and held it up.

'God bless my soul!' he ejaculated. 'It's a red stone out of one of the cracker brooches.'

'You permit?' Very deftly, M. Poirot took it from his fingers and examined it attentively. As the Squire had said, it was a big red stone, the colour of a ruby. The light gleamed from its facets as he turned it about.

'Gee!' cried Eric. 'Suppose it's real.'

'Silly boy!' said Jean scornfully. 'A ruby that size would be worth thousands and thousands and thousands—wouldn't it, M. Poirot?'

'Extraordinary how well they get up these cracker things,' murmured Miss Endicott. '*But how did it get into the pudding?*'

Undoubtedly that was the question of the hour. Every hypothesis was exhausted. Only M. Poirot said nothing, but carelessly, as though thinking of something else, he dropped the stone into his pocket.

After dinner he paid a visit to the kitchen.

The cook was rather flustered. To be questioned by a member of the house-party, and the foreign gentleman too! But she did her best to answer his questions. The puddings had been made three days ago—'The day you arrived, Sir.' Everyone had come out into the kitchen to have a stir and wish. An old custom—perhaps they didn't have it abroad? After that the puddings were boiled, and then they were put in a row on the top shelf in the larder. Was there anything special to distinguish this pudding from the others? No, she didn't think so. Except that it was in an aluminium pudding-basin, and the others were in china ones. Was it the pudding originally intended for Christmas Day? It was funny that he should ask that. No, indeed! The Christmas pudding was always boiled in a big white china mould with a pattern of holly-leaves. But this very morning (the cook's red face became wrathful) Gladys, the kitchen-maid, sent to fetch it down for the final boiling, had managed to drop and break it. 'And of course, seeing that there might be splinters in it, I wouldn't send it to table, but took the big aluminium one instead.'

M. Poirot thanked her for her information. He went out of the kitchen, smiling a little to himself, as though satisfied with the information he had obtained. And the fingers of his right hand played with something in his pocket.

'M. Poirot! M. Poirot! Do wake up! Something dreadful's happened!'

Thus Johnnie in the early hours of the following morning. M. Poirot sat up in bed. He wore a night-cap. The contrast between the dignity of his countenance and the rakish tilt of the night-cap was certainly droll; but its effect on Johnnie seemed disproportionate. But for his words, one might have fancied that the boy was violently amused about something. Curious sounds came from outside the door, too, suggesting soda-water syphons in difficulty.

'Come down at once, please,' continued Johnnie, his voice shaking slightly. 'Someone's been killed.' He turned away.

'Aha, that is serious!' said M. Poirot.

He arose, and, without unduly hurrying himself, made a partial toilet. Then he followed Johnnie down the stairs. The house-party was clustered round the door into the garden. Their countenances all expressed intense emotion. At sight of him Eric was seized with a violent choking fit.

Jean came forward and laid her hand on M. Poirot's arm.

'Look!' she said, and pointed dramatically through the open door.

'*Mon Dieu!*' ejaculated M. Poirot. 'It is like a scene on the stage.'

His remark was not inapposite. More snow had fallen during the night, the world looked white and ghostly in the faint light of the early dawn. The expanse of white lay unbroken save for what looked like on splash of vivid scarlet.

Nancy Cardell lay motionless on the snow. She was clad in scarlet silk pyjamas, her small feet were bare, her arms were spread wide. Her head was turned aside and hidden by the mass of her clustering black hair. Deadly still she lay, and from her left side rose up the hilt of a dagger, whilst on the snow there was an ever-widening patch of crimson.

Poirot went out into the snow. He did not go to where the girl's body lay, but kept to the path. Two tracks of foot-marks, a man's and a woman's, led to where the tragedy had occurred. The man's footprints went away in the opposite direction alone. Poirot stood on the path, stroking his chin reflectively.

Suddenly Oscar Levering burst out of the house.

'Good God!' he cried. 'What's this?'

His excitement was a contrast to the other's calm.

'It looks,' said M. Poirot thoughtfully, 'like murder.'

Eric had another violent attack of coughing.

'But we must do something,' cried the other. 'What shall we do?'

'There is only one thing to be done,' said M. Poirot. 'Send for the police.'

'Oh!' said everybody at once.

M. Poirot looked inquiringly at them.

'Certainly,' he said. 'It is the only thing to be done. Who will go?'

There was a pause, then Johnnie came forward.

'Rag's over,' he declared. 'I say, M. Poirot, I hope you won't be too mad with us. It's all a joke, you know—got up between us—just to pull your leg. Nancy's only shamming.'

M. Poirot regarded him without visible emotion, save that his eyes twinkled a moment.

'You mock yourselves at me, is that it?' he inquired placidly.

'I say, I'm awfully sorry really. We shouldn't have done it. Beastly bad taste. I apologize, I really do.'

'You need not apologize,' said the other in a peculiar voice.

Johnnie turned.

'I say, Nancy, get up!' he cried. 'Don't lie there all day.'

But the figure on the ground did not move.

'Get up,' cried Johnnie again.

Still Nancy did not move, and suddenly a feeling of nameless dread came over the boy. He turned to Poirot.

'What—what's the matter? Why doesn't she get up?'

'Come with me,' said Poirot curtly.

He strode over the snow. He had waved the others back, and he was careful not to infringe on the other footmarks. The boy followed him, frightened and unbelieving. Poirot knelt down by the girl, then he signed to Johnnie.

'Feel her hand and pulse.'

Wondering, the boy bent down, then started back with a cry. The hand and arm were stiff and cold, and no vestige of a pulse was to be found.

'She's dead!' he gasped. 'But how? Why?'

M. Poirot passed over the first part of the question.

'Why?' he said musingly. 'I wonder.' Then, suddenly leaning across the dead girl's body, he unclasped her other hand, which was tightly clenched over something. Both he and the boy uttered an exclamation. In the palm of Nancy's hand was a red stone that winked and flashed forth fire.

'Aha!' cried M. Poirot. Swift as a flash his hand flew to his pocket, and came away empty.

'The cracker ruby,' said Johnnie wonderingly. Then, as his companion bent to examine the dagger, and the stained snow, he cried out: 'Surely it can't be blood, M. Poirot. It's paint. It's only paint.'

Poirot straightened himself.

'Yes,' he said quietly. 'You are right. It's only paint.'

'Then how—' The boy broke off. Poirot finished the sentence for him.

'How was she killed? That we must find out. Did she eat or drink anything this morning?'

He was retracing his steps to the path where the others waited as he spoke. Johnnie was close behind him.

'She had a cup of tea,' said the boy. 'Mr Levering made it for her. He's got a spirit-lamp in his room.'

Johnnie's voice was loud and clear. Levering heard the words.

'Always take a spirit-lamp about with me,' he declared. 'Most handy thing in the world. My sister's been glad enough of it this visit—not liking to worry the servants all the time you know.'

M. Poirot's eyes fell, almost apologetically as it seemed, to Mr Levering's feet, which were encased in carpet slippers.

'You have changed your boots, I see,' he murmured gently.

Levering stared at him.

'But, M. Poirot,' cried Jean, 'what are we to do?'

'There is only one thing to be done, as I said just now, Mademoiselle. Send for the police.'

'I'll go,' cried Levering. 'It won't take me a minute to put on my boots. You people had better not stay out here in the cold.'

He disappeared into the house.

'He is so thoughtful, that Mr Levering,' murmured Poirot softly. 'Shall we take his advice?'

'What about waking father and—and everybody?'

'No,' said M. Poirot sharply. 'It is quite unnecessary. Until the police come, nothing must be touched out here; so shall we go inside? To the library? I have a little history to recount to you which may distract your minds from this sad tragedy.'

He led the way, and they followed him.

'The story is about a ruby,' said M. Poirot, ensconcing himself in a comfortable arm-chair. 'A very celebrated ruby which belonged to a very celebrated man. I will not tell you his name—but he is one of the great ones of the earth. *Eh bien*, this great man, he arrived in London, incognito. And since, though a great man, he was also a young and a foolish man, he became entangled with a pretty young lady. The pretty young lady, she did not care much for the man, but she did care for his possessions—so much so that she disappeared one day with the historic ruby which had belonged to his house for generations. The poor young man, he was in a quandary. He is shortly to be married to a noble Princess, and he does not want the scandal. Impossible to go to the police, he comes to me, Hercule Poirot, instead. 'Recover for me my ruby,' he says. *Eh bien*, I know something of this young lady. She has a brother, and between them they have put through many a clever *coup*. I happen to know where they are staying for Christmas. By the kindness of Mr Endicott, whom I chance to have met, I, too, become a guest. But when this pretty young lady hears that I am arriving, she is greatly alarmed. She is intelligent, and she knows that I am after the ruby. She must hide it immediately in a safe place; and figure to yourself where she hides it—in a plum-pudding! Yes, you may well say, oh! She is stirring with the rest, you see, and she pops it into a pudding-bowl of aluminium that is different from the others. By a strange chance, that pudding came to be used on Christmas Day.'

The tragedy forgotten for the moment, they stared at him open-mouthed.

'After that,' continued the little man, 'she took to her bed.' He drew out his watch and looked at it. 'The household is astir. Mr Levering is a long time fetching the police, is he not? I fancy that his sister went with him.'

Evelyn rose with a cry, her eyes fixed on Poirot.

'And I also fancy that they will not return. Oscar Levering has been sailing close to the wind for a long time, and this is the end. He and his sister will pursue their activities abroad for a time under a different name. I alternately tempted and frightened him this morning. By casting aside all pretence he could gain possession of the ruby whilst we were in the house and he was supposed to be fetching the police. But it meant burning his boats. Still, with a case being built up against him for murder, flight seemed clearly indicated.'

'Did he kill Nancy?' whispered Jean.

Poirot rose.

'Supposing we visit once more the scene of the crime,' he suggested.

He led the way, and they followed him. But a simultaneous gasp broke from their lips as they passed outside the house. No trace of the tragedy remained; the snow was smooth and unbroken.

'Crikey!' said Eric, sinking down on the step. 'It wasn't all a dream, was it?'

'Most extraordinary,' said M. Poirot, 'The Mystery of the Disappearing Body.' His eyes twinkled gently.

Jean came up to him in sudden suspicion.

'M. Poirot, you haven't—you aren't—I say, you haven't been spoofing us all the time, have you? Oh, I do believe you have!'

'It is true, my children. I knew about your little plot, you see, and I arranged a little counterplot of my own. Ah, here is Mlle. Nancy—and none the worse, I hope, after her magnificent acting of the comedy.'

It was indeed Nancy Cardell in the flesh, her eyes shining and her whole person exuberant with health and vigour.

'You have not caught cold? You drank the tisane I sent to your room?' demanded Poirot accusingly.

'I took one sip and that was enough. I'm all right. Did I do it well, M. Poirot? Oh, my arm hurts after that tourniquet!'

'You were splendid, *petite*. But shall we explain to the others? They are still in the fog, I perceive. See you, *mes enfants*, I went to Mlle. Nancy, told her that I knew all about your little *complot*, and asked her if she would act a part for me. She did it very cleverly. She induced Mr Levering to make her a cup of tea, and also managed that he should be the one chosen to leave footprints on the snow. So when the time came, and he thought that by some fatality she was really dead, I had all the materials to frighten him with. What happened after we went into the house, Mademoiselle?'

'He came down with his sister, snatched the ruby out of my hand, and off they went post-haste.'

'But I say, M. Poirot, what about the ruby?' cried Eric. 'Do you mean to say you've let them have that?'

Poirot's face fell, as he faced a circle of accusing eyes.

'I shall recover it yet,' he said feebly; but he perceived that he had gone down in their estimation.

'Well, I do think!' began Johnnie. 'To let them get away with the ruby—'

But Jean was sharper.

'He's spoofing us again!' she cried. 'You are, aren't you?'

'Feel in my left-hand pocket, Mademoiselle.'

Jean thrust in an eager hand, and drew it out again with a squeal of triumph. She held aloft the great ruby in its crimson splendour.

'You see,' explained Poirot, 'the other was a paste replica I brought with me from London.'

'Isn't he clever?' demanded Jean ecstatically.

'There's one thing you haven't told us,' said Johnnie suddenly. 'How did you know about the rag? Did Nancy tell you?'

Poirot shook his head.

'Then how did you know?'

'It is my business to know things,' said M. Poirot, smiling a little as he watched Evelyn Haworth and Roger Endicott walking down the path together.

'Yes, but do tell us. Oh, do, please! *Dear* M. Poirot, please tell us!'

He was surrounded by a circle of flushed, eager faces.

'You really wish that I should solve for you this mystery?'

'Yes.'

'I do not think I can.'

'Why not?'

'*Ma foi*, you will be so disappointed.'

'Oh, do tell us! How *did* you know?'

'Well, you see, I was in the library—'

'Yes?'

'And you were discussing your plans just outside—and the library window was open.'

'Is that all?' said Eric in disgust. 'How simple!'

'Is it not?' said M. Poirot, smiling.

'At all events, we know everything now,' said Jean in a satisfied voice.

'Do we?' muttered M. Poirot to himself, as he went into the house. '*I* do not—I, whose business it is to know things.'

And, for perhaps the twentieth time, he drew from his pocket a rather dirty piece of paper.

'Don't eat any plum-pudding—'

M. Poirot shook his head perplexedly. At the same moment he became aware of a peculiar gasping sound very near his feet. He looked down and perceived a small creature in a print dress. In her left hand was a dust-pan, and in the right a brush.

'And who may you be, *mon enfant*?' inquired M. Poirot.

'Annie 'Icks, please, Sir. Between-maid.'

M. Poirot had an inspiration. He handed her the letter. 'Did you write that, Annie?'

'I didn't mean any 'arm, Sir.'

He smiled at her.

'Of course you didn't. Suppose you tell me all about it?'

'It was them two, Sir—Mr Levering and his sister. None of us can abide 'em; and she wasn't ill a bit—we could all tell that. So I thought something queer was going on, and I'll tell you straight, Sir, I listened at the door, and I heard him say as plain as plain, 'This fellow Poirot must be got out of the way as soon as possible.' And then he says to 'er, meaning-like, 'Where did you put it?' And she answers, 'In the pudding.' And so I saw they meant to poison you in the Christmas pudding, and I didn't know what to do. Cook wouldn't listen to the likes of me. And then I thought of writing a warning, and I put it in the 'all where Mr Graves would be sure to see it and take it to you.'

Annie paused breathless. Poirot surveyed her gravely for some minutes.

'You read too many novelettes, Annie,' he said at last. 'But you have the good heart, and a certain amount of intelligence. When I return to London I will send you an excellent book upon *le ménage*, also the Lives of the Saints, and a work upon the economic position of woman.'

Leaving Annie gasping anew, he turned and crossed the hall. He had meant to go into the library, but through the open door he saw a dark head and a fair one, very close together, and he paused where he stood. Suddenly a pair of arms slipped round his neck.

'If you *will* stand just under the mistletoe!' said Jean.

'Me too,' said Nancy.

M. Poirot enjoyed it all—he enjoyed it very much indeed.

BIBLIOGRAPHY

Agatha Christie's short stories typically appeared first in magazines and then in her short story books, which tended to be different collections in the UK and the US. This list attempts to catalogue the first publication of each, and gives alternative story titles when used.

Christmas at Abney Hall

Excerpted from *An Autobiography* (1977).

Three Blind Mice

Originally broadcast as a radio play in the UK by the BBC in May 1947. First published in the US in *Cosmopolitan* magazine Vol. 124, No. 5, in May 1948. Reprinted in *Three Blind Mice and Other Stories* (US, 1950).

The Chocolate Box

First published in the UK as 'The Clue of the Chocolate Box' in *The Sketch* Number 1582 on 23 May 1924, and in the US in *Blue Book Magazine* Vol. 40, No. 4, in February 1925. Reprinted in *Poirot Investigates* (US edition, 1925) and *Poirot's Early Cases* (UK, 1974).

A Christmas Tragedy

First published in the UK as 'The Hat and the Alibi' in *Storyteller* Vol. 46, No. 273 in January 1930. Reprinted in *The Thirteen Problems* (UK, 1932) aka *The Tuesday Club Murders* (US, 1933).

The Coming of Mr Quin

First published in the UK as 'The Passing of Mr Quinn' in *The Grand Magazine* No. 229 in March 1924 and in the US as 'Mr Quinn Passes By' in *Muncey magazine Vol.* 84, No. 2 in March 1925. Reprinted in *The Mysterious Mr Quin* (1930).

The Clergyman's Daughter

First published in the UK as 'The First Wish' in *The Grand Magazine* No. 226 in December 1923. Reprinted in *Partners in Crime* (1929).

The Plymouth Express

First published in the UK as 'The Mystery of the Plymouth Express' in *The Sketch* No. 1575 on 4 April 1923, and in the US as 'The Plymouth Express Affair' in *Blue Book Magazine* Vol. 38, No. 3 in January 1924. Reprinted in *The Under Dog and Other Stories* (US, 1951) and *Poirot's Early Cases* (UK, 1974).

Problem at Pollensa Bay

First published in the UK in *Strand Magazine* No. 539 in November 1935, and in the US as 'Siren Business' in *Liberty* on 5 September 1936. Reprinted in *The Regatta Mystery and Other Stories* (US, 1939) and *Problem at Pollensa Bay and Other Stories* (UK, 1991).

Sanctuary

First published in the UK in *Woman's Journal* in October 1954, and in the US as 'Murder at the Vicarage' in *This Week* in September 1954. Reprinted in *Double Sin and Other Stories* (US, 1961) and *Miss Marple's Final Cases and Two Other Stories* (UK, 1979).

The Mystery of Hunter's Lodge

First published in the UK in *The Sketch* Number 1581 on 16 May 1923, and in the US as 'The Hunter's Lodge Case' in *Blue Book Magazine* Vol. 39, No. 2, in June 1924. Reprinted in *Poirot Investigates* (UK, 1924; US 1925).

The World's End

First published in the UK as 'The World's End' in *Storyteller* magazine No. 238 in February 1927 and in the US in *Flynn's Weekly* Vol. 19, No. 6 on 20 November 1926. Reprinted in *The Mysterious Mr Quin* (1930).

The Manhood of Edward Robinson

First published in the UK as 'The Day of His Dreams' in *The Grand Magazine* No. 238 in December 1924. Reprinted in *The Listerdale Mystery and Other Stories* (UK, 1934) and *The Golden Ball and Other Stories* (US, 1971).

Christmas Adventure

First published in the UK as 'The Adventure of the Christmas Pudding' in *The Sketch* No. 1611 in December 1923. Reprinted in *While the Light Lasts and Other Stories* (UK, 1997). This is its first official publication in the US.

ABOUT THE AUTHOR

Agatha Christie is the most widely published author of all time, outsold only by the Bible and Shakespeare. Her books have sold more than a billion copies in English and another billion in a hundred foreign languages. She died in 1976, after a prolific career spanning six decades.

agathachristie.com
Facebook: /OfficialAgathaChristie
Twitter: @agathachristie
Instagram: officialagathachristie